The Legacy of the Sky Pendant
By Jonathan Crayford
Published 2018 by Your Book Angel
Copyright © Jonathan Crayford

Printed in the United States

Interior design by Christi Koehl

Edited by Keidi Keating

ISBN: 978-1-7320268-7-2

For my little brother and sister, Daniel and Caitlyn.

And also in loving memory of my Grandfather, David Ronald 'Roy' Harris, (Tadcu) – 04/09/2012 – my partner. – The most kind and inspiring man I ever knew, and forever in our hearts.

THE LEGACY
OF THE *Sky*
PENDANT

BY

JONATHAN CRAYFORD

Acknowledgements

Firstly, I would like to thank my good friend Emyr Thomas, who read one of the earliest drafts of my novel and who I must have bored senseless with my constant thinking out loud and brainstorming ideas. Thank you, my old friend.

To my friend Gareth James, for his constant words of encouragement when I lacked motivation and came close to giving up, and also for his help as a musician and a songwriter for the lyrics to the song 'Marcus the Swift' in book 2 chapter 19 and also for helping out with the setting up of my website www.jonathancrayfordauthor.co.uk.

To my Grampa, John, for being the very first person to proofread my first draft of the novel and who encouraged me to continue writing.

To Keidi Keating, who edited and helped to publish my manuscript. Her engagement and guidance to a first-time writer was invaluable to me and was one of the reasons why I ended up finishing writing the story.

And last but not least, special thanks to my parents Carolyn and Matthew for supporting me not only through the process of writing my first book, but throughout my whole life. Also. Thank you to everyone else that helped me along the way.

Book One - Part One
THE ACCOUNTS
OF MARCUS
THE SWIFT

Chapter One

The Plague Approaches

'Do you see anything yet, Marcus?' echoed a voice from behind him.

Marcus stood still and silent, firmly gripping an ashen spear and vigilantly gazing towards the golden horizon from his post at the castle wall. He was bound in his late father's old heavy steel plate armour and fumbling with a strange, bizarre-looking pendant, which he had found while playing down by the river when he was only a small child. Back then he had fastened it securely onto a length of leather cord and he had worn it around his neck ever since.

It was angular in form and crafted from an unknown marbled and silver metal, which glowed faintly when in the moonlight. It fit snugly into the palm of a grown man's hand.

Marcus had always been drawn to it and had often pondered its origin and crafter. More than two decades had passed since he had found it, and it now held great sentimental value to him, as it had been through so much with him. It had been a source of comfort to him through difficult times, and he never took it off, not even while he slept.

Marcus was quite a serious young man, and an average height and build.

He lived in the old mining village of Soulwind, and he was about to defend her with his life, for a deadly threat, and war it seemed, was fast approaching.

It had happened so unexpectedly, it could not be explained by either himself or by anyone else that lived in his peaceful little village.

But there had been a lot of talk between the folk of the village of mysterious looking strangers that had appeared in and around many of the villages of the Kingdom and set up their camps just outside each village.

These Strangers had been dressed in bizarre clothing, which had never been seen nor worn by any of the natives before.

The Strangers wore dirty, sooty, long, tattered robes, with dark veiled hoods that shadowed the wearers' eyes and most of their faces but displayed enough of it to show that they were human.

The Strangers seemed harmless enough to everybody at first.

'Distant travellers,' some of the villagers passively commented.

'Exotic traders, perhaps,' others remarked to reassure themselves.

The Strangers offered gifts to the natives of the villages in which they were now quickly occupying and settling near: small trinkets and curious knick-knacks.

These items were of great value and fine

craftsmanship, but the more the villagers thought about it, they realised it was rare, almost even unheard of to encounter either distant travellers or exotic traders in the peaceful Kingdom of Termelanor.

Soon after the docile villagers had grown accustomed to the Strangers' presence about the villages, some of them received unusual requests from them.

Queer demands and tempting offers of joining a strange sounding cult and promises of riches and luxury if they did so.

However, the people of Termelanor were a peaceful and simple folk and they had no interest in partaking in such suspicious sounding activities.

As the sightings of the Strangers increased further, they began to cause serious disturbances in the villages they had recently occupied.

Homes were discovered by their owners trashed and overturned and innocent people were commonly assaulted and robbed in the streets, often in broad daylight in the presence of numerous witnesses.

Many people suspected that the Strangers were looking for something or someone, but nobody ever discovered whom or what that was.

The violence gradually escalated and before long the Strangers began to pillage and plunder the villages they had established a foothold in. With superior numbers, and the villagers' trust in their favour, the Strangers took full advantage of the villagers' naturally relaxed nature, and any man woman and child who refused to join them or answer their questions were either, enslaved, imprisoned or slain.

And so, terrified, the villagers submitted to their captors' will.

Chapter Two

Of the Strangers

The now enslaved villagers and what remained of the free people whispered between each other with regards to the Strangers' recently evil actions, movements, and of course, their reputation.

They discussed plans of escape and even ways they could fight back against them.

The prisoners were under constant watch by their captors, so they had little choice but to use secretive code names to refer the Strangers to.

The name 'Malignant' seemed to stick and suit the Strangers rather well and happened to be the most commonly used amongst prisoners, although slightly more colourful code names were used by angrier prisoners.

However, the Strangers soon realized what the imprisoned were up to, and they quickly adopted this code name as their official title.

And so, there the imprisoned remained, unaware of their fate.

Although, a few free-standing people remained in Termelanor whom did not take the news of the Malignants' terrible and unforgivable actions very well.

Companies of volunteer resistance fighters rose from the lesser villages, farmlands, and the small holdings that had so far remained untouched by the Malignants' presence.

These included bitter fathers of butchered children and angry sons of slaughtered parents. Together they united and formed a specialized deployable unit of passionate, battle-ready fighters, prepared to counter-attack the Malignants' next movement without hesitation.

They were dubbed 'the Benigns' by the Kingdom's free inhabitants, a fitting title they had all agreed, for the brave warriors that would cleanse their beloved land from the evil hostile presence that now plagued it.

The Benign Warriors were commanded under their Captain and battle commander, Varrick, a retired yet well-respected and skilled ex-combat trainer. Under his command they led their resistance company to counter any possible hostile Malignant attack, wherever intelligence may indicate so.

After many failed campaigns and unsuccessful liberation attempts, The Benigns were now so few in number they had little choice but to retreat and resort to ambush and guerrilla tactics to fight against the ever-advancing Malignant swarm.

The Benigns' actions merely delayed the Malignants' advancements for so long, until intelligence reached Captain Varrick that the Malignants were planning a relentless assault on the peaceful village of Soulwind, the last free-standing Greater Village that remained in the Kingdom.

Word was urgently sent to Soulwind for the women

and children to be evacuated from the village, and for every able-bodied man who lived there to arm himself and make his way to man and defend Soulwind Castle, where they would rendezvous with the last of the Benign Warriors, whom were also prepared to fight to the death to defend the castle in a desperate last stand against the Malignants.

Marcus was approached by a balding middle-aged man named Raymond.

'They should be here soon,' said Raymond, turning to face Marcus, a slight tremble in his voice. 'Don't you think?'

Raymond was a retired foot soldier from the Kingdom's Capital's army, the only professional fighting force that had existed in Termelanor before the Malignants invaded, and that for some unknown reason, had thus far remained absent from this entire brutal conflict.

Raymond had once served in the army with Marcus's father, Argyle.

Both of them were once in the same battalion as each other, and they were dear friends. They had grown up together in the village of Soulwind, before enlisting and serving together in the Capital's army.

Regrettably, during their unit's return from a patrol in the north one evening, their battalion was brutally ambushed by a large force of outlaws and bandits.

The battle was narrowly won by the Capital's army, however many of the soldiers were tragically killed and fatally wounded during the ambush, including Marcus's father, and few men returned to the safety of the Capital with their lives.

Ever since that day, Raymond had kept a close eye on the newly orphaned Marcus, for Marcus had also lost his mother to childbirth.

Marcus was only a young boy when Argyle was killed, and Raymond had been like a father to him ever since, for Raymond had no living family of his own.

Marcus nodded, his eyes still transfixed on the horizon.

'I've heard from Varrick and his men that it isn't in a Malignants' nature to delay an attack once they've set their dark hearts on it,' said Marcus.

'I must say, I don't like our chances, Marcus,' said Raymond anxiously. 'Not even with Captain Varrick and the others here to reinforce our defences.'

'Never doubt the spirit of any free man whom is prepared to fight for that which is dearest to him, my old friend,' replied Marcus as he smiled bravely at Raymond before diverting his sharp eyes back towards the horizon.

'Even so,' said Raymond, now also joining Marcus, and looking towards the horizon, 'our scouts have reported that their forces have us outnumbered by more than ten to one, and even in a siege situation, those numbers aren't favourable for us.'

'You know better than any man here that I was never good with numbers, Ray,' Marcus joked as he suppressed a little smile.

'I wish I had your courage,' smiled Raymond nervously, his lips twitching with apprehension. 'You always were a brave young soul, just like your father.'

Marcus turned to Raymond and smiled warmly as he placed his steady hand on Raymond's armoured shoulder.

Soulwind Castle was now garrisoned with around one hundred able-bodied men from the village of Soulwind, and several of these included men from Soulwind's trained village militia.

The men of Soulwind were both poorly protected and armed, and their ages varied from young lads to old men.

Most of their armour consisted of little more than their everyday garments, mostly working clothes made out of cloth or linen.

The trained militia wore slightly better protection, including variations of soft and hard leather armour, mostly worn by the men whilst hunting, and even less wore chain and plate armour; in fact, only Marcus and Raymond did.

Raymond wore his old heavy steel plate armour and Marcus donned his late father's armour, left to him after he died.

The armament of the combined motley force of the men of Soulwind and Soulwind's Militia, both included and consisted of anything that ranged from farming tools to woodcutting hatchets and mining picks, (which were plentiful in the village of Soulwind), hunting bows and makeshift wooden shields, and practically anything they could use as a weapon.

Marcus and Raymond were lucky enough to own more formidable weapons. Raymond fought with a standard army issue sword and shield whereas Marcus wielded his father's two-handed steel sword, which was a little too big and heavy for him to use effectively, but it was sharp, and a good size for keeping the distance between him and his enemy. He made up for his lack of shield by wearing his father's full steel helmet.

The men of Soulwind were fortunate enough to be supplemented by an equal number and what remained of the allied Benign force whom had arrived to aid Soulwind in the defence of her castle.

The Benign Warriors were no doubt better armed than the men of Soulwind.

Although only the highest-ranking officers wore plate and chain armour, all of what remained of these men wore good quality studded hard leather armour, and each of them was equipped with a steel long sword, reinforced banded wooden shield, and a good quality yew long bow.

Each and every one of them brave and battle-hardened men, and their mere presence lifted the Soulwind men's spirits, and gave them greater confidence that they could successfully defend their castle from this advancing monster.

Soulwind Castle was merely a simple and basic fortification.

It was a sturdy castle, constructed from the finest quality hard stone, the same that was used to build and fortify the Kingdom's Capital and all of its buildings, and sourced from the now-exhausted quarry south of Soulwind.

It wasn't a very large castle, in comparison to the Capital, however it was designed so it could be easily defended with a small number of inexperienced militia in the unlikely event that the need ever arose.

The remaining Kingdom's villages, however, were not so fortunate in their defences as Soulwind was with her castle, save for their respective militia and the terrain and landscape, which naturally protected them. This might have been the reason why those villages fell sooner, and why the Malignants attacked them before they attacked Soulwind.

This behaviour told Marcus that the Malignants showed frighteningly advanced war and invasion tactics and knowledge of the local landscape, far above any that of a typical common invader, if it had not been for an unlikely coincidence.

Argyle had always spoken to Marcus about the art of war and of battle tactics even when he was a young child, and it had always both interested and fascinated him.

He could recall playing for hours on end outside as he drew the battle formations into the dirt using sticks and stones as his play armies. Even at that age he thought of fresh and innovative ways to potentially win battles, even when grossly outnumbered.

'See, Dad?' said the young Marcus to his father, pointing down at the dirt as he tugged on his sleeve, 'even though they have twice as many men as I do, it doesn't matter as long as I send my some of my men around to attack them from behind as they're attacking my army head on.'

His father Argyle was impressed with the young Marcus and told him he would make a fine commander in the King's army one day, although nothing ever came of it.

After Soulwind, the last remaining stronghold in Termelanor was the Kingdom's Capital itself, thus leaving Soulwind Castle the only solid manmade fortification that existed outside of the Capital.

More than anything, the castle was built as a comforting precautionary foundation, many centuries ago by the late King Norman, as a gesture of thanks to the people who lived in the village of Soulwind for allowing him to mine stone from its quarry to build and fortify the Capital.

This was very typical of King Norman. Even though it was his stone to take as King in the first place, he had always ruled fairly, and encouraged others to follow by example.

The mined stone left over after the construction of the Capital was later used to erect Soulwind Castle.

Soulwind Castle consisted of a main solid wooden gate on the left-hand side of an eastward facing battlemented wall, a courtyard that was located behind the main gate and a dual flight of stone steps led up to a simple, square central and secure keep.

Finally, three tall thick walls reinforced the remaining cardinal points.

And there, as the sun set on Soulwind Castle, the men waited, pondering whether they would live out the night, or join the other villages in their fate.

Chapter Three

The Desperate Last Stand

The black silhouettes of the enemies' spears scraped the sky on the horizon as the sun set behind them. Marcus gripped his spear tight and gazed coldly at the oncoming advancement through the narrow eye-slit in his father's old steel helmet.

The Malignant force was soon in plain sight, and they struck fear into the hearts of even the bravest warriors inside of the walls of the castle.

The typical Malignant Warrior wore dark hard-leather armour, stained and almost soaked black by the blood of their countless innocent victims. Their thin, curved and black steel sabres and scimitars were jagged and notched and their bows were short, crude, and stout.

The Malignant Warriors sought victory by sacrificing reliability in their weapons and armour for the sheer fear that their appearance struck into the hearts of their victims. Marcus recalled his father once telling him that few weapons were as effective as terror; it seemed now as though that he may have been right.

Just as the men predicted, the Malignants did not delay their attack for one second, and as they reached the range of the castle's arrow fire, the siege immediately commenced.

The enemy's battle cries were terrifying; their faces were grim, scarred, and intimidating and black war paint patterned the bare areas of their skin.

Marcus could only ponder what could possibly drive men to turn this way, but for now his mind could be nowhere else but in the defence of Soulwind Castle.

The Malignants brought up many shoddy ladders to scale the high walls of the castle and a sheltered battering ram to shatter down the solid wooden gate.

Their archers hurled wave upon wave of black flaming arrows at the castle's battlements, screeching taunts at the men behind the walls, while allied forces tried to return fire from the cover of the walls.

Marcus's post was located at the dead centre of the castles eastward facing wall, and the men were spread sparsely along it, and there he was ready to greet the first invader that dared to climb the ladder in front of him with cold and bitter steel.

Marcus had never been a brave soldier or a heroic warrior, but his father had taught him a lot about sword combat when he was alive, and Raymond had also taught him a thing or two.

As the arrows whistled over Marcus's shoulders, he launched his spear over the battlements and drew his father's great sword from the sheath on his back, gripping it with both hands high over his right shoulder.

The ladders were set, and without hesitation the first Malignant Warrior quickly scaled it and leaped over the battlements with a blood chilling battle shriek, his sabre held high above his head. And with one fell swoop, Marcus had slain one of the first of the many victims of Soulwind's siege, black blood splattered all across his face, as he unintentionally tasted and smelt the metallic dark blood of his kill.

The battle seemed to be going well, and the keen-eyed Benign archers picked out vulnerable hostile targets, while the defenders on the wall held back the scaling Malignant force.

Suddenly, Marcus heard his name being called out from down in the courtyard below, just behind the castle's gate.

'Marcus!' yelled a veteran with cropped grey hair. It was Captain Varrick, 'Marcus, I need another sword down here, the bastards are about to smash down the gate!'

Varrick was right… Marcus was focusing so hard on the defence of the wall that he had forgotten all about the ram, and it was fast approaching the gate.

Marcus witnessed frustratingly as the allied arrows clattered feebly off the ram's thick and protective leather hide.

He called out to Raymond, whom was also defending the wall a short distance away from him.

'Raymond!' yelled Marcus in a deep, commanding voice. 'I'm needed down at the gate!'

Raymond nodded toward him and continued desperately with the defence.

'Keep holding them back men,' cried Marcus. 'Let them experience a taste of hell themselves before they send us there.'

Marcus now fought his way down towards the g quickly as he could, where Varrick and a few dozen or so Benign Warriors were anchored to the spot, gripping their weapons and staring terrified at the gate as the iron head of the enemy's ram thudded loudly against the thick oaken doors of the castle.

'Thank you, Marcus,' Varrick sighed.

'There's no need to thank me,' said Marcus. 'We're all in here together.'

The thuds of the ram grew ever louder as the solid oak gate splintered, and then without warning the gate gave way and smashed open with what seemed like the force of an erupting volcano, and in poured the enemy.

Marcus and the gates' defenders fought desperately as the two forces collided and their blades clanged together, but the weight of the attacking force was too great for the defenders to handle as the Malignant Warriors flooded the stone courtyard like a thick black tar.

'Marcus,' cried Varrick, 'this is no good. We can't fight them like this. You have to take the men and fall back, and I'll hold them here.'

'No,' said Marcus, 'I won't leave you alone to die down here.'

'That's an order soldier,' yelled Varrick exposing his yellow teeth and shoving Marcus towards the direction of the keep.

While the battle at the gate had been raging on, the defenders on top of the wall were broken and overrun, already desperately retreating towards the castle's keep.

'Fall back!' Varrick yelled, loudly enough so that every man in the castle could hear him. 'Fall back to the keep!'

Marcus, along with what was left of the gates defenders, fell back towards the castle's keep, fighting the enemy off as they retreated.

Many were slain quickly as they retreated; the Malignant Warriors killed mercilessly as they slashed at the throats of the castle's defenders and forced their blades through their chests violently in a vicious bloody onslaught, taunting their victims as they did so.

Marcus was a surprisingly strong defender. He parried the foe's blades skilfully as he retreated, and when he finally reached the stairs to the keep, he turned on his tiptoes and sprinted like a flash towards the stronghold, his legs pounding and pumping hard like a pair of furnace bellows on the solid stone steps.

As Marcus exhaled blasts of hot air through the narrow slit in his steel helmet, he felt and heard the clang of steel blades biting at his heels as he desperately tried to reach the keep in one piece.

The Malignants had now taken the wall and were picking off the fleeing castle's defenders as they retreated, brutally taking out their victims with forceful arrow shots, still taunting and howling as they killed.

Nothing could have prepared the men for this massacre; their fate was sealed the very moment they had entered the castle.

As Marcus neared the keep, a young warrior from the

village was waiting at the top of the stairs wielding a short sword, holding the thick keep's door ajar for him.

'Hurry, Marcus!' he trembled.

Marcus recognised the warrior as he got closer to the keep; it was Wyatt, the tanners' boy.

Marcus was merely feet away from him when suddenly a black arrow thumped into the side of Wyatt's calf, and he cried with pain.

Marcus supported Wyatt and they both retreated inside the keep.

As they stumbled inside, Raymond was there to meet them.

'Marcus!' cried Raymond in disbelief, both out of breath and bloodied.

'Help me with the door!' pleaded Marcus.

Marcus set Wyatt down nearby and Raymond moved swiftly to help him bar the door shut.

The door was barred with seconds to spare, and they heard the Malignants slamming, clawing, and hacking at the door from the outside.

Marcus slid down the wall on his back exhausted from his retreat.

'That should buy us some time,' said Raymond, eyeing up the door.

'Time for what?' said Wyatt, grasping his leg, 'they'll eventually break in here and kill us all.'

The remaining Malignant force now hacked and smashed against the door of the keep, while the remainder of Soulwind's defenders, Marcus, Raymond, and Wyatt were trapped inside it.

Marcus could not even try and comprehend the horror that was still going on outside as he heard the screams of the trapped defenders who didn't make it to the safety of the keep.

'Wyatt's right, it's hopeless Ray,' sighed Marcus, shaking his head. 'We're trapped in here.'

'I wouldn't say trapped,' said Raymond as he walked forward and slid over a table in the centre of the room, pulling back a rug, and opening a hidden trapdoor.

'Well that's conveniently original, Raymond,' Marcus joked, still heavily out of breath, 'just like in the story books.'

'Marcus,' said Raymond, 'it's up to you now. You have to alert the King, and tell him that the last greater village has fallen to these monsters. The Capital will be next, for certain. This trapdoor leads to a hidden gate that emerges behind the castle. Make for the Capital and don't stop until you get there.'

'Raymond,' said Marcus, 'I don't think I can. I can't leave you.'

'Marcus,' said Raymond as he knelt down and held him by his shoulders. 'I'm far too old. I'll never make it and look at poor Wyatt. He's in no shape to retreat. Do you understand? It must be you; we'll distract them for long enough for you to make your escape.'

'Raymond,' said Marcus, looking into his old friends' milky eyes, 'I promise that I won't let you down.'

The thuds and the hacks against the strongholds door grew louder.

'You're a lot like your father, Marcus,' said Raymond, 'I know I don't speak of him much but I saw a lot of him in you, and that day we were ambushed, well….' Raymond nodded his head and put on a sorry smile.

'I understand, Raymond,' said Marcus as he placed his forehead against Raymond's, 'it's all right.'

'I promised him that I'd look out for you, my lad,' said Raymond, as his eyes watered. 'I guess that ends here. Go now, quickly!'

As Raymond helped Wyatt to his feet and shoved a blade into his hand, Marcus leaped down the trapdoor and Raymond quickly sealed it behind him. Seconds later, he heard the keep's door breaking through, and feared the worst for Raymond and Wyatt, but there was no turning back for him now.

Marcus now found himself facing a long, dark, narrow stone tunnel.

The only source of light was a small lit hand torch in the iron wall bracket to his right, which presumably had been lit by Raymond shortly before the siege had commenced.

Marcus sheathed his sword into his back scabbard, gripped the torch's wooden shaft, and with his left hand felt his way steadily along the narrow passageway, holding the torch out in front of him as he squinted into the dark.

The tunnel was cold and damp and had a sharp musty smell, and it had rarely been used, known to very few people, if not only to Raymond.

Information perhaps disclosed only to the Kingdoms' soldiers or a select few from Soulwind, or maybe discovered from pure inquisition, as Raymond naturally was.

The high seeping ceiling dripped icy droplets of dank water down the back of Marcus's neck, and he shivered with disapproval.

Before long, Marcus neared the end of the passageway and reached a dead end.

Marcus placed the torch in the empty wall bracket next to him and took a closer look at the stone wall in front of him. Upon closer inspection, he discovered it was not a stone wall, but in fact a sealed door.

Sealed from the inside using a wooden plank supported along its width by two iron brackets.

Marcus carefully lifted the wooden plank off of the iron wall brackets and grasped the door's large iron ring handle.

The gate's door, although constructed from lumber, matched the surrounding castle's stone in colour, much like the trapdoor inside the keep.

This now explained how the passage was kept so effectively hidden.

The tree to which this timber would have previously belonged to must have been extremely rare, for Marcus had never before seen such a stony hue to wood before.

He pulled on the iron ring as he strained to open the door, and then he slowly peered his head out.

The coast seemed clear.

He exited the castle and the hidden gate closed with its own weight behind him so it was flush once again with the wall outside.

Marcus was ever so careful not to make the slightest sound.

He hugged with his back to the wall of the castle, and quietly made his way around it.

He peered his head around the first corner of the castle's wall, still with his back tight to it, side stepping slightly to cover ground.

He still had no idea what he was doing; all he knew was that the most direct route to Kingdom's Capital lay to the north-east, and that was the direction where he would head, which unfortunately meant heading past the direction in which the Malignants arrived.

He checked to see if the coast was clear. It was not.

Many of The Malignant foes still cluttered the anterior of the castle, arrogantly celebrating their victory. Marcus was so angry at them that he wanted to fight them all by himself there and then, but that would jeopardize his mission, his duty, and he would never let Raymond down.

He took a deep breath.

It was up to him now. He would not let the deaths of his friends and allies be in vain nor would he let the Malignants get away with all of the horror they had caused him, plus, he would not let the Kingdom fall. It was now down to him alone.

It was now or never.

Marcus bolted out from behind the cover of the stone

wall and ran with all of his remaining energy towards the north-east and headlong towards the Malignants. It was not long before he drew dozens of Malignant Warriors' attention.

As the Malignant Warriors charged towards him with their sabres held high, screeching their deafening shrieks, he made right for them. As they swiped and slashed hungrily at him, hoping to retrieve a limb or to claim his head, they collided with nothing but thin air as Marcus ducked and dodged and bobbed and weaved through the countless Malignant Warrior's attacks.

It was not easy for the Malignants; Marcus was simply too swift and agile for any one of them to come close to landing a single strike on him.

Marcus made it through the Malignant ranks and into the clear, and a few desperate Malignant Warriors feebly attempted a chase, but to no avail.

A few others tried to take him down with arrow fire, but Marcus continued to run, and the arrows thudded into the ground, inches away from his heels.

As Marcus sped towards the Capital, the remaining Malignant force had long since captured the castle, and had slain the remaining defenders inside of it, and not once did Marcus look back.

Chapter Four

The Great Capital of Termelanor

Marcus had been running for what seemed like hours and the darkness of the night had long since set in.

The waning gibbous moon provided him with enough light to see well enough ahead of him as he journeyed onward towards The Capital.

He was lucky it was such a clear and dry night, as Marcus could roughly estimate the general direction of the Capital from navigating the landscapes and the night's sky.

His surroundings transformed as he pressed forward.

Marcus splashed through icy cold streams and pounded through pine tree woodlands and rocky tundra.

His father's armour was heavy now, and the battle had long since diminished his energy.

Yet something from within still carried him forward.

He thought of abandoning the armour on more than one occasion, but it was all he had left to remember his father by, and so its sentimentality clung to him like a tick on a wild dog.

He was shattered and drained, but still he persisted, that one objective burning inside him like a blacksmith's forge.

At certain times during the night he thought he felt a faint warmth radiating from his pendant. He also thought he had felt it earlier whilst he was evading the Malignant's swipes as he fled from the castle, but he put it down to delusion on account of his fatigue.

Many more hours passed and then the sun rose, and finally he made it. He arrived exhausted over the brow of the hill, with The Kingdom's Capital soon in plain view.

He had never been to see the Capital before, but he had heard many tales of its undeniable magnificence and staggering beauty.

He took a moment to admire its wonder in the lazy morning sunshine.

Marcus stood unsteadily on what had long ago been his last legs, the larks' chorus drowned by his throbbing eardrums, and there he stood, deluded and smiling weakly as his blurred vision struggled to focus on the colossal structure.

The Kingdom's Capital was protected by four gargantuan battlemented stone walls, much like the walls of Soulwind Castle, but on a far larger scale, with four strong square towers in each corner, a flag on each drooping down their tall poles from the lack of morning breeze. These walls protected the inner city. On the far north-western corner of the city lay The King's Palace, also protected by strong stone walls and mighty stone towers.

Marcus had spent more than long enough standing idly; it was time to move once again.

Marcus approached ever closer to the Capital,

preparing to enter the main gate. This was easy enough for him, as the city's doors opened freely each morning to merchants and traders to do business in the market district of the city, and the main gate would normally be bustling with comers and goers, but not today.

He passed through the gate and ran up the streets while the Capital's dwellers looked on at what they were witnessing with confusion.

The Capital was normally a slow-paced way of life, as was much of the rest of Termelanor, therefore to see a worn and haggard warrior, pounding the streets in full battle armour at that time in the morning, was a rare sight to behold.

Some whispered amongst themselves while children pointed and giggled. The City Guard did not know whether to give chase or to stand back and simply spectate.

'Where do you reckon that one's off too in such a hurry, Jasper?' one guard pointed casually towards Marcus as he ran past them.

'He was probably halfway to the market when he realised he had left his house dressed in his armour,' chuckled the other as they laughed between themselves.

Marcus passed clothing stores and raced through narrow streets, running into dead ends, still searching for the palace.

It soon occurred to him that he was now lost, and he did not have any idea how to get to the King's Palace. He had also forgotten the general direction of it while he was running through the city's maze-like streets. An elderly lady kindly pointed him in the right direction and he continued on his hunt.

Before long, Marcus finally made it, and he stumbled towards the gates of the King's Palace, but he was swiftly approached by two of the Palace Guards.

'Halt!' said one of the guards, gripping a mighty looking spear and pointing it towards Marcus' throat. 'In the name of King Heath, state your business with the Palace of the Kings.'

'The Castle...' Marcus whispered feebly. 'Soulwind...'

Marcus suddenly blacked out and collapsed in a metallic heap on the hard stone floor.

Chapter Five

Of Stern and Heath

Marcus finally came around a few hours later in a very clean and comfortable white down bed. He instantly noticed his father's armour through his sleepy eyes, placed idly in the corner of the room. He had been left in only his tunic and undergarments.

It was a simple square stone room, containing nothing more than a single bed and a wooden bedside cabinet, topped with a silver jug on a white crochet doyley, presumably filled with water, or wine Marcus wishfully hoped, a silver cup and a small glass vase with a single lonely white flower in it, and a marble fireplace near the foot of the bed in the centre of the room with a beautiful painting of a waterfall hanging above the mantelpiece.

His heart skipped a beat as he felt for his pendant, and he sighed with relief as his warm hand met its cool, marbled silver.

He attempted to rise, but immediately let out a growl of pain. His whole body felt like it had been trampled upon by a dozen stampeding bulls and then another dozen for good measure.

With his helmet now removed, he was a rather good looking young man, although he did not think so himself.

His medium-length shiny jet-black hair was partly tied

back into a lazy knot and curtained his pale skinned face as two shy clear blue eyes peered nervously from behind.

He had a small scar over the bridge of his slightly turned up button nose, although he could not recall how he had acquired it, probably a fall as a child or a silly accident.

His small, sad mouth gave him a permanently troubled expression, and coupled with his highly arched black eyebrows, he appeared much younger than he truly was.

At that moment, a pretty young lady dressed in white appeared in the open doorway of the room he was in, accompanied by a tall Palace Guard wearing very decorative looking armour. She appeared to be a nurse of some kind.

'Oh!' she gasped in disbelief. 'You're awake!'

'We cannot delay,' said the Guard to the lady, and then turning immediately to face Marcus, he said, 'King Heath has ordered that he's to see you at once in the throne room.'

Before Marcus could utter a word, he was swiftly helped up out of his bed by the Guard. Marcus winced as the Guard lifted his arm over his shoulder to support him as he hoisted him out of the bed.

'Please,' said the nurse holding up her hands to the guard, 'he must rest.'

'There'll be time enough for that later,' said the Guard.

'My armour,' whispered Marcus weakly struggling to point back as they left the room.

'Don't worry,' said the Guard reassuringly, 'I won't let you leave the walls of the Palace without it. Come.'

Marcus, now with the aid of the Palace Guard, made his way towards the direction of the throne room.

He wondered what would be in store for him. Why did the King want to see him so urgently?

Perhaps he wished to question him simply because he had learned that a stranger had collapsed in full battle armour unexpectedly at the gates of his palace.

Marcus thought to himself that if he was the king, and this was his palace, that he personally would be curious to know why somebody had collapsed outside his gates.

Or maybe it was possible that he had heard the rumours about the Malignants and was curious to know if Marcus could provide some information for him.

Marcus thought that even given the circumstances, if he would explain himself to the King then surely he would understand, even if he was not generally an understanding person.

Marcus knew very little about the King, and not one single person he knew from Soulwind had seen him before, not even Raymond, but whatever kind of king he was, Marcus would soon find out.

From the little Marcus had seen from the Palace so far, mostly being corridors and a hospital bed, it was everything he imagined a Royal Palace might have looked like.

Everything was so clean and spotless, gigantic golden picture frames held paintings of royalty, and great leaders of men hung up high on the great stone corridor walls. Plus, a perfect scarlet carpet trimmed with gold, plotted its way through the great halls of the palace, and impressive chandeliers hung from the high ceilings as wall mounted torches and lanterns lit the way.

Every so often they passed a fine table supporting a rather expensive looking, ornament, trinket, sculpture or vase. Some of the vases were filled with sprigs of lavender, and the perfume of the wildflower filled his nostrils.

As Marcus approached the throne room, the Guard neared two great doors with two palace guards on either side. The Guard that Marcus was with nodded at the other two, and the pair of guards opened the two doors, allowing them entry to the throne room.

With no surprise to Marcus, the throne room was enormous. Several giant cylindered stone pillars helped to support a several-storey high ceiling, with a palace guard standing in between each one, wielding a tall and mighty decorative looking spear, complete with scarlet tassels. It seemed to Marcus that scarlet was becoming a theme in the palace, as every palace guard also wore a cape of scarlet trimmed with gold to match the carpet.

At the far end of the throne room he noticed a grand golden throne with scarlet cushions on top of a stone stair, and on the throne, sure enough, sat a noble looking figure.

Marcus' initial thought was that it was such a privilege to meet the King himself, for few must have ever had the pleasure. But why did he feel frightened? He hadn't done anything wrong, had he?

Marcus and the guard helping to support him came to a halt just in front of the throne. There was a long silence, and then finally the King spoke out, in a loud, booming, echoing voice that carried all the way across the throne room.

'Who are you?' asked the King eyeing up Marcus, 'and what are you doing here?'

Marcus thought King Heath was indeed a forthright king, even if this was only based on a brief first encounter.

King Heath was a portly man and not incredibly tall either. Even though he sat slouched in his throne, Marcus could still tell he wasn't.

Perhaps it was an early mock or a double bluff that he played on people who did not know him very well, a mental edge that he gained upon a first meeting with a stranger, or the more Marcus thought about it, maybe King Heath simply liked to slouch.

Marcus also thought that slouching in one's throne was a very un-kingly thing to do, but who was going to tell him off? He was the King after all.

King Heath continued to sit in this slouched position, one elbow rested upon his throne's arm rest, his free hand fumbling with his big bushy brown beard.

Upon his head sat a heavy and expensive looking solid gold crown.

Marcus now thought it must have been the crown that was responsible for King Heath's slouching, as it looked as if it weighed as much as a small child.

Marcus paused for a moment, paralyzed, stunned, and stricken by the sight of the King, the situation that he found himself in, and also by the tone of his voice. And then finally, after another a brief pause, Marcus mustered up the courage to return with some words of his own, trying his best to remember his manners.

'Your highness,' trembled Marcus, freeing himself from the guard's support, 'I've come here to deliver some urgent news to you.'

'And what,' said King Heath, 'pray tell, would that be?'

Marcus swallowed his fear, 'The last greater village of Termelanor, Soulwind, has fallen. The Malignants attacked us during the night, and I came here because I feared that they may soon decide to assault the Capital, unless something is done soon to stop them.'

The King stared sarcastically at Marcus.

'The Malignants, you say?' snorted the King, 'that mindless rabble of brigands that I've been hearing so much about?' He looked around the room towards his Guards, appealing for laughs, as one or two painfully struggled to humour him. 'Do not make me laugh boy! I control the finest army in Termelanor. What makes you think that my city can be so easily overthrown by these, rebellious, interloping foreigners?'

Marcus could not believe the ignorance he was hearing from the man who was supposed to be responsible for the protection of the Kingdom, his Kingdom.

'My King,' said Marcus desperately, 'I do beg of you not to make the grievous mistake of underestimating the Malignants, as so many have done before you. As far as I am aware, they have taken and now control every single village, holding and farmstead in Termelanor, and despite the efforts of the allied Benign Warriors, and the villages militia combined, they proved no match against them, and now most of our men lay slain or enslaved as a result of their brave efforts. And what's more, Varrick, Captain of the Benigns, now also lies slain at their hands, along with what remained of the Benign Warriors.'

The King stared once more at Marcus. He held his gaze longer this time before he spoke.

'It would intrigue me greatly to discover as to how you have come about this information, stranger?' questioned King Heath suspiciously, continuing to busily fumble his bushy brown beard.

Marcus paused, looking around the throne room nervously as he suspected that no matter what he told the King, he would not be believed.

'I was there, my Lord,' said Marcus. 'I fought in the defence of Soulwind Castle. I watched as my life's friends and village folk died defending it, and just when it seemed that all of our deaths might have been in vain, a small window of opportunity opened that allowed me to escape the castle unharmed. I then journeyed here in the hope that you would not turn a blind eye towards these actions any longer. Your Kingdom needs defending. Do not wait for them to come knocking on your Palace doors. Do not let your city's walls inspire ignorance any longer. If you respond quickly, you may be able to put an end to them once and for all. I have seen what they can do first hand, and please believe me when I say they are a force to be reckoned with. They are strong and numerous, yes, but that's not all of what I saw. There is something different about them. They are no mere invaders, and do not behave as men normally should. And I fear it is only a matter of time, as to whatever their goal may be, that they will aim to target the Capital next. It would make perfect sense to anyone else carrying out their actions up until this point, and it is certainly what I would do if I were in their situation, and I'm pretty sure you would agree with me by saying that it is also what you would do. We have to resolve this now. It is high time that they were stopped before their evil spreads any further.'

There was a long dead silence following Marcus's speech, and then the King finally spoke once again.

'If the Malignants truly are exactly as how you have just described them,' said the King, 'how did you so easily escape? Tell me, exactly how were you the sole survivor of Soulwind Castle's siege?'

'I did not manage it alone,' said Marcus, 'a dear friend aided me in my escape, and he guided me to a secret passage that led to a hidden door that exited from behind the castle. I was then able to make my way here.'

'Hidden doors and secret passage ways? Is that what you would have me believe?' said King Heath. 'I'll have you know that my ancestor built that castle, and such things do not exist. I see through your charade, stranger. You're a Malignant spy, sent here as a cheap tactic to draw out my forces into the open so that you lot can swoop in and ambush us, leaving my city unguarded so that it is ripe for the picking.'

'No, I-.' said Marcus.

'Guards,' said the King, cutting across Marcus with an air of pleasure, his heavily ringed and jewelled hand signalling and waving around in the air, 'do we have any cells free at this moment in time in the dungeons for our new friend here?'

Marcus looked both outraged and confused at the same time.

'Oh, absolutely my liege,' replied a nearby guard smiling with glee, staring cruelly at Marcus.

'Very good,' said King Heath, 'lock him away until I decide what to do with him. Alert Walter in the torture chamber. I expect he shall be busy tonight.'

'At once, my lord,' said the Guard as he went to grab Marcus.

'No!' said Marcus as he shrugged off the guard, 'you're making a grievous mistake. I'm not a spy, I'm here to help you! Please, you must listen to me. The future of your Kingdom depends on it. The future of all of us depends on it. Get your hands off me, you bastard!'

The King said nothing and watched half smiling as Marcus was dragged across the scarlet carpet of the throne room, kicking and flailing feebly, as two members of his Royal Guard took him to the dungeons.

'How long do you think your City will survive without the support from its surrounding villages?' Marcus yelled at the King across the throne room as he was being dragged away. 'They'll wait you out and starve you inside your very own walls, if they don't lay ruin to them first!'

The King's advisor, Stern, who had been standing nearby throughout the recent events of the throne room, approached the King once Marcus's cries were out of earshot. The guard closest to the door could have sworn he had heard Marcus shouting at him something derogatory about his mother before he closed the door behind him.

'Did you think that was wise, my King Heath?' asked Advisor Stern, 'why did you not believe him? What if he had been telling you the truth?'

Advisor Stern was a fairly tall man; he had medium length, smart dark

hair, sarcastic eyebrows, a beaked nose, and small pursed lips. He seemed to make a habit out of rubbing his front teeth a lot with his tongue behind his somewhat permanently closed mouth, as though he was always deep in thought.

Undoubtedly handsome, he stood with his arms behind his back almost constantly, grasping one hand with the other, his keen, piercing blue eyes occasionally darting around the throne room. Normally, when somebody looked in his direction, he would catch their eye immediately, almost as if he saw it coming. The man must have had excellent eyesight and field of view and seemed sharp and on a constant state of alert with the throne room and all of its occurrences, but on this occasion, when he was in the room, he focused only on Marcus, standing behind the throne to the left-hand side of the King, keenly studying Marcus's every development.

At first impression, he gave off an air of intelligence

that Marcus could not explain, for Marcus had noticed him standing there when he was present in the throne room. He had a mild arrogance about him. It seemed to Marcus that Stern did not really want to be there, or that he thought he was too good for his job as the King's personal advisor, but of course Marcus knew very little of the King, and he could not judge Stern's actions accordingly.

'My dear Stern,' said King Heath, 'you have to understand that I must treat all strangers as potential spies. I cannot afford to be too careful, especially during this current state of security, and I must remain wary in the case of spies, trespassers, and even worse, assassins. I admit now that I have done the grave mistake in underestimating this enemy, never dreaming they would ever get this far. I openly admit my error. I did not see them as an initial threat and should have acted earlier on at their source, and now I must pay the price and await their next move, lest I risk the safety, security, and the future of my Capital, and worse, my Kingdom.'

King Heath rose from his throne, unsteady on his feet.

'Careful, m'lord,' said a palace guard as he helped him towards an open window, and there he stood, gazing outward for hours on end, scanning the horizon, ready to give the word to defend his city.

Chapter Six

Gemstones in the Dark

It had been a few long hours since Marcus had had his ankles and wrists shackled together in heavy chains and been slung into his dark, grim, cold and damp cell of the palace dungeons. Although, even after a few short hours of lying down on his damp straw pile he felt the soreness of his body from the morning strangely fade away and begin to leave him. He placed his hand over his pendant and then shook his head thankfully with disbelief at the fact that he was still wearing it.

Single-roomed and dark, with no window, and not much more in it than the pile of straw for his bed, and an old wooden bucket for his waste, he wasn't too sure if it had been emptied from the prisoner before him, as a grim odour emanated from it and tormented his nostrils. Marcus expected a little better from a palace dungeon.

He lay on his side on his straw pile, resting his head now on the palm of his hand, as he squinted at a small mouse nibbling on something in the corner of his cell. He could hear it better than he could see it. He thought of names he might call it, being the only potential company he would ever share down here for the rest of his life, if the torture chamber that evening didn't kill him first.

Nibbles? No, he thought, he was annoyed with himself,

that was too obvious, unimaginative, and lazy. He had not been in the cell for long and already he was starting to lose his mind.

Suddenly, he heard voices as the dungeon doors opened a short distance away from his cell.

'Just a check,' said the first voice, 'everything in order?'

'One fresh in cell three,' said the second, 'he came in not four hours ago.'

'I'll make it quick then,' said the first.

Marcus thought he recognised the first voice from somewhere, but he had

been through so much in the past twenty-four hours that he thought he had been   imagining a lot of things. Maybe he should try and get some sleep.

Marcus heard footsteps approaching his cell, and the amber torchlight illuminated and navigated the grooves in the damp cold cobbled ground as they approached nearer. Yet he did not rise from his straw pile; he just lay there, hands interlocked and resting upon his midriff, staring blankly at the cold dripping and damp stone ceiling.

He heard the footsteps halt outside the door of his cell.

'Is this the one?' said the first voice.

'Yes, that's him,' said the second.

'Get up prisoner, and come here,' said the voice that sounded familiar to him.

Marcus looked back and then rose slowly from the straw pile. A tall silhouetted figure stood before his cell door, clutching a lit torch. Marcus approached the man, staring at the ground as he unenthusiastically shuffled towards him, dragging his clanging chains along the cold damp cobblestones of his cell.

'What's your name?' requested the man.

'Marcus,' he replied flatly.

'Then you must be the Malignant spy that the King informed me about,' said the man.

'Now you listen here, mister,' said Marcus sternly looking up at the man, and rekindling his anger from the throne room, 'I made myself perfectly clear earlier on back in that throne room. I'm not a Malignant, and I'm certainly not a sp-.'

Marcus's sentence was cut short as he caught a glimpse of the man's large bridged nose, a deep scar cut over his left eye and down his cheek, and he noticed his pitch black pupils constrict through the gleaming flicker of the amber torchlight.

Marcus had seen those eyes before.

He had never forgotten the time he had first set his own eyes on them, and he had never seen such eyes like them since, not until now. As grey as the hardest stone, yet as clear as water from the purest spring, and fused with blue from the clearest summer sky, never thinking that the sight of them would still mesmerize him, and for a short moment, he felt lost and dissolved in their natural beauty.

'Slade...?' Marcus whispered as he exhaled.

The man said nothing for a while and stared obnoxiously at Marcus.

'How is it that you know my name, prisoner?' replied Slade suspiciously, almost with a hint of anger to his tone.

Marcus said nothing and remained gazing almost mindlessly into Slade's eyes, and it immediately took him back to the time where he had first met him.

Slade had at one time trained Soulwind's village militia, around about the time when Marcus was a still a young boy. Marcus could recall heading over to the training grounds to watch the village's men in action. Able bodied volunteers from the village would turn up by the dozens to train with Slade and his men.

Slade was an expert combat trainer, and he had developed unique and bespoke combat styles for each of the Kingdom's village's militia, taking into account not only what weapons would be freely at hand but also how to use the natural surrounding terrain and landscape to their advantage should their village come under attack.

Slade was always a happy and sociable fellow despite his military background.

He came across as a naturally powerful and dangerous person, but at the same time, a friendly and gentle human being. A tall strong man, everyone in Soulwind respected him, and he was always pleasant to all, especially the children whom he adored.

Slade would often joke around and play tricks on the children. Marcus's favourite joke was when he would approach them very slowly and sternly as if they were in serious trouble or as though they had done something wrong, before he would stop mere feet away from them and suddenly pretended to draw out his sword quickly to frighten them, before letting out a loud and infectious laugh and ruffling up their hair after he had seen them flinch. Sometimes one or two of the younger ones would trip and stumble onto their backsides.

His men would always leave treats and gifts behind for them whenever they came, and Marcus looked forward to it, even though they did not come around as often as he would have liked them to.

Slade's duty at the time was to journey to all of the greater villages in the Kingdom and train each of their villages' militia respectively, in case of any potential hostile attack. At least then the villages and its people would have some form of defence and protection and a chance to fight back if they ever were attacked.

Slade was particularly fond of the young Marcus. He knew he was an orphaned child, and he had learned about the death of his father, Argyle. Raymond was not around to take care of Marcus while he was away with the army on campaigns, patrols, and training.

Slade respected Marcus's courage, as even from a very young age Marcus would attempt to join in with the men and try to pick up a sword or a shield while they practiced on the grounds. Slade would chuckle and take the weapon off him and then escort him back to the safety of the spectators before telling him,

'When you're older lad, I'll teach you how to fight.'

That was many years ago, and now Slade was the Captain of the Guard in the Kingdom's Capital.

'Slade, don't you remember me?' said Marcus, sounding surprised, even though he was now all grown up. 'I remember you. It's Marcus from Soulwind. Argyle's boy.'

Slade stopped to think for a moment, moving his torch light closer to Marcus to get a better look at his face. He must have recognised him after a while.

'You can't be?' said Slade, 'not little Marcus from Soulwind?'

'Yes,' said Marcus, nodding and smiling with relief. 'You remembered. Slade, please, you have to get me out of here.'

'It is you,' said Slade, still a little shocked, 'I would, Marcus, but it's a little more complicated than that. There's a lot of paperwork to fill in and-.'

'Please Slade,' said Marcus, 'you know I don't belong in here. This is a complete misunderstanding. You must have heard what the King said. Now you know the truth, you can let me out. Every minute counts now.'

'You're right Marcus, this is a mistake,' said Slade. 'All right, I'll let you out but know that this will be on my head if this goes sideways.'

'It won't Slade,' said Marcus, 'I promise.'

'So be it,' said Slade. 'Guard, open up this cell.'

'But sir,' said the guard, 'King Heath has ordered that he isn't to be released at any cost.'

'Leave it with me,' said Slade, 'I know this young man. Now open the door, I won't ask you again.'

'At once Captain,' said the guard as he nervously fumbled with his large ring of keys and finally opened the cell door.

'Come with me, Marcus. Stay close and let me do the talking,' said Slade as he escorted Marcus back to the throne room.

'Thank you, Slade,' Marcus smiled.

Marcus thought that he had been spared in the nick of time from Walter and his torture chamber, however he feared that a fate worse than torture or even death would be in store for him should Slade's sure word fall short.

Chapter Seven

A Royal Hearing

Shortly after Marcus's release from the prison cell, Slade approached the King and explained to him all about Marcus and his past. He told him who Marcus's father was, and all about how Argyle had served in the army, how he was killed in action, and how both he and his son had always been natives to Soulwind. He assured King Heath that Marcus was not a spy or an assassin, and certainly not a Malignant.

Slade had always thought logically and dealt in facts. He was an intelligent man and had a natural gut feeling for anything suspicious. It did not matter which King he served, he always believed in the truth in everything he did.

'Are you sure of this, Captain Slade?' asked the King.

'Beyond any doubt,' said Slade, smiling at Marcus, 'I knew Marcus's father very well, and an invaluable soldier he was indeed. The bandit ambush that their battalion met with on their return from a long campaign in the north was most unfortunate. Raymond, Marcus's guardian, a casualty in the siege of Soulwind was with Marcus's father during that ambush, and very few of them made it back here alive.'

The King stared deeply at Marcus with a piercing sharp gaze, again curiously, stroking his bushy brown beard. 'I am extremely grieved to hear about the news of your late father Marcus, and indeed of your dear friend and guardian, Raymond. They both served in my army well, and of course, I have always trusted and have never doubted Captain Slade's sure word and solid judgement. Guards, release this man.'

The guard released Marcus from his heavy shackles and they thudded onto the stone floor of the throne room, and Marcus massaged his wrists whilst inhaling through clenched teeth.

'Marcus,' said the King, 'I am truly deeply sorry for my decision. You must understand that I had to do what was in the best interests for the safety of my Capital. Can you ever forgive me?'

'There is no need for forgiveness, my King,' smiled Marcus, 'I would have done the very same if it had been my Kingdom under threat and I apologise for my inappropriate behaviour earlier on in the throne room. I should not have acted that way in front of royalty.'

'Not at all,' smiled the King, 'although Marcus, I must say that I was considerably impressed to hear about the great distance in which you travelled to arrive here, particularly after participating in such a brutal sounding battle. Please tell me, why did you not shed the armour on your long journey here? Surely it would have been easier if you had abandoned it?'

'That armour belonged to my father, your highness,' explained Marcus, 'it's all I have left of him now, so you must understand that it holds great sentimental value to me. I could not bear to part with it, not if I was being hunted by a pack of wolves and shedding the armour alone could save me.'

'I understand,' smiled the King before signalling behind him. 'Advisor Stern.'

'Yes, my lord?' approached Stern, his arms behind his back.

'Send word to the royal armoury,' said the King, 'young Marcus's armour is to be restored at once, and better than new.'

'Very good my Lord,' bowed Stern before pointing at two nearby palace guards. 'You two there, have this man's armour taken to the armoury at once.'

'Excellent work Stern,' smiled the King. 'Marcus, you are welcome to stay here at the palace as my honoured guest for as long as you need to until you're back to your old self again.'

'Thank you, my King,' said Marcus with a hint of shock.

'Not at all. It's the least I can offer for falsely imprisoning you. Take it as a small gesture of my forgiveness,' smiled King Heath. 'Now, Captain Slade.'

'My King,' replied Slade.

'Prepare your army to leave at once,' ordered King Heath, 'Soulwind Castle is to be retaken immediately, and with no further delay.'

'At once, my Liege,' bowed Slade with his right hand upon his chest plate and then he turned to leave the throne room.

'Excuse me for interrupting, my King,' said Marcus,

'but I would like to volunteer myself to aid Captain Slade in the recapture of Soulwind Castle.'

King Heath, Advisor Stern, and Captain Slade all turned to Marcus, flabbergasted at what they had just heard.

'May I suggest,' said Stern looking Marcus up and down, 'that one rests for the time being.'

'Advisor Stern is right, Marcus,' said Slade, 'you've only just returned from Soulwind Castle yourself, not to mention covering that great distance you ran to get here, wearing your full heavy armour and spending the night in a cold dark cell with no food in your belly and having next to no sleep. To say that you must be beyond exhausted would be a grave understatement.'

'I feel fine,' said Marcus, 'trust me Slade, plus you know nothing about the Malignants. You'll need me there with you. I have more experience fighting them in my little finger than every soldier in the Capital combined. I'm not meaning to sound arrogant or disrespectful, but my experience and advice could prove invaluable to you.'

'Well if you are sure,' said King Heath, 'then you are more than welcome to join them, and I very much agree Captain Slade that Marcus's experience fighting the Malignants would be more than valuable to both you and your men. However little that may be, it would be far better than going in and fighting an unknown enemy cold.'

Slade paused for a moment, a concerned look on his face.

'Very well,' said Slade, 'Marcus may join us in the recapture.'

'Very good,' said King Heath, 'he will make a fine battle advisor, I'm sure, not to mention a capable warrior. Captain Slade, take Marcus with you to the barracks. There is no time to lose. Marcus, please teach Slade everything you know about the Malignants and brief the men. It's time to quell this invasion before it is too late.'

But at the back of Marcus's head, he feared that it was, indeed, already too late. By now, the Malignants had all the villages well and truly under their control and would surely now be planning on mounting their final imminent attack on the last target that was available to them. The Great Capital of Termelanor.

Chapter Eight

Near-Blind Preparation

The pair stepped outside into the warm sunshine and Slade guided Marcus towards the barracks located in the far corner of the palace grounds.

Marcus saw more of the palace now he was free to roam it in the company of the Captain of the Guard.

On closer inspection, the Capital's stone was undoubtedly of the same kind as Soulwind Castle's if not a little better maintained.

Marcus noticed statues of past kings carved out of huge, single blocks of the stone, placed at different locations around the palace grounds. The largest of these was in the palace gardens… fifty feet high, a smiling king wielding a fine blade and a large tome.

'That's King Norman,' said Slade as they passed it, 'he was the very first king of Termelanor, and the man who founded our Kingdom, King Heath's Ancestor.'

'Where did he come from?' asked Marcus, for few commoners knew the true history of Termelanor. 'Why did he choose to settle here?'

'The thing is, nobody knows the full story, not even King Heath,' said Slade. 'All we know is that he fled with what was left of his people from a distant place to find new and fertile lands, and that they finally settled here and founded Termelanor. There aren't many records regarding the journey they took, not even in our palace libraries.'

The palace gardens were beautiful. Vines of morning glory climbed the exterior walls of the grounds, and rare flowers and plants were arranged beautifully in raised beds. There was also a sculpture of a tree in the centre of the gardens that looked like it had been carved out of the same stone as the statues.

Soon, they arrived at the barracks and the soldiers were all busy in the middle of combat practice. Some sparred one-on-one with blunt edged and wooden swords, while others carried out various strength exercises, and ran laps around the training grounds. New recruits struck at hay dummies with their wooden training weapons and others practiced sword combinations with their drill instructors. Some marched in full armour while others stood at attention.

Everything ceased when Slade approached and held up his hand signalling for silence.

'Attention, everyone,' yelled Slade, 'gather 'round.'

Every single man in the training ground immediately stopped what they were doing and did what he was told, quickly forming a large semi-circle around their Captain to listen attentively.

'Now I'll cut to the chase men, as we're extremely short on time, and every second is precious to us now. As you may or may not be aware, there have been a lot of rumours floating around lately regarding the arrival of certain 'strangers' whom have arrived in our beloved

Kingdom. Well men, I can now confirm to you all that the rumours are true. These Strangers call themselves *The Malignant Warriors*, and they've been rather busy of late to say the least. As of last night, they managed to capture and control every single greater village in Termelanor.'

The men turned to face one another and a murmur of whispers kindled from their ranks.

'Listen in,' said Slade, 'last night, Soulwind Castle was attacked by a large force of Malignants, and this man standing here beside me was the sole survivor. His name is Marcus, and now from fear that the Capital may be the next target for the Malignants, the King has no choice but to finally issue formal war upon this enemy. No longer will we sit back and witness how their actions unfold. The enemy may sound terrifying and seem to have accomplished much in only a short space of time, but you are the Capital's finest, the Kingdom's finest, and not one man here has ever let me down. We may live in a peaceful Kingdom, and many of you have yet to see true battle, but I know what you all can do, and I'd trust my very life to each and every one of you. Fight for me now, and fight for your King, and your country, for today this mockery ends. Today the enemy advances into our Kingdom no further. Today we take back our homeland!'

'Yeah!' yelled the soldiers. 'Slade, Slade, Slade!'

'Ready yourselves, my brothers,' said Slade, 'for we march within the hour.'

'Sir, yes Sir!' cheered the soldiers with broad smiles upon their faces, as they all scrambled in different directions to prepare for battle.

'Now Marcus,' said Slade, 'please join me in my quarters. I think you've deserved something to eat. Tell me everything you know.'

Marcus caught a hungry glint in Slade's curious eye. It was a look that told Marcus that Slade was eager not only to discover a new enemy, but rather the only true enemy that he would ever likely both encounter and confront in his lifetime. The raw and pure look of excitement in the eye of a true and wild warrior, he was about to become sincerely satisfied in himself from facing this new foe. A worthy adversary to test his commanding skills against in combat.

Chapter Nine

A March to Certain Danger

Marcus and Slade spoke long and intensely with each other during their hour in Slade's quarters.

A small, simple and basic room for a Captain of the Guard, the focal point was a large and detailed map of Termelanor mounted on a large wooden table in the centre, with models of allied and enemy forces that you could move around the map, and points of interest such as the greater villages highlighted and pinned.

Marcus and Slade spoke about everything from tactics to battle plans and the strengths and weaknesses of the Malignants to the best of Marcus's knowledge.

Slade sent word for his sergeants to brief his men and within the hour, a battalion of Slade's finest soldiers were fully equipped and ready to move out to counterattack and recapture Soulwind Castle, consisting of a unit of over three hundred strong men and siege equipment.

Slade's soldiers wore fine steel-banded, high-quality hard leather armour, with thick and strong metal helmets, rectangular polished steel banded oaken shields and long sharp spears to match, a longbow and quiver on their backs with a short sword at one side and a sharp dagger on the other.

The battalion was stationed ready outside the Capital's

front gate, and Marcus and Slade made their way out to meet them.

'Listen up men,' said Slade approaching the battalion, 'as I briefly mentioned to you all earlier, not twenty-four hours ago, Marcus here was the sole survivor of the siege of Soulwind Castle, and despite his exhaustion and fatigue he has bravely volunteered to join us. The King believes that any information and guidance that he can provide us on this enemy will benefit us greatly, to which I wholeheartedly agree. He has more experience fighting this enemy than all of us combined and to this day he remains the only person to have ever faced a Malignant Warrior in battle and not ended up either captured or killed. He also informs me that many Malignants were killed by allied forces during the siege, so despite some of the tall tales and wild rumours you may have heard, rest assured that they are not invincible. Do not fear them – they can be killed just like any man. Prepare to move out.'

The soldiers turned face and marched forward when from towards the city's gate, Marcus heard a faint shout.

'Wait!' yelled a voice.

In the distance, Marcus witnessed a rather comical sight.

It was Advisor Stern, running towards Marcus and the men, purple faced and out of breath, clutching his side with two large burly men coming up from behind him, carrying between them what looked like a suit of armour.

Advisor Stern stopped just feet in front of Marcus with his hands on his knees, trying his best to catch his breath, when he finally straightened himself out, brushed off his fancy clothes and struggled to speak.

'I think you might need this, Marcus,' he wheezed, as the two burly men brought the armour forward, 'if you're planning on marching with Captain Slade to reclaim Soulwind Castle.'

'It can't be, can it? It is... that's my father's armour!' said Marcus in disbelief as he was passed the helmet and gripped it in his hands. 'How did you manage to finish it so soon? I didn't think that I'd see it again for a very long time.'

'My boy,' said Stern proudly, 'we have the finest blacksmiths in the entire Kingdom. Our smiths pride themselves on their efficiency and professional handiwork, and with the whole forge's manpower behind the job, between them they made very short work of it, without sacrificing any of the quality, of course.'

'Well, I don't know what to say. Thank you, Mr. Stern,' said Marcus.

'Oh, and how could I forget,' said Stern, 'I have your sword here too, Marcus. The blacksmiths have altered it slightly to better suit your size under my instruction. You'll also find that it's a lot lighter and sharper, but the scabbard design has been left as it is so you can still wear the sword on your back, as I'm sure that's what you're used to.'

'It is what I'm used to,' smiled Marcus, 'and again, I can't thank you enough.'

'Well that's quite all right,' said Stern, 'it's the very least we could do for falsely imprisoning you. Now then,

I imagine Captain Slade would like to make a hasty start to his long march? You'd better put this on, Marcus. You'll be a mighty tempting target for the Malignants if you're wearing nothing but your tunic, don't you think?'

'Thanks again, Mr. Stern,' said Marcus as the rest of his newly restored armour was brought forward to him. It was certainly his father's old armour, there was no doubt about that, however it had been greatly improved.

It felt lighter somehow, and the metal looked brighter and had a shine to it, not like the dull dark iron that it had once been. The dents and nicks had been beaten out of it, and it had a very attractive looking trim around the edges, plus Soulwind's sigil had been engraved into the breastplate.

'I love it,' said Marcus, still inspecting the helmet, 'I wish my father was still alive to see it.'

'I'm sure he'd be very proud and I'm glad you like it,' smiled Stern. 'The smiths will be pleased to have heard of your praises, I'm sure. I'll pay them your compliments, now, Mr. Slade, as you were.'

'Very good advisor,' bowed Slade.

'Best of luck,' said Stern, 'oh, and Marcus, try not to get yourself killed, dear boy. The King really does seem quite fond of you. It's my job to pick up on these things, you know.'

And with that, Stern trod back towards the main gates of the city, with the two burly men bumbling at his heels.

Marcus equipped his newly improved armour, and Slade spoke to him about his unit.

'Speaking about your father, Marcus,' said Slade, 'did you know that this is the very battalion that your father served in when he was with the army? This particular infantry battalion forms the backbone of the Kingdom's Army is primarily used as a patrol, campaign and skirmish unit wherever they're needed, and they're usually the most experienced and deployed unit used in any circumstance.

Within no time, Marcus was soon all kitted out in his newly improved armour and all set and ready to go. Together with Captain Slade and his men, they all marched their long march to Soulwind Castle.

Chapter Ten

Fates Among Leaders

The battalion approached Soulwind Castle when it was in plain sight to them, and as they got nearer to it they found it was very quiet, but there was still an obvious presence there.

The Soulwind banners had already been torn down from the castle's flagpoles, and the gate had been barred and blocked up with flimsy makeshift materials.

Broken arrows and ladders still littered the ground outside of the castle, but there was not a soul in sight. Slade raised his hand and ordered the unit to halt.

'Stay here,' Slade whispered to Marcus, 'I'm going to go and scout it out.'

'I'll come with you,' said Marcus.

'No,' commanded Slade, 'stay with the men.'

'You can't go alone,' said Marcus, 'it's far too dangerous.'

'Very well, Marcus,' agreed Slade, 'The King did not gift us with your presence here for you to merely stand idle and spectate. I must listen to your instincts. I know that it'd be foolish of me not to. You two come as well.'

Marcus, Slade, and two of Slade's soldiers cautiously approached the gate of the castle, shifting across the ground and gripping their swords at their sides. When all of a sudden, a black arrow whistled past Slade's ear and thudded into the ground behind him and all four of them came to a sudden halt.

'That's quite far enough,' said a voice from above the gate.

Slade's entire battalion immediately drew their bows tight with an arrow primed.

'Hold!' commanded Slade, raising his hand to his soldiers. 'Hold your fire!'

Slade turned back to face the gate and standing above it was a very tall, muscular man grasping a crude black bow in his hand. He was covered in black war paint, patterned all over his face and bare torso.

'Who are you?' Slade asked the man.

The man chuckled to himself but did not answer for a while.

'No, no, no, Captain, I presume?' said the man, 'That's not how things work around here now. I'm the one that will be asking the questions.'

Slade growled unapprovingly.

'Slade,' whispered Marcus subtlety, 'I don't remember seeing this man at the siege.'

'Now,' said the man, 'let's try that again. Who dares to approach this castle?'

'I will not partake in your pathetic authority game, Malignant,' said Slade boldly and sharply.

'I'd watch my manners if I were you, Captain,' said

the man, 'if you valued your head, something your Benign ally did not.'

The man signalled to one of the Malignant Warriors behind the wall and up he brought to the man, a wooden crate. The man reached inside the crate and pulled out a bloodied head and threw it down at Slade's feet.

'Varrick...' sighed Marcus.

'Too long had the Benign scum inconveniently delayed our advances,' said the man, 'but not any longer.'

'You monster,' growled Slade, shaking his head before speaking up loud and clear enough so that every man inside of Soulwind Castle could hear him, 'Malignant Warriors! I will say this once and only once, so take heed and listen well. For crimes committed against King Heath and the Kingdom of Termelanor, each man will be punished accordingly; however, any man who steps out here now and lays down his arms will have his freedom granted and made to vow never to set foot in the Kingdom of Termelanor again for as long as he should live and as a result he will be permitted to return to his homeland with his life. These are the King's terms. If you choose to ignore them, not a single man's life will be spared at the hands of myself or my men, as we rightfully claim Soulwind Castle back in the name of our King.'

The Malignants howled from behind the wall like a pack of laughing hyena.

'You are indeed a brave man, Captain of Termelanor,' said the muscular man, 'but I also have a proposition for you.'

The man signalled to his men once more, but this time around they did not bring up a wooden crate; instead, they brought up to the top of the gate two prisoners, blindfolded and gagged.

'Take your men,' said the man, 'turn around, and march back to your precious Capital, and we will set these prisoners free.'

'Raymond!' shouted Marcus as he immediately recognised his old friend.

As Raymond heard Marcus's scream, his muffled voice attempted to cry out. Raymond's face was bloodied and he looked like he had been badly beaten.

'A friend of yours?' said the man to Marcus, 'maybe he'd like to see you once again before he dies?'

The man removed Raymond's blindfold and Raymond looked out towards Marcus with tears streaming down his bloodied face. He was breathing heavily, his teeth clenching his cloth gag.

'You'd better not hurt him,' threatened Marcus, gripping the hilt of his sword and taking a step forward towards the man.

'Or what, little man?' he laughed.

'I'll fight you myself,' said Marcus, 'and if I defeat you, you have to let them go. Both of them.'

The Malignants howled even harder and cried with laughter from the castle once more.

'Marcus,' said Slade, 'don't be so rash. We can find other ways to settle this.'

'Yes, why not?' the man chortled. 'I could use a

little sport.'

'You will do no such thing,' ordered Slade. 'Very well, then, if you will not comply with the King's terms, here are my revised terms. As Captain of the Guard of the Kingdom of Termelanor, you will fight with me, one-on-one, and if you defeat me, I will order my men to stand down and return to the Capital, as you requested. If I defeat you, however, you must release the prisoners unharmed and stand your army down, and then leave and surrender Soulwind Castle to the crown. We can end this all now, one man to one.'

'Very good Captain,' nodded the man, 'and how will I know that your men will not attack once I have slain you?'

'You don't,' said Slade, 'but I could say the same to you and your men. But I promise you that you have my word, on a Captain's honour, a man's honour.'

There was a pause and the man loosened Raymond's gag.

'Don't listen to him, Marcus!' cried Raymond immediately, 'they can't be reasoned with! Don't worry about us, just attack! Do what you have to do!'

The man punched Raymond hard in the gut, winding him. 'Won't somebody shut this fool up? All right Captain,' said the man, 'we will do it your way.'

The man descended the wall without hesitation and collided with the ground with an almighty thud, then rose and walked slowly towards Slade, drawing two long, crude black curved blades. A rusty black metal brassard protected his large and muscular left shoulder, but it looked to

Marcus as if it had been strapped onto him so tightly for so long that the serrated metal ate into his infected flesh, it almost looked like it was a part of him, and the man seemed unbothered by it.

The Malignants now appeared at the battlements for a better view, and a few others remained guarding Raymond and Wyatt.

'Marcus,' said Slade drawing his longsword in response and gripping it tight, 'no matter what happens, please stay out of this.'

'Are you ready to die, Captain?' said the man.

'It's considered polite in Termelanor to know the name of the man that you are about to duel,' requested Slade.

'Well,' said the man circling Slade, 'we're well-mannered in the south, aren't we? Very well, you can call me Vorak for what it's worth.'

'Right you are, Vorak,' said Slade, now also circling him, skilfully flipping his blade around in his hands, 'you can call me Slade. Now Vorak, tell me who you are, and what your business is here in Termelanor.'

'Demanding also,' said Vorak, continuing to circle Slade, 'we were sent here, and that's all you need to know.'

'Sent here from where?' Slade asked, 'by whom, and what for?'

'Questions, questions, questions,' said Vorak shaking his head and smiling arrogantly, 'from the north, and we're here looking for something we were sent to retrieve.'

'What are you here for?' asked Slade. 'What do you need?'

'Enough of your questions,' said Vorak, hungrily licking his lips, 'I grow tired of waiting. It's time for you to show me how well you bleed, Captain of Termelanor!'

Vorak charged towards Slade like a rabid beast and raised one of his blades high above his head and struck down hard at Slade. Slade was a tall man, but Vorak towered over him. Marcus had almost forgotten how magnificent a sword master Slade truly was. Of course, he was very young at the time and he only saw him during practices, but this was for life and death, one on one.

Slade wore very decorative plate armour, which sacrificed no practicality, probably among the best in the Kingdom, but he wore no helmet, his long greying hair blowing in the breeze, his scarlet cape sweeping at his ankles, and he carefully watched his footwork.

Slade parried each and every one of Vorak's heavy blows and was very nimble for an older warrior; it was clear to see why he was Captain of the Guard. Vorak battled like a wild animal, throwing his weight around and swinging relentlessly, desperately trying to claim Slade's head, and yelling out loud with each attack. Vorak had just swiped at Slade's midsection when Slade caught his heel on something sticking out of the ground and fell over backwards, as cheers arose from the castle's battlements.

'Slade!' cried Marcus as he ran forwards.

'Back!' ordered Slade. 'Get back.'

Slade rolled across the dusty ground and back onto his feet, avoiding yet another one of Vorak's rabid swipes. The two continued the duel, as the swings and the parries grew more intense.

Marcus's heart was in his throat the entire time as the cheers arose from the men on both sides for their champions. Vorak was about to unleash a tremendous slash with his blade, but it did not meet its target.

As Vorak was pulling back ready to strike, Slade had unloaded a thunderous right cross with his sword's hilt square across Vorak's nose and jaw, and Vorak crashed to the ground, trembling the earth.

The Capital's soldiers cheered loudly as Slade advanced towards the fallen beast.

Vorak lay panic-stricken on the hard ground, grasping at his shattered nose with both of his hands, blood cascading out from between his fingers, his blades scattered. As Vorak noticed Slade approaching, he desperately looked around and scrambled for a weapon.

'It's over, warrior,' said Slade as he pointed his sword down towards Vorak, 'this is your final warning. Release the prisoners and come quietly, and I'll let you keep your pitiful life.'

Vorak laughed, now missing a few of his teeth, choking and spluttering as blood dripped down from his mouth and onto his chest. 'Do you seriously think that you've won? Fool! We have warriors all over your kingdom now, and your precious villages still belong to us. Take back your castle if you can Captain, but mark my words, your flimsy kingdom will crumble. You have no victory here today, Captain of Termelanor, and you were foolish to ever come here, and an even bigger fool to trust me, and more of us are coming... Slit their throats!'

'No!' cried Slade as he darted his gaze towards the gate.

'Raymond!' cried Marcus.

The Malignants above the gate brought Raymond and Wyatt to the edge of the wall.

'Marcus!' cried Raymond.

'Raymond, no!' cried Marcus.

Raymond and Wyatt's throats were slashed mercilessly by the Malignants and they were both kicked off the side of the castle wall.

In Slade's anger and disbelief, he lanced Vorak through his heart with one mighty thrust of his longsword, and the Malignant archers up on the walls fired their arrows down at Marcus and Slade.

Slade's bodyguards were both struck down by arrow fire before Slade and Marcus retreated towards the safety of the ranks of Slade's men.

When Marcus and Slade were out of range of the arrows, the battle commenced.

'Attack, loose your arrows!' yelled Slade at his soldiers as his men charged forwards and initiated the siege. 'Marcus, we'll stand a much better chance if we can outflank these bastards, even if it is with only a few men.'

'Flank them?' said Marcus, 'But this is a siege, Slade. They have the protection of the walls surrounding them. How are we supposed to do that?'

'Aren't you forgetting about something already,

Marcus?' said Slade, 'your hidden gate. The chances are, the Malignants still don't know that it even exists, so it must still be open.'

'It's worth a shot,' said Marcus.

'Hann!' yelled Slade, 'get over here!'

'Yes sir,' said a tall, dark, fit-looking man with olive skin, wearing the plate armour of the capital, wielding a longsword at his side.

'Fetch me Lars, Erid and Lemy, and meet me back here as fast as you can,' said Slade.

Hann nodded and disappeared back into carnage of the advancing ranks.

A short while later, Hann returned with the men Slade had requested. Lars, a tall, slender and shady looking man wearing full padded leather armour and tall thick leather boots, wielding two sharp, deadly looking daggers; Lemy, a scruffy looking man wearing medium steel plate armour and wielding a round shield and a short sword; and Erid, a stout looking man with a square jaw wearing heavy iron plate armour with his village sigil inlaid with gold on the chest, and wielding a large and heavy broadsword.

'Marcus,' said Slade, 'these men will be perfectly suited for the job in hand. I've personally trained them to specialize in operations such as this. The men and I will keep the Malignants occupied from the front, while the five of you sneak in from behind and do the damage from the inside. It could very well win us the battle. Marcus, these men are now under your command. Show them to the gate and good luck.'

'Yes, Captain,' said Marcus nervously before turning to the men. 'We'll have to be quiet and remain out of sight. Follow me.'

Slade and his men pressed the siege from the front of the castle, and Marcus led his squad out of view and around to the rear in an attempt to enter the hopefully still open still hidden gate.

They took as much cover as they could and trod lightly until they were out of sight of the Malignants.

Marcus guided the men and repeated much of what he had done the previous night himself but in reverse, and they all clung tight to the castle walls. Sure enough, they eventually came to the hidden gate, still flush with the castle wall, exactly how he had left it.

Marcus stood in front of the gate and carefully pushed up against it.

Ever so carefully, he pushed open the door, until the space was now large enough for a fully grown man to pass through, and the four men gasped with surprise.

The torch Marcus had left there the night before had long since burned out, and the tunnel was pitch-black once again.

'Do any of you have a torch that you can light for me, please?' asked Marcus as he turned to the men, 'the tunnel is quite dark inside.'

'I have several,' said Lemy, as he reached a skinny arm into his rucksack and lit one for each of the men.

'Thanks Lemy,' said Marcus, accepting a torch, 'come on, keep the noise down and follow me.'

Marcus led the men back through the cold, damp tunnel.

They navigated the dark passage until eventually they stopped a short distance from the trapdoor above them.

'Wait here a second,' whispered Marcus, 'let me check if the coast is clear.'

Marcus approached the trapdoor. He waited and listened out for any sound.

Dead silence.

'Who would you say is the stealthiest out all of you?' whispered Marcus as he turned again to face the men. 'I need somebody to quietly open the trapdoor that's above me.'

'That would be Lars,' nodded Hann.

'Okay Lars,' whispered Marcus, 'do you think you could open up the trap door for us and secure the room?'

'I think I could manage that,' said Lars with a hint of cockiness in his voice as he slicked back his mousey hair.

'All right,' said Marcus, 'but be careful though, as there may be a rug pulled over it, and you'll have to be quick and quiet as they may have someone standing guard up there.'

'Like a whisper,' winked Lars.

'Good luck,' said Marcus.

Lars approached the trap door, and before Marcus could say anything, Lars had climbed up and flung open the trapdoor in one perfectly fluid motion that if any of the men would have blinked they would have missed it. But strangely very little sound was made and the trapdoor took the rug with it and all, leaving a perfectly clear opening for the men to climb up.

Lars hoisted himself into the room of the keep and signalled that the coast was clear, then he gave an arm down to help Marcus and the others up.

'How did you do that?' asked Marcus in shock as Lars helped him up out of the trap door.

'Don't ask,' said Lars shaking his head and walking towards the door of the keep.

'Colourful past,' said Lemy to Marcus as he shut the trap door behind them.

The room was quite dark and empty, and the battle was raging on outside.

They knew nothing of the outcome so far, but there was a small paned window facing outward that Lars was peering through to assess the ongoing situation.

'Ah,' said Lars, 'we'd better not go out just yet; Slade and his men have yet to breach the gate nor scale the walls. We won't last long out there with just the five of us fighting.'

Hann noticed something from the corner of his eye, a large bundle of Malignant bodies piled up high in the corner of the room, fully clothed. He attracted the attention of the others and they all gathered around the bodies, except for Lars who was still keeping an eye out of the window.

'Casualties from the siege?' questioned Erid, kneeling down.

'Yes,' said Marcus, 'some of the few we managed to slay. I imagine they didn't have enough time to burn or bury them just yet.'

Lemy looked towards Erid with a suggestive facial expression and then he turned to Marcus and did exactly the same.

'No,' said Marcus quickly realising what Lemy was thinking, 'that's a foolish idea. Don't think about it, not even for a second. To start with, we'd get mistaken for one of them by Slade and his men, and secondly, how long do you think it'll take before The Malignants notice their own men turning on each other? They'll realise that something is out of place and attack us for sure.'

'They'll be far too focused on the siege to take any notice of that,' said Lemy.

'All it takes is one of them,' replied Marcus.

'I agree with Marcus,' said Hann, 'however, I do think that Lemy may be on to something here. Marcus, would it sway your decision at all if we partly dressed ourselves as one of them? Over our own attire, I mean, at least well enough to keep us hidden until Slade breaches the castle, then we can quickly ditch the disguises. We can take up separate positions behind the enemy and then take out any unwary Malignant Warriors when we can, whilst keeping out of sight of the allied arrow fire.'

'I think that would be easier said than done,' said Marcus.

'I think it could work,' said Lemy, 'and besides Marcus, Slade and the men know we're in here, so they're going to be keeping an eye out for us anyway,' Lemy continued in a slightly happy-go-lucky manner without a hint of worry.

'And just before Slade and the men breach the walls and the gate, we ditch the disguises and join the attack, we can overwhelm them; in fact, I think it will definitely work. It's flawless.'

Marcus paused for a moment to think. 'What do you think, Erid?' said Marcus.

'I don't think we have much choice,' said Erid, rubbing his stubbled jaw with his broad hand, 'if we burst out that door right now, with our swords held high, we'd get taken out in a heartbeat, and if we go out in full Malignant attire and start hacking away at them we'd either get spotted eventually or killed by mistake when Slade and the men break in.'

'I think we can all agree then,' said Hann, 'that this is a good happy medium, even if I do say so myself.'

'It seems we have little choice,' said Marcus, 'we'll do it your way, Hann.'

Marcus and the others stripped the clothes from the cold, dead, rigid bodies of the fallen Malignants, carefully choosing the least bloodied items of clothing and armour. They were lucky that the bodies didn't smell of death just yet. They all dressed themselves well enough so they would not get noticed and easy enough for them to remove the clothes at the right time.

'Hey Erid,' said Lemy as he lifted a blade over his head and pretended to stab him, 'you look just like one of them, argh!' he continued, laughing loudly.

'Will you stop fooling around Lemy!' said Hann through gritted teeth, 'there are men dying out there.'

'Sorry Boss,' said Lemy.

'Are we all set?' asked Marcus. 'We'll have to be quick. How is it looking out there, Lars?'

'I think Slade is covering a bit of ground now,' said Lars, 'but it's difficult to tell through this misted window, and I don't want to draw any unwanted attention by wiping it clean.'

'All right,' said Marcus, 'when it's safe to do so, we all descend the steps quickly without drawing too much attention to ourselves, and then we split up and take up our positions around the castle. Slade entrusted your skills and lives to me so I have every trust in you. Just follow your instincts like we planned, wait for the breach, and please be careful, all of you.'

'Right,' said the men nodding as they each put on a stern concentrated face.

The men took their positions by the door of the keep ready to exit, while Lars continued to keep watch out of the small window, occasionally putting on some Malignant clothing and armour that Erid was handing him.

'All right,' said Lars, 'nobody seems to be looking this way. Go now, quickly.'

'Okay,' said Marcus, 'last one out, shut the gate behind them. We don't want any of them falling back into here.'

Marcus opened the door and the five dashed out as swift as shadows, lightly padding down the stone steps, making little sound and being ever so careful not to draw any unwanted attention to themselves.

When they reached the bottom of the steps, the group

all split up and blended into the Malignant ranks to find a suitable spot to take up their position.

Marcus shuffled past many Malignant Warriors, each and every one obsessing over the defence of the castle. Not one of them looked twice at him. Marcus took up his position behind a group of Malignants standing with their crude black spears pointing towards the gate on the left-hand side of the courtyard and he stood there waiting, imitating the warriors and taking up a similar stance to them. There was no chance he could take out anyone without the others noticing, not even in a stealthy manner, so he would just have to remain there for now until Slade and the others breached the gate.

He had a quick look around to see if he could spot any of the others. He saw Hann take a similar position to himself but on the right-hand side of the courtyard, however he saw no sign of Lars, Erid or Lemy; he assumed they had taken up positions behind men on the wall.

Marcus could see over the heads of The Malignants and through the gaps in the shored-out gate. The gate had merely been shut and barred using scrap and rubble and anything else that The Malignants could get their hands on, Marcus suspected that it would not be long until Slade's men would breach it.

By now there were a good number of ladders at the wall, and the thud of the allied soldiers ram could be heard behind the already weakened and damaged gate.

This was it. He knew the others would be waiting for the moment the gate smashed open before abandoning their disguises and attacking.

With an echoing crash, the gate flung open, and the Malignants charged forward to meet Slade and his men. Meanwhile, a good number of Slade's soldiers had also scaled the ladders and fought their way onto the wall, in almost perfect synchronisation and timing to the gate's attackers.

'Now,' Marcus thought to himself. There was no one behind him, and an inviting wall of ill-protected backs facing him.

Marcus shed his disguise and drew his newly improved steel two-handed great sword. It now felt much lighter in his hands compared to his father's old oversized and cumbersome weapon.

Marcus gripped the blade in both hands, and as he held the hilt up to his face. He closed his eyes and took a single deep breath before slicing across the backs of four Malignants in one single devastating slash.

The Malignants fell to the ground, screaming in agony and grasping behind at their freshly cleaved and bloodied backs. He swung his sword at another and another and soon, after some confusion, the Malignants had realised what was happening behind them, but Marcus did not stop or slow up his relentless attack. He continued to hack as long as he had easy targets lined up in front of him, giving his enemy no chance to turn around and face him. He sliced and hacked like a mad frenzied butcher as he was engulfed by a red mist, feeling no remorse for the value of the lives in front of him.

The Malignants did not know whether to continue facing the soldiers pouring in through the gate or to turn around to deal with Marcus, but whatever their decision, they would have eventually had a sword in their back.

Hann had been doing much the same nearby, and the Malignants at the gate were thinning as more and more of Slade's men poured into the courtyard and engulfed the enemy while Marcus and Hann continued to cut them down from behind.

The Malignants panicked and formed into a phalanx formation as the allied forces surrounded, encircled and overwhelmed them. They squeezed themselves into a tight circle with their shields and spears facing outward like a gigantic black porcupine. Some begged for mercy as Slade's soldiers cut them down where they stood with powerful strikes, hacks and shield bashes.

A similar scene was unfolding up on the wall, as Malignant Warriors were being forced and thrown off the side of the battlements by Slade's experienced soldiers.

It was over, Marcus knew it. The plan had worked and Marcus had his beloved Soulwind back once again.

As the soldiers finished off the remaining broken Malignants, Slade ordered that any still breathing be captured alive and brought forward to him later for questioning.

Slade approached Marcus in the courtyard as his men heaved up and bound the remaining Malignant prisoners.

'Are you all right?' Slade asked Marcus as he wiped the blood from his sword before sheathing it.

'I'm fine,' smiled Marcus out of breath and drenched in blood, 'how are you?'

Hann approached Marcus and patted him on the back.

'Not bad lad,' he laughed, 'not bad.'

At that moment, Lemy and Erid burst through the ranks, holding up a slouched and spluttering Lars.

'Lars!' cried Hann as they laid him down on the ground.

'Shit,' cried Lars, choking on his own blood, 'the sneaky bastard shanked me.'

'He sprung too soon,' said Lemy to Slade, 'the guy turned around and thumped a dagger into his throat.'

'Even after that I still took a few of the bastards on, didn't I?' wheezed Lars as he smiled proudly, 'don't you worry about that.'

'It's all going to be all right, my friend,' said Hann as he knelt over Lars. 'We'll get you back to the Capital and get you patched up.'

'Spare me the bullshit, Hann,' choked Lars, 'I can see it in your eyes, and I saw it in theirs.' He nodded towards Erid and Lemy. 'I've had it. Hey, lad,' said Lars smiling at Marcus, 'you did good.'

Lars screamed and held his throat as blood gushed out all over him.

'Lars, you don't do this to me, do you hear?' said Erid holding his friend's arms.

Lars let go and released one final rattling breath and

his eyes rolled back into his skull.

'How many more did we lose?' asked Erid.

'One was too many at the hands of these cretins,' said Lemy looking down at Lars. 'Damn it, he was like a brother to me, to all of us.'

'I'll take the register,' said Slade, 'help tie up the rest of the prisoners.'

Marcus sensed a change in Slade, one he had not seen before. He was not himself.

Slade ordered the remaining men to line up in the courtyard and he produced a scroll from his pack and took attendance of the remaining men, marking off as he went with a small stick of charcoal.

'Daryl…'

'…'

'Fargo…'

'…'

'Gento.'

'Here, Sir,' said an old soldier with an eye patch, stepping forward before falling back into line.

'Manny.'

'Sir.'

The register continued, until Slade had reached the end. Slade exhaled, and grasped the list in his palm. 'At ease soldiers,' he said before he walked towards the stone steps and retired into the keep alone.

Shortly after, Marcus and Hann followed Slade up into the keep and found him sitting at the table with his hands in his face.

'How many did we lose, Sir?' asked Hann.

'Eighty-seven,' replied Slade flatly.

'What of the wounded?' asked Hann.

'Forty-two,' replied Slade. 'They were my men Hann, good men. I let them all down.'

'They did their duty to their Kingdom, Slade,' said Marcus, 'they fought well, and they were victorious. Soulwind is finally free once again.'

'Don't you preach to me at the lives of my fallen men,' snapped Slade as he pounded the table with a clenched fist and stared daggers towards Marcus.

'Come now,' said Marcus nervously.

'This is your fault,' said Slade as he stood up from his seat, 'if you'd just died here and hadn't escaped and retreated to the Capital then I never would have found you in that wretched cell, and I wouldn't have been sent out here to win a battle that Soulwind couldn't win by themselves. All those years I trained the village's militia, and for what? All useless and a complete and utter waste of time, and now Lars and my men are dead because of you.'

Slade grabbed Marcus by the throat and forced him up against the stone wall of the keep.

'The Malignants would have arrived at The Capital eventually, Slade,' said Marcus, struggling to speak and gripping Slade's strong hand with both of his, 'and who knows what they might have done to you all. For all we know, what we did was the best move, and you would have lost many more men if it wasn't for your flanking idea.

And you heard what Vorak said, there are more of them out there. The Malignants here would have regrouped and attacked the Capital with the Malignants from the other villages, and they would have killed everyone inside without mercy.'

Slade slightly loosened his grip and Marcus fell to the ground.

'So you see Slade, it isn't my fault,' said Marcus picking himself up and rubbing his neck, 'it isn't anybody's fault. We fought a good fight, and now it's our responsibility to take back and free the other villages too.'

There was a silence and Marcus saw Slade return to his old self.

'Oh my god,' said Slade coming back to his senses. 'I'm so sorry, Marcus. I don't know what came over me. I'm Captain of the Guard for god sakes, and here I am crying like a baby at my losses. Marcus, thank you, you're a better man than I am and than I ever will be.'

'Don't worry about that now,' said Marcus putting on a serious face, 'we have to decide on our next move, while we have the upper hand on the enemy, and we have prisoners, don't we? Let us question them.'

'Yes,' said Slade, 'yes, you're right Marcus. Hann bring up the prisoners to me, at once.'

'Very good, Captain,' said Hann.

'Wait a second, Hann,' said Slade, 'I've just thought of something. All of these bodies here, they're the Malignant casualties from the initial siege. Is that right, Marcus?'

'Yes,' said Marcus, 'that's right.'

'So where are the others?' said Slade, 'the men of Soulwind, and the Benign Warriors?'

'They must be nearby,' said Marcus, 'they wouldn't have had enough time to shift them too far if they all had to be dragged or carried.'

'Marcus,' said Slade, 'I think you should take Lemy and Erid and search the surrounding area for the dead. They'll need something to do to take their mind off Lars. I suggest heading south. We passed nothing on the way here, and I trust you saw nothing behind the castle. Erid is a fair tracker; he'll be able to spot the signs of any recent disturbance to the ground, and I imagine he'd be able to pick up on the signs fairly easily if they happened to be lugging a large number of dead bodies back and forth.'

'Right you are, Slade,' replied Marcus, 'I'll go and find them. We shan't be long.'

'Good lad,' smiled Slade. 'Hann, bring me the first prisoner.'

Chapter Eleven

In Search of the Lost Souls

Marcus exited the keep and descended the stone steps yet again and back down into the courtyard. He saw no sign of Erid and Lemy, but a nearby soldier told him he had spotted them walking out of the front gate.

Marcus passed through the front gate and spotted two figures in the distance whom he presumed were Erid and Lemy.

As he got closer to the figures he could see it was in fact them. Erid was puffing on a gold trimmed short wooden pipe and Lemy was sitting on a rock, unenthusiastically sharpening his blade.

The two turned to Marcus and said nothing and he did not know what to say back to them at first either.

'Slade has tasked us to search for Soulwind's dead,' said Marcus finally. 'Erid, I hear you're a fair tracker. Do you think you could find where the Malignants took them?'

'I can't see why not,' said Erid as he exhaled a large puff of smoke, 'the weather's been fairly dry the last twenty-four hours and the tracks shouldn't have been too disturbed.'

'Fantastic,' said Marcus, 'Slade suggested we should head south. We passed nothing obvious on our march here.'

'I agree,' said Erid, clearing his throat and tapping his pipe on a rock before putting it away, 'let's go.'

The trio made south, as Erid occasionally knelt down and studied the ground to study the disturbances.

'Do you notice anything, Erid?' said Lemy.

'The ground has been recently disturbed quite obviously here,' said Erid, 'but it comes and goes depending on the hardness of the earth. If we just head in this general direction though, we should be on to something.'

'They'd still be far too fresh for us to smell anything,' said Lemy, 'keep your eyes peeled, it'll be dark soon.'

The three continued for a short while longer until Lemy's keen eyes noticed something up ahead.

'Ah,' said Lemy, 'I think we've found your friends, Marcus.'

The sky up ahead was teaming with crows, some circling, others descending to the ground.

'Come on,' said Marcus staring coldly ahead.

The three steadily picked up their pace until before long they were faced with a dozen or so piles of mounded bodies being pecked at by some crows. The three stood there idly for a while unable to speak or move.

'Poor souls,' whispered Lemy, 'such a sad waste of life.'

The three split up and walked between the piles of bodies and the surrounding area. Marcus spotted a distinct looking body and called out to the others.

'Over here!' cried Marcus.

'What is it?' questioned Erid.

'This must be Varrick,' said Marcus as they looked down at a lone body that was dumped away from the rest of the bodies and had been beheaded.

'We'll have to arrange for the bodies to be brought back to Soulwind castle for now,' said Erid. 'We can't leave them here for the crows. Their families will surely want to give them a proper burial.'

'Come on, we did what we set out to do. There's no use lingering here any longer,' said Lemy, 'let us return to Slade and the others.'

Why did the Malignants drag Varrick's body away from the pile of the dead before beheading him instead of doing it beforehand while he was back at the castle? thought Marcus. Could it have been that they had recognised him somehow as the leader of the Benigns? Marcus feared that the Malignants may have found something on Varrick's body that could have been significantly useful to them. As leader of the Benigns, Varrick must have had a fountain of knowledge and intelligence regarding the Malignants and would have kept them close at hand at all times. Marcus shuddered at the thought of the Malignants getting their dark hands on information and plans that would have been of use to them in their advancement. But either way, it didn't matter now, the damage had already been done. They had already come this far and Marcus hoped that they wouldn't have had the chance to act upon anything they potentially could have found on Varrick. Intelligence, or victory at Soulwind castle or otherwise, the Capital was next.

Chapter Twelve

A Regretful Report

Marcus, Erid, and Lemy slowly trod back to the castle, their heads slumped and the heavy weight of the emotion and the sight of the deceased upon their shoulders. None of them said a word the entire way back.

As the three neared the castle once more and stamped up the steps back into the keep to meet Slade, he was still sat at the table, softly conversing with Hann.

'Ah, gentlemen,' said Slade, 'did you have any luck finding the fallen?'

'We found them sir,' said Erid, 'they're stacked up in piles a short distance directly south of here, just as we thought.'

'Very good Erid,' nodded Slade, 'all of you, well done. We'll make arrangements to identify them and have them returned to their respective families in good time.'

'What of the captives?' asked Marcus, 'what did they say?'

'Neither of them would speak a word,' said Slade. 'They'll need to be sent back to the Capital for interrogation.'

'So what do we do next, Captain?' said Lemy.

'Soulwind is now free,' said Slade, 'and the men need to rest. We should return to the Capital and replenish our numbers before we mount the next attack on the Malignants, especially if we're likely to be outnumbered again, and I highly expect that we shall be.'

'Captain Slade,' said Marcus, 'I'm sorry but I must interfere and disagree. I don't think we should wait another second before we mount the next attack.'

'Marcus,' said Slade, 'I admire your persistence, but we simply don't have the numbers, and even if we did, the men are absolutely exhausted from the battle, and as much as I'd like to press on the advancement myself, we have little choice but to regroup at the Capital.'

'Which would also allow the enemy enough time to regroup their army and mount their next attack on us,' interrupted Marcus, 'don't you see, Slade? We don't have the luxury right now of taking our time assessing each battle in your traditional manner. No disrespect to you, but we have to take the fight to them while we still can. We must adapt to fight this foe in order to defeat them.'

Slade looked half annoyed, but he also knew Marcus had a strong point.

'Look,' said Marcus, 'we don't think that any of them escaped the battle, am I correct? Which means the chances are that the Malignants in the other villages have no idea what even happened here, so I think it'd be a foolish idea not to immediately mount the next attack. An element of surprise would give us a far greater advantage against an off-guard enemy than regrouping and gathering reinforcements ever could. Please don't feel that I'm trying to insult your honour as a captain, or disrespect your commanding skills,

Slade, but I'm just thinking what would be best for the survival and future of the Kingdom.'

'I knew it would annoy me when the King assigned you to be my battle advisor for the siege Marcus,' said Slade, smiling humbly.

'Let's say for arguments sake that we did press on with the next attack,' said Lemy, 'the question we have to ask ourselves then is how do we decide which village we're going to free next?'

'Well, Bridgewood is directly north of here and the next closest village to Soulwind,' said Slade. 'I have a dear friend who lives there. His name is Buck and he's a good man. There's a chance he may be alive if he was taken captive.'

'Then we should head there at once sir,' said Hann with a concerned look on his face. 'I can prepare one hundred and fifty of your finest remaining soldiers to be ready to march north on your command.'

'I don't know, Hann,' said Lemy, 'what if one did manage to somehow slip off and escape from the battle and alerted the Malignants at Bridgewood? Then we'd be in serious trouble.'

'That's the risk we're going to have to take, Lemy,' said Marcus. 'If there's the slightest chance that we can catch them off guard there, or even better, ambush them, then the odds will tip in our favour.'

'Then it's settled,' said Slade. 'Hann, just as you suggested, gather one hundred and fifty of the men who are best fit for battle and have them ready to march out at once, gather what rations and supplies we can spare, and have a few soldiers remain here to tend the wounded and assign the rest to make for the Capital with the prisoners. The dead will be reunited with their families and put to rest in good time, but for now have word sent to Lieutenant Aaron at the barracks to meet us north of Bridgewood as soon as the request is received with whatever reinforcements they can spare.'

'Very good sir,' smiled Hann as he bowed and left the keep.

'Marcus,' said Slade, taking a deep breath, 'I thank you for the priceless services you've offered to both me and my men, and of course to the Kingdom of Termelanor. Your village is free now. You've done more than anyone in your village could ever ask of you. You're free now to return to your beloved village. Leave the rest to me and my men. I do not ask you to come with us.'

'If you thought you were going to get rid of me that easily,' smiled Marcus, 'then I'm afraid you're horribly mistaken, captain.'

Slade smiled back at Marcus and shook his head.

'I guessed that might have been your answer,' said Slade. 'Your spark and your courage amaze me, Marcus.'

'I wouldn't deserve to live in Termelanor if I didn't help fight for her freedom,' stated Marcus, 'and if the Malignants succeed in taking Termelanor, there won't be a Soulwind for me to go back to.'

'Well Marcus,' said Slade, 'with Lars gone, Hann, Erid and Lemy are a man down. I'm sure they'd be pleased to have you in our ranks, as would I. If your mind is made up and that is what you truly want, you've proven yourself a more than capable soldier.'

'I'd be more than honoured to,' smiled Marcus, 'thank you, Slade.'

'Then we must leave immediately for Bridgewood to ascertain the fate of the inhabitants there,' said Slade, 'if we travel through the night and attack first thing at dawn hopefully we should catch the Malignants there while they sleep and save any captors that they may have locked up. Erid, Lemy, arrange for the men that are staying behind at the castle to also have the Malignant corpses searched and salvaged before they're piled and burned. I shall meet you outside the castle gates with the others for the night's march.'

'At once, Sir,' said the pair.

Marcus felt great pride being accepted within Slade's ranks, for the Capital's men were some of the finest that the land had to offer, and he had always dreamed of being a warrior. But more so, he now felt closer to his father than he ever did, serving in the same battalion and both protecting and defending his beloved homeland.

Chapter Thirteen

Moonlit March

It was a clear evening and there was not a cloud in the sky. The moon hovered over the castle like an almost-perfect giant pearl pulsing out a band of light, which illuminated the valiant violet sky.

The rest of the men vacated the castle, aside for the select few that were chosen to remain behind to tend to the badly wounded and the rest of the selected soldiers made out for the Capital with the Malignant captives.

Slade tasked a couple of the younger, fitter soldiers to abandon their armour and rush ahead to the capital to deliver the urgent message to the barracks. Marcus did offer himself to do this, however Slade was adamant that he should stay with the men.

Meanwhile, Marcus was stood within the ranks alongside the one hundred and fifty or so of Slade's chosen men that were selected to march north to Bridgewood.

He overheard a few of the soldiers getting anxious and speaking between each other, and they had heard that Bridgewood was their next target and were wondering why this was the case.

'I have a cousin in Greystone Ridge,' said one soldier, 'what if she's still alive and is in need of our aid?'

'Aye,' said another, 'my mother is back home in Sycamore

Valley, I have not heard from her in months.'

Marcus understood the questioning of the captain's decision amongst the soldiers with friends and family at the other villages, however he quietly agreed with Slade's decision of heading to Bridgewood next, being the nearest and the most direct village to Soulwind, but he continued to stand in silence and kept himself to himself.

'Soldiers,' said Slade, 'you are the chosen men who have been selected to mount the next immediate attack to liberate the village of Bridgewood from Malignant infestation. Now, just to brief you all very quickly, the most direct route to Bridgewood is if we follow the waning crescent river north of here. We should remain and stick close to the west bank and move towards the forestry cover on our approach to the village. Hopefully they won't know that we're coming, so light and noise discipline on our approach please, all of you. Is everything set and ready, Hann?'

'Yes sir,' said Hann, 'the men have already left for the Capital with the prisoners and the runners are on their way to request for reinforcements. The others are going to remain here with the wounded. We're all ready when you are, Captain.'

'Excellent, Hann,' said Slade, 'let us not waste another second. Move out men. The march should take us the best part of the night, and we attack at first light.'

The soldiers moved out and marched forwards, heading northeast in single file, grasping their lit torches towards the west bank of the waning crescent river.

It was a few hours march to Bridgewood, but the night was

fairly clear and the men were lucky enough that the moon was so high and bright and they had plenty of torches between them. Slade led the pack and the rest of the men followed suit.

A short while into the march, already bored, Marcus caught up to and walked alongside Slade.

'Captain,' said Marcus, 'what do you suppose we'll discover when we get to Bridgewood?'

'I don't know, Marcus,' said Slade, 'your guess is as good as mine, although I think it'd be safe for us to assume that the Malignants will have the place well and truly under their control by now, and that we should prepare for the possibility that they may be expecting us, and as you know there has been no word from the other villages for weeks.'

'I don't think the other villages were so lucky to have the luxury of evacuating the women and children as Soulwind did,' said Marcus, 'we have Varrick and his men to thank for that.'

'We can't abandon the hope that the Malignants have taken live captives,' said Slade, 'it's imperative that we prioritise the safety of the villagers if any have indeed been taken prisoner.'

'How many do you suppose will be there waiting for us?' asked Marcus, 'with over two thousand at the initial siege, do you think we're probably looking at similar numbers?'

'We have good men with us, Marcus,' said Slade, 'and they all fought well at Soulwind. Providing that we do not alert them on our approach, we should have the upper hand on them, outnumbered or not.'

Marcus spoke long with Slade, and after a while longer into their march, the shroud of the forest to Marcus's left immediately caught his eye, and he glanced sheepishly towards it, gripping his torch tightly as a slight shudder came over him.

Marcus could not help but be drawn to the forest, although he tried his hardest not to look at it.

Tales from his youth flooded back into his memory as the forest frowned at him, tales that he remembers the villagers used to speak of when he was a child.

It was a shady forest, dark and very quiet, and no birds sang in it or flew over it. It was silent and hazy, and no leaves grew on the skeletal branches of the trees, and a carpet of mist blanketed the forest floor.

It was the forest of Darkshade, and it lay in between the south of Bridgewood and the north of Soulwind.

Once a lush and vital part of Bridgewood's forestry rotation and lifeblood, it was immediately cut off from the rotation when reports of the lumberjacks that were felling in that area mysteriously began to disappear.

Some folk swear to this very day that they can still hear terrifying noises echoing out of Darkshade Forest if they wander too close, and others had even claimed that they had witnessed shadows and ghostly figures drifting through the forest.

'That's one forest I can safely say we won't be using as cover, Marcus,' whispered Slade, 'and I intend to stay as far enough away from it as possible. I've heard from the

Bridgewood folk that it's haunted, and not a pleasant place to drift too near to.'

'I know,' said Marcus, 'I've heard enough about that place to stay well away.'

'Very wise,' said Slade, 'we should keep our voices down for now. Marcus, you'd better fall back in.'

'Yes Sir,' said Marcus, taking one final look at Darkshade as they passed.

The march was long, and the men continued to trudge north, single file and hugging the bank of the river in the darkness, a torch each in hand, the light reflecting on the water's surface like a long flowing snake of flame.

Marcus quickly grew bored of the single filed silence and apprehensiveness once again.

He thought they were probably far enough from Darkshade by now to at least keep a conversation down to a whisper and he looked around to see who he could pester.

Hann was behind him, so Marcus slowed down his pace slightly and deliberately allowed Hann to catch up with him.

Hann looked pleased to have somebody to talk to, and Marcus thought they were far enough from Slade so they wouldn't get into trouble for talking.

They spoke long until the conversation turned to the background of Hann and the other men, and Marcus was curious to hear their story.

'I was an orphaned boy when Slade found me all those years ago,' said Hann, 'I can't really remember my parents. All that I remember is living on the streets and in the alleyways of the Capital's poor district. I ate scraps of food and waste, and rats, and sometimes worse, just to get by. I slept rough on the streets when I couldn't find a place to sneak in to at night. I often found myself getting beaten up by the bigger lads and sometimes even by the city guard. I had nothing, and that's when I met Lars. He took me under his wing and taught me how to pickpocket and he even watched over me. I was still very poor but I was better off than I was. I had rags on my back and half decent food in my belly for once, and to top it all off I wasn't getting beat up as often. Unbeknownst to me at the time, Lars was a highly wanted man and a renowned thief in the Capital going by the name of Haze. Then one sunny Monday morning, the city guard and the King's men found him, with me in his company. He was destined for the stocks, but Slade put a stop to it and demanded we were sent to the barracks. He gave us both a second chance. We eventually met Lemy who came to the army from Bouldershore, and Erid from Goldstream. After years and years of intense training we made the cut and earned Slade's respect and trust. When Slade put us all together, our pasts and our skills seemed to complement each other, and the missions and campaigns that Slade sent us on only proved to sharpen our skills, and eventually we were used by Slade mostly for sabotage and behind enemy line missions. He also taught each of us personally in combat.'

'You mentioned that Lemy was from Bouldershore,' said Marcus. 'How did he end up in the army?'

'Lemy was caught smuggling rum into his village

of Bouldershore,' said Hann, looking back at Lemy who was walking close to Erid and watching his footing as he walked. 'He was captured by the harbour guards and sent to the Capital for trial. He was then given three options: prison, death, or the army. Slade noticed his skills early on and he quickly picked him out of the ranks.'

'I'm going to visit all of the villages if we ever make it through this,' said Marcus.

'As will I,' smiled Hann. 'Fall in Marcus, we'll be in Bridgewood soon.'

Marcus's heart was in his throat on the approach to Bridgewood, and it was evident in the faces of the rest of the soldiers that they had already accepted their fates. Certain death awaited them under what would soon be the shroud of the tall canopy of the gargantuan pine forest. But no matter what they would face there and no matter what the likelihood be of their defeat, they would still fight, even if a graveyard of roots and limbs awaited.

Chapter Fourteen

Forestry Façade

The men entered the forestry of Bridgewood and extinguished their torches on Slade's command. It was still quite dark, so the men turned in for a little rest under the large pine trees for what remained of the last few hours before dawn, save for Erid and Lemy who both kept a watch on the surround.

As the sun rose at first light, the men awoke slowly and quietly shifted and shuffled through the undergrowth until they were on a ridge overlooking the village of Bridgewood. They crouched there and quietly overlooked the village from the shadow and cover of the forest.

Positioned due west of the Capital, and placed at the heart of the thick forestry which surrounded it, the village of Bridgewood supplied the Kingdom with much of its most plentiful resource; lumber.

Bridgewood was built amidst a colossal pine forest and acquired its name from the large bridges that had been constructed from its famous timber to cross the rivers that flowed through the forest. The bridges were beautifully carved by local craftsmen and the bridges held shapes and designs that even told the history of the village.

The inhabitants of Bridgewood lived in cosy log cabins and exported logs to the Capital for trade. The people of

Bridgewood were master lumberjacks and woodsmen, passed down their skills from generation to generation. They were no strangers to the skill that was woodcutting and had developed efficient ways to maximize the harvest of their precious and primary trade resource.

There did not seem to be any movement down below as the entire village slept. Malignant tents were visible in the dim light and the faint glow of the dying fires littered the ground around the enemy camp. No silhouettes were visible around the campfires, which implied that the whole village was still asleep or waiting for them.

'What do you think, Captain?' whispered Marcus to Slade.

'It looks like they had no idea that we were coming, after all,' said Slade. 'Can you make out any movement down there at all, Hann?'

'Not at the moment,' said Hann, 'but providing that the tents are at full capacity, I'd say we're going to be outnumbered by at least ten to one.'

'Ten to one?' said Marcus. 'How are we meant to contend with that? We're one hundred and fifty strong.'

'I say we burn the bastards alive in their tents,' said Erid, 'it's the least they deserve for everything they've done.'

'Erid is right… it's better than they deserve,' said Lemy, 'and burning them while they sleep should even out the score for us at least.'

'Perhaps it'd be a good idea if we set a couple men at the end of each bridge that enter and exit the village,' said Marcus, 'that way we can prevent any from escaping.'

'Or better yet, burn the bridges at the same time as we light up the tents and keep them trapped in here,' said Lemy. 'I don't want a single one of those bastards getting away.'

'No, that's far too destructive,' said Slade, 'I understand your emotions are running high Lemy, but we can't let them distort our plan. Those bridges are over a hundred years old, and we may need them ourselves should we need to fall back.'

'And we may have to resort to that,' said Marcus, 'however, I'd be happy to volunteer and wait at one of the bridges to prevent any stragglers from escaping.'

'Right you are, Marcus,' said Slade. 'Erid, you go with Marcus and wait at the eastern bridge. Hann and Lemy you take the western bridge and wait for my command. And as much as I hate the idea, you may have to resort to burning them.'

'Yes,' smiled Lemy, exposing a silver tooth. 'Here Marcus, Erid, take these,' said Lemy handing Marcus a large thick, corked glass bottle filled with a dark liquid. 'Don't spill it and keep it away from any fire until you need it.'

'What is it?' said Marcus, taking the bottle and inspecting it.

'It's pitch,' said Lemy, 'well, my own recipe to be exact, it's about a thousand times more volatile. Pour that on your end of the bridge when Slade gives the order and try not to get any on your hands. Make sure you throw your torch into it if you don't want your arm to catch fire.'

'There still doesn't seem to be any sign of movement down there,' said Hann.

'Make ready men,' said Slade. 'Prepare to move out.'

'Perhaps we should use a little of this undergrowth and brush to help disguise us against the forest background,' said Marcus, 'it should make us a little harder to detect. It won't be much but it should give us a little light cover.'

'Sharp thinking, Marcus,' smiled Slade. 'Pass the word back to the men and order them to stuff the gaps of their armour with undergrowth.'

'They still appear to be asleep, Captain,' said Hann, 'if we move out now we should still catch them off-guard.'

'I'll take the men and spread out position ourselves around the tents,' said Slade, 'just like we planned. Marcus, make for the bridge and wait for my signal.'

As Slade and his soldiers quietly moved into position, Marcus and Erid made it to the eastern bridge and crouched down out of sight while they waited for Slade's command.

Marcus was about to ask what was taking them so long when suddenly they saw the tips of the enemy's tents ignite into flames, one by one, like a hundred burning candles.

The deafening screams of the Malignants erupted immediately as they were burned alive in their tents.

'Hann!' yelled Slade in a booming voice that carried across and echoed over as far as the bridges, 'get over here now!'

'Slade's in trouble,' said Marcus, 'we have to go and help him, Erid.'

'Wait,' said Erid grabbing hold of Marcus's arm, 'our

orders were to wait here.'

'You heard him, Erid,' said Marcus pulling Erid along, 'we have to get over there.'

Slade was obviously in trouble and Marcus and Erid sprinted across the wooden bridge and into the village Bridgewood, where the scene of extreme carnage awaited them.

The Malignants were in a panic-stricken state and ran in every direction like frightened sheep screaming and howling as their skin was toasted by the flames. They scrambled for buckets of water and rolled in the dirt to try and douse the flames.

Meanwhile, Slade's men hacked away at whatever they could. Most of the Malignants had been burned in their sleep or as they retreated in panic. Both enemy and ally seemed utterly confused as to what was happening and fought desperately for their survival.

'The shamans predicted this would happen!' Marcus heard one Malignant scream in terror, 'the forest is alive with anger and is fighting back!'

Initially outnumbered by ten to one, those numbers were suddenly reduced to a more favourable odd after a large portion of the enemy was scorched alive.

The light of the rising sun still hadn't quite risen above the branches of the giant pine trees, but the torches and the dying embers of the campfires helped to illuminate the village as the allied soldiers hunted down the fleeing Malignants.

Marcus and Erid wasted little time in joining in with

the bloody and fiery mayhem as they slashed at and cut down the fleeing enemies.

The battle raged on, and the embers of the extinguished campfires that were still smouldering on the ground were kicked into the air as the intensity of the fighting increased.

Marcus spotted Slade in the heat of the battlefield and made right for him.

'Marcus,' said Slade, 'quickly, the men tell me they have prisoners held up in the clearing just over there. They overheard one of the Malignants shouting at one of his comrades to kill them before we get to them. You have to help them, Marcus.'

'Right away, Slade,' said Marcus rushing off towards the clearing.

Marcus fought on through the village until he came to a blatant gap in the forest, and in the clearing, sure enough, was a long line of prison cages, full of prisoners.

Marcus approached the cages, when out of the forest emerged two Malignant warriors, holding a knife to the throat of a pretty young woman.

'That's close enough, scum,' said the Malignant, 'step any closer and we slit her throat.'

Marcus held his sword out towards the Malignants and stood with his legs apart, ready to fight.

The Malignants chuckled as Marcus stood there, outnumbered and pathetic. They tossed the young woman to the ground, and they both advanced forward to attack Marcus.

Marcus parried the first attack and made short work of

the first Malignant before quickly finishing off the second, and he immediately ran over to check if the young woman was unharmed.

At that moment, a large group of Malignants approached Marcus from behind and he found himself trapped inside the clearing.

The next thing, Erid and Lemy arrived from out the cover of the forest and instantly dispatched the large group of Malignants.

'Marcus, free the rest of the prisoners,' said Lemy, 'we'll make sure no more get past us.'

Marcus hurried over to the prisoners and tried to force open the cage.

'Who are you?' said a frightened old man, trembling as Marcus tried to force open the lock.

'My name is Marcus. I'm here with Captain Slade from the Capital and we've come to set you all free. Now stand back while I try and break open this lock.'

While Marcus was struggling with the lock, Hann showed up from behind him and bust it open with a large woodcutting hatchet. Marcus opened the gate and Hann continued to unlock the remaining cages as the battle continued raging on behind them.

'Women and children,' shouted Hann after he had finished breaking open the locks, 'make for the thick of the forest and hide somewhere out of sight. Any man who has the strength to fight, pick up whatever weapon you can find and follow me and help us take back your village.'

Marcus ushered the women and children to safety

and the now free men of Bridgewood took up whatever weapons they could muster and followed Hann into the thick of the battle.

As soon as the women and children were safely hidden away, Marcus rushed back over to rejoin the battle.

The men fought on hard for the remainder of the battle, and they finished off what was left of the retreating Malignants. The rising sun now fully illuminated the village through the cover of the branches of the colossal pine trees.

In the full light of the morning, after all of the Malignants had been taken care of, the survivors of the battle met with Slade and his men at the centre of the village.

Slade once again took the battalion register and found that miraculously, he had sustained very light casualties, and had only lost eight men. The rest had only sustained minor injuries, if they had any at all.

The men all praised each other at how well the battle had gone as they took in the aftermath of the carnage around them, but Bridgewood was a free village once more.

Chapter Fifteen

Malignant Motives

Amidst the aftermath of the battle, Slade was talking beside a large campfire with a hard, rugged looking man. They spoke as old friends and they seemed very happy to see one another.

The man was none other than Buck, Slade's dear friend.

'Did the Malignants ever mention what they had in store for you?' said Slade. 'Did they say what they were planning to do with the captives?'

'If I knew all the answers, I'd tell you, Slade,' said Buck. 'I remember the day that they stormed the village and overpowered our militia. Our men put up a fight but they were quickly overwhelmed. Most of them were killed, but they captured the rest of us and locked us up. We had no choice but to surrender, Slade, they were slaughtering us like animals. We had no opportunity to prepare, and we had no idea that they were coming.'

'I'm so sorry to hear that, Buck,' said Slade. 'What did they do after they captured you?'

'That was pretty much it,' said Buck, 'they threw us scraps every so often and they spat on us if we ever tried to speak to them, or worse, we had no idea what they had planned for us, possibly slavery? Your guess is as good as mine. They would rape women in front of their husbands to get them to speak, and torture and butcher children in front of their parents to achieve the same desired effect. They'd kill once in a while, when we wouldn't answer their questions, but we never told them anything.'

'What sort of things did they ask you?' said Slade.

'Always the same thing,' said Buck, *'we know it's here, so tell us where you're hiding it.'*

'Tell us where you're hiding it?' repeated Slade, 'what did they mean by that? What were they talking about?'

'We never found out,' said Buck, 'they'd just kill us if the answer wasn't what they wanted to hear.'

'Once again, I'm sorry for the loss for your people, Buck,' said Slade, 'and I wish we could remain behind here and help what is left of your people, but it's imperative that we continue on with the fight while we still have healthy numbers. It should be safe enough for all of you to remain here in the village for now, however I'm afraid I can't spare the men to remain here to aid you right now. We can spare some rations and some field dressings for your sick and wounded, but after that I'm afraid you're on your own, until this is all over and the Capital can help Bridgewood rebuild.'

'We completely understand, Slade,' said Buck, 'the village can spare you a few able bodied young men to continue on with your march. There are a few here who can still fight, and I'm confident that they'll volunteer. I would volunteer myself, but I'm not as young as I once was, so I'm afraid I wouldn't be much use to you.'

'I understand, my old friend,' said Slade. 'I'll accept any aid that your village can offer us.'

'The women can tend to our sick and wounded,' said Buck, 'Bridgewood will recover from this, as will all of Termelanor.'

'I also have the confidence that it will,' said Slade, 'just one more thing before we leave, Buck. Did you happen to receive any word from any of the other villages before you were attacked?'

'I'm afraid not,' said Buck.

'I feared that that may have been the case,' said Slade, 'farewell for now, Buck.'

'It was good to see you again, my old friend,' said Buck, 'best of luck to you, and please, stay safe.'

Marcus was helping the men prepare for the long march north to Goldstream, when he was approached by a shy young lady clutching a small package in her hands. He recognised her as the girl he rescued from the two knife-wielding Malignants earlier on in the battle.

'I wanted to give you a little something,' said the girl, 'for saving my life.'

'Oh, don't mention that,' smiled Marcus, 'we were just doing what needed to be done.'

'Please,' said the girl, 'take it, it isn't much, just a few rations that I was sparing. I'm sure you'll need them for the many battles ahead.'

'Thank you,' said Marcus, accepting the package.

'Will you come back and visit us one day when all this is over?' said the girl.

'I will,' smiled Marcus. 'I plan to visit all of the villages when this is all over, but I'll make sure I visit Bridgewood first.'

'I hope you do,' said the girl approaching Marcus and rubbing a smudge of dirt off his cheek. She kissed him tenderly on the lips and smiled as she looked deep into his eyes before she turned away and headed back into the village.

Slade's men welcomed the young men of Bridgewood into their ranks. They were all strong, sturdy men wielding great big two-handed woodcutting hatchets, and all hungry for revenge.

Chapter Sixteen

The March Continues

The men wasted little time in continuing their march north and left the village of Bridgewood behind them remarkably Malignant-free.

The men were bedazzled at the fact that they had somehow managed to leave the shroud of the forest with their lives and sustaining such light losses.

Slade witnessed proudly as many of his men smiled at Marcus and patted him on the back as they passed by him and continued their long march to Goldstream.

With the cover of the forest behind them, they came back out into the fresh, cool breeze of the open plain.

They had marched onward for a fair distance when one of the soldiers noticed a cluster in the distance.

'Be wary men,' said Slade, 'it could be a scouting party of the enemy.'

As the men approached closer to the cluster, they soon found it was not an enemy scouting party; it was none other than the unit of reinforcements that Slade had sent for shortly before their departure from Soulwind Castle. They had travelled west to meet them from the Capital along the Open Pass Road.

'Captain Slade!' yelled a voice from the ranks of the cluster.

A young, pale, blonde, intelligent looking man approached the company and spoke without delay.

'Here are the men you that you sent for, Captain,' saluted the young man, 'it's all that's left of your unit sir, as you requested.'

'Aaron,' smiled Slade, 'it's so good to see you again, my friend, but were there no extra men to spare at The Capital?'

'The King demanded that both the city and the palace guard remained at the Capital, and that his personal unit of Sterling Guard remain behind in reserve in case they came under attack themselves,' said Aaron. 'I pleaded with Advisor Stern but he could not persuade the King to leave the city so undermanned.'

'That's understandable,' said Slade, 'did the men make it back with the Malignant Captives?'

'The runners that were sent ahead arrived first with your message, Captain. We prepared to leave as soon as we'd received your word,' said Aaron. 'I presume that the men arrived with the prisoners shortly after we left. We haven't been waiting here too long. We were surprised to see you so soon, and still in such healthy numbers?'

'Let us say that the fortune of battle swung in our favour Lieutenant,' smiled Slade. 'Aaron, allow me to introduce to you Marcus of Soulwind. Marcus, this is my first lieutenant, Aaron.'

'Pleased to meet you, Marcus,' said Aaron taking Marcus's hand. 'I've heard so much about you already.'

'My reputation is beginning to precede me it seems,'

joked Marcus as he shook Aaron's hand.

Slade's men and the cluster of reinforcements all came together like old friends as they were reunited. They all traded news and tales of their recent battles and spoke of rumours they had heard from back home. Marcus smiled as two brothers shared a long embrace nearby and cried out with joy and disbelief at the sight of seeing the other alive.

Slade briefed his Lieutenant and his men as they regrouped and explained that they must all continue to Goldstream immediately.

Along with one hundred and forty-two of Slade's original soldiers from the battle of Soulwind, over one hundred and fifty of the reinforcements who arrived with Lieutenant Aaron, and around fifty of the volunteers from Bridgewood, as well as Marcus, Hann, Erid and Lemy, the unit was now looking like a fairly formidable force, and they all continued for Goldstream.

Chapter Seventeen

Panning for Gold

The land south of Goldstream was flat and thin with cover. The sun rose higher and shone brighter than ever and beat down on the men as they trod across the wide open land. The sunrays pierced the tumbling cascades of the river, which was so loud now that the men did not have to tread as lightly as they once did, although they remained on their highest guard.

Very soon, Marcus could see the sun reflecting off the roofs of the tin shanties in the distance.

'There it is,' said Erid, 'my hometown.'

Goldstream was an unusual village due to the fact that it had been hastily erected and constructed out of scrap sheets of metal and flimsy wooden supports.

A makeshift shanty-town, built in haste by its settlers to attend to more pressing matters, for the wealth of Goldstream lay within the Livid River that flowed through it. Large chunks and nuggets of pure gold specked the river bed and were collected by portly bearded men and their families that settled there. The precious yellow chunks were washed down from the Snow Dust Hills in the north and transported from the hills by a series of streams. These streams naturally eroded these nuggets from the gold rich hills directly to Goldstream via the Livid River, which meant there was no need to mine in these hills. The wealth in the streams meant that the people had settled there for far longer than expected, but the villagers still did not bother to erect more permanent structures, except only to maintain the village.

The men did not only collect the gold, skilled smiths and crafters also settled there.

On the approach into Goldstream, the men, as ever, remained alert and vigilant as they paced through the village, but there was not a single Malignant in sight. In fact, there was nobody in sight. It was like a ghost town, upturned and trashed.

The men split up to search for any sign of life when suddenly Marcus heard a cry for help, which appeared to be coming from the direction of the river.

Marcus signalled to a few of the soldiers and they rushed towards the river.

It was a sickening scene, seeing dozens upon dozens of steel box cages stuffed full of prisoners littered the shallows of the river. The cries of the captives erupted even louder when the soldiers came into view.

Marcus and the men all dropped their weapons and rushed into the shallows of the livid river to help free the prisoners, some of whom were unfortunate enough to be stuffed at the bottom of the cages and appeared to have already drowned.

The rest of the soldiers all waded in to the river towards the cages and tried with all of their might to break open the locks.

Marcus desperately clamped his palms around the metal bars to try and pry them open, but to no avail. The cages gave way slightly as the weight of the soldiers disturbed the stony riverbed.

'Help us!' cried the villagers.

Some soldiers managed to drag a few of the cages towards the bank while others tried to smash open the locks.

Marcus plunged his arm into the icy river and retrieved a large stone. He smashed the lock of a cage open and pulled the villagers out to safety.

Many of the other soldiers did the same, until finally the villagers were helped to the safety of the bank, some coughing and some too weak to stand. Sadly, many had lost their lives to the river.

'What happened here?' said Slade, panting for breath, as he dragged an old man onto the bank.

A nearby woman spoke out as she helped a young boy out of the shallows.

'It happened all of a sudden,' said the woman. 'One minute everything was calm and quiet, and then for some reason the Malignants all started to panic and stampeded out of the village, but before they did, they pushed the cages off the banks and into the river on their retreat in an attempt to drown us, and then as quickly as it all happened, they were all gone.'

'Do you suppose they knew we were coming, Captain?' asked Lemy.

'It's quite possible,' said Slade, 'I can't think of any

other reason why they'd leave in such a hurry. Maybe they heard of our recent victories after all, and it frightened them off.'

'The Malignants attempted to drown their captives as they fled,' said Hann, 'so they must have been in a serious rush if they didn't have time to execute them all individually. It's all very strange. Why would they do that? Do you really suppose that they knew we were coming?'

'Did you notice which way they were heading?' Slade asked the woman.

'They seemed to be heading South,' said the woman, 'possibly South-East, but I can't be certain.'

'Do you suppose they'll make to attack the Capital?' Lemy asked Slade, sounding concerned.

'Not right away,' said Slade, 'and besides, they'd have crossed paths with Aaron and the men if they were planning on that.'

'We saw no movement on our march here,' said Aaron, 'we must have just missed them if they were heading South-East.'

Once the drama of the river had died down and the villagers conversed with the soldiers regarding the Malignants, a man yelled above the voices of the others and the attention of the village was immediately diverted to him.

'Erid!' yelled the man, 'you damned murderer! How dare you show your face back here!'

A few more villagers also raised their voices and they hurled torrents of abuse towards Erid.

'Murderer!' they all yelled.

'Get a hold of him!' shouted another as the group of villagers advanced towards Erid.

'Stay away from him.' said Lemy as he shoved the man to the chest.

'Stand back!' howled Slade, 'cool it, Lemy.'

Slade and his men immediately drew their swords and pointed them towards the Goldstream villagers.

'Explain yourselves,' shouted Slade sternly, 'Erid is now under my command, and anyone who harms him answers to me.'

The villagers took a step back from Slade and then the man shouted again.

'That man murdered my wife!'

'Wesley,' said Erid, 'I tell you now as I've told you all before, it wasn't me. I was trialled for this, and I was framed. It was that scumbag, Titus. I was wrongly accused and punished for a crime I didn't commit, and I was sentenced to serve in the army and I've been here ever since. Titus murdered her in her sleep, Wesley. He claims he is innocent, but where is he now?'

'You liar,' yelled Wesley, 'I loved her, we all loved her, and if it wasn't you, then explain her blood on your hands!'

The mob yelled even louder and demanded answers as they advanced towards Erid, Slade, and his men.

'Do as you will, Slade,' said Wesley, 'we finally have him here in front of us again, and this time we'll have our revenge.'

'This is your last warning,' said Slade, 'I'll defend my men Wesley, so stand back.'

Marcus suddenly stepped in fearlessly between the two advancements.

'What the hell are you all thinking?' cried Marcus, 'we're all at war. The fate of Termelanor hangs in the balance and here you all are preparing to fight your fellow men. Now I'm sure you all have questions, but they can't be answered now. Our priority is those bastards who have only just left here, who attempted to drown you and your loved ones not a few hours ago. Have you all forgotten that we're at war? Erid fought for your freedom, as we all have, and now the duty of the Kingdom's survival belongs to you as well as us. This is our home and if we don't use every ounce of our strength to defend it right now, then we'll lose it forever.'

There was a long silence.

'All right soldier,' said Wesley to Marcus, 'have your way for now, but mark my words Erid, you'll hear from me once all of this is over.'

Once all of the commotion had subsided, both Slade and Aaron decided between themselves that it was most likely that the Malignants were potentially routing and regrouping somewhere in the south, in a possible attempt to mount one final attack on the Capital, so they decided to follow the tracks of the Malignants that fled from Goldstream and see where they would lead.

'Do you really think it's worth the risk, Captain?' said Lemy. 'Why don't we continue our march north to

Greystone Ridge? If there's any change that there may be live captives there, then we should head there at once.'

'What if there aren't?' interrupted Hann, 'and by the time we get there to find out it'll be too late to make it back to the Capital to fight, if that's what these bastards are intending on doing.'

'But surely we can't just leave the other villages to their fates?' said Lemy, 'what about Sycamore valley, Eastvale, Birchwood Grove? What about the prisoners there? We can't just forget all about them?'

'Sadly, we have little time and resources to help everyone,' said Slade, 'and we have to accept the fact that they may already be dead. If the Malignants from the other villages did the same as they did here and attempted to kill their prisoners too, then there may be no prisoners left for us to free once we make it to the next village. And if the Malignants also retreated like they did here, then there will also be no enemy there for us to fight, and that would be a wasted journey for us. That's why our best lead is to follow the Malignants that fled from here while the trail is still hot. They must have known that they were going to lose to us here, otherwise why would they have fled? I think they were scared of another defeat.'

'Or it's all one big trap that they're luring us into,' said Lemy.

'Either way,' said Slade, 'we're going after them. Erid, do you think you can make a start at the tracking?'

'Right away, Captain,' said Erid.

'Men of Goldstream,' said Slade, 'I ask this of you just

as I asked your brothers in Bridgewood, if there's any man here with the strength to fight, please lend me your arms and march onward with me and my men. You'd be more than welcome in our ranks.'

Every single man from Goldstream turned to face one another, and then silently raised their hand in respect to their new Captain.

The soldiers all watched from the corner of their eyes at the Goldstream villagers as they kept a close watch over Erid as he led the pack. Slade's men subtly shifted and stood to fill the gaps between them to ensure they kept their distance from him. Without order, each and every one of Slade's men guarded Erid quietly with their lives. Erid was their best hope in finding the common enemy now, their bloodhound of the pack.

Chapter Eighteen

March with Haste

Slade led his army and marched as fast as they collectively could, following the tracks of the Malignants who had fled south from the village of Goldstream.

'Erid,' Slade yelled, 'how's it looking up there?'

'The tracks still lead south-east, Captain,' he yelled back, 'they can't be too far from here. If these tracks were any fresher, we'd be trampling on the bastards right now.'

The unit advanced forward and followed Erid for a while longer, until finally they all faced a vast and open meadow.

'The tracks are spread out here,' said Erid, 'they're not in single file anymore, and they've faded out a little and have disappeared into the grass.'

'These meadows once served as farm land for the Capital,' said Slade, 'but they were abandoned when the farmers found more suitable lands to plough nearer to the Capital's gates, but the Capital is still visible from here, in the distance. Have the tracks faded out entirely, Erid?'

'Not entirely,' said Erid, 'although it's very difficult to track through here surprisingly, but they've definitely passed through.'

'Where could they have gone?' said Lemy, 'they couldn't have just disappeared?'

'These meadows are acres wide, Lemy,' said Slade, 'it's quite possible that they're lying low, maybe in the patches of grass, ready to ambush us, but we're going in regardless. Have your wits about you men; these meadows extend for miles and miles, and they may spring on us at any moment.'

'It might be wise if we send someone to get word to the King, Captain,' said Aaron, 'he may be able to spare us further reinforcements. If we face the brunt of the Malignant army here alone as we are, there's no way that we can fight them in this open meadow. We're far too exhausted and I suspect we shall be severely outnumbered.'

'I need every man here with me, Aaron,' said Slade, 'and besides, we have many good men in our company, who are worth at least a dozen Malignant Warriors, even exhausted and in open combat. We shall hold here for now. Let's enter the meadow and set up camp.'

'I hope you're right, Captain,' thought Aaron.

The men all set to work. With not an ounce of energy left between them, they all dug deep like men possessed and stood firm, strengthening their position, their lifeline, their future.

Chapter Nineteen

The Battle of the Crimson Meadows

The tracks had faded out and Erid had difficulty continuing the tracking.

The meadows had been abandoned for so long that all that was left were patches of grass and dry earth, almost a barren wasteland.

'We'd best make a start with what we have,' said Slade, 'we'll wait them out here. We can still retreat to the Capital if we need to.'

'Very well captain,' said Aaron.

'Have your men set up an encampment, lieutenant,' said Slade, 'we may be here for quite some time. Send out a few men to scout the area and set a watch about the camp. The rest of the men can get some rest while they can, especially the ones who originally marched out with me from the Capital… they must be exhausted.'

'At once, Captain,' said Aaron saluting him.

'If we're to battle them here we'll need every ounce of our strength. Make sure that the men have something to eat,' said Slade, grasping Aaron firmly and pulling him close, speaking just loud enough for them both to hear. 'If we don't defeat this enemy, it'll surely spell the end for all of us.'

Meanwhile, Hann was busy guiding some of the men to prepare for the potential upcoming battle.

'We shall dig a few light trenches here,' said Hann, 'and start work on a few sharpened stake lines, here and other one here. It'll give us a little defence from an oncoming charge. The enemy is likely to approach from the south, so we'll prepare to expect their attack from there.'

Marcus was standing nearby feeling a little useless as the rest of the men were allocated tasks and preparing for an upcoming battle. He wondered if he was better at sharpening stakes or digging trenches?

'Marcus,' said Slade, 'can you come here for a minute, please?'

'What is it, Captain?'

'How are you feeling lad?' said Slade as he put a hand on Marcus's shoulder.

'I'm fine,' said Marcus, 'why do you ask?'

'You looked as if you needed something to do,' smiled Slade.

'I'm sorry,' blushed Marcus, 'I haven't been much use to you for a while, Captain.'

'Don't be ridiculous,' said Slade, 'you've already done far more than has been asked of you, but I think it's time that I call upon your help one final time.'

'Anything,' said Marcus, 'what is it?'

'There's an old ruined farmhouse in the distance,' pointed Slade, 'do you see it?'

'Yes, I see it.' said Marcus, gazing in the direction

Slade was pointing.

'Take the men, Marcus,' said Slade, 'and secure the farmhouse. Perhaps you'll be able to hold it with just the four of you if the enemy passes through that way, and if my men and I have to make a stand here, you may be able to take a few of them out before they get to us. What do you say?'

'I won't let you down, Captain,' said Marcus.

'Marcus,' said Slade, 'I'll see you when this is all over, one way or another.'

Marcus nodded at Slade as he turned and made his way towards the trenches.

Marcus searched amongst the soldiers and tried to locate the men.

Lemy was easy enough to find standing waist deep in a trench he was helping to dig, looking even dirtier and scruffier than he normally did, and Erid was nearby sitting on a rock sharpening a stake.

The trio relinquished Hann from Aaron and they all made for the farmhouse, and Marcus ran them through Slade's plan.

'Does he have a head injury?' was Lemy's first question, 'it's a suicide mission.'

'It's a shot in the dark, but it may sway the battle for us if they come through that way,' said Marcus.

'Yes, and we MAY get our heads lobbed off our shoulders in the process,' said Lemy.

'Stop your whinging Lemy,' said Erid. 'What do you think, Hann?'

'This place looks pretty run down,' said Hann, inspecting the ruin as they approached it, 'although it should provide us with enough cover for a light defence, even with just the four of us, especially if we catch them by surprise.'

'I'll get a fire going,' yawned Lemy, ignoring Hann, 'and make us some stew.'

The ruined farmhouse had no roof save a small portion of the ruin, which was thatched and had fallen through into one of the rooms. All that remained of the rest of the farmhouse were the foundations and the pillars; there was little cover from the outside save for the low crumbled waist-high walls and the ruined stone pillars once held up the now non-existent roof.

After the others had checked out the ruin, Marcus, Erid, Lemy, and Hann all sat around a large cooking pot at the centre of the ruined pillars. Slade's men were visible in the distance, moving about like a small swarm of worker ants going about their business, carrying and shifting objects around their camp.

Lemy stirred the cooking pot with a large wooden spoon and Erid sprinkled some sort of woody smelling herb into the stew. It wasn't much but it was something to fill a hole.

'Do you think any of the king's men will come to our aid?' said Lemy. 'He commands the Sterling Guard. Now is as good as any a time to use them, or if not, surely he can spare us a few of the city's men? Or even the Palace Guard?'

'Those throne room fairies?' said Erid, 'I wouldn't

bank on it, and besides I don't think they'd be much use. Rumour has it that their decorativeness outweigh their functionality. A steak or two wouldn't go amiss here, though. Maybe he can send a wagon or two of red meat and malt beer.'

'What's wrong with my stew?' said Lemy.

'I didn't say that there was anything wrong with your stew,' said Erid, 'it's actually not bad for a change.'

'It's better than what you can cook, Erid,' Lemy grinned.

'Do you think this plan will work?' said Marcus, cutting across.

'Well, if the enemy don't end up coming through this way at least we aren't too far away from Slade and the men to join the battle if they're attacked,' said Hann, 'however, if they do pass through here at least we can take a few of them out before they get to Slade, and it may even the numbers up for us a little.'

'Do you suppose it's likely that the Malignants went back to where they came from on account that they'd suffered a defeat?' asked Marcus.

'I doubt it,' said Hann, 'no, I think they're still around here somewhere. I don't think they're going to let us off that easily. I suspect they'll want some revenge for what we did to them at Bridgewood.'

'I suppose you're right,' said Marcus. 'What's the plan if they do come this way?'

'There isn't much we can do,' said Lemy. 'We can pick a corner of the ruin each and try hold them off as best as we can. The ruined pillars at the centre of the farmhouse will provide good cover if we're cornered and have to fall back for any reason.'

'God, if I ever live through this I swear I'm going to get so drunk that I won't even remember my own name,' smiled Erid.

'That's every other day for you though isn't it, Erid?' laughed Lemy.

Marcus laughed out loud as Lemy and Erid took it in turns to banter one another other.

'At least I can handle my drink, you lightweight!' said Erid. 'Remember that time at The Crow and Kite when-.'

Erid cut his sentence short as a bewildered look suddenly crossed his face.

'Erid?' said Marcus, 'what is it?'

'Can any of you feel that?' said Erid.

'Feel what?' asked Lemy.

'The ground,' said Erid, 'it's shaking.'

'I feel it too,' said Marcus.

'It could be an earthquake?'

'It's no tremor,' said Erid, 'the earth is rumbling. I can feel it in my chest.'

'It's getting stronger,' said Marcus, 'do you feel it Lemy?'

'Now I feel it,' said Lemy, looking nervous and breathing heavily, 'I can hear it.'

'It's stopped now,' said Hann.

The four rose from their seats and approached the

edge of the southern wall.

There, from across the meadow facing them was the host of the Malignant army. It was just like Marcus had recalled at the battle of Soulwind, only far, far worse.

There must have been thousands of them, all standing in a long line gazing towards the direction of Slade and his men.

'Oh my god,' said Hann, passing by Marcus, 'they must have regrouped with the Malignants from the other villages.'

'What are we supposed to do against that?' cried Lemy. 'We've barely a few hundred men, Hann.'

Marcus looked back towards Slade's army. The farmhouse stood in between the two armies, however, luckily the allied army was closer to the farmhouse than the Malignant army, at the moment.

Slade and his soldiers had also spotted the Malignants and each and every one of his men stood frozen as they stared down the Malignant host.

'How many do you count?' said Marcus to Hann as both their eyes darted from side to side eyeing up the enemy.

'A good few thousand at least,' said Hann, 'but it's difficult to be certain, as I can't see how far back their line goes.'

'We have a few hundred men at best, Hann,' said Marcus, 'a few hundred, exhausted and battle worn men.'

'There's no way we can fight that,' said Lemy, panicking.

'We don't have much choice in the matter,' said Hann, 'we fight against that, or we die against that.'

'People will sing of this day if we ever make it out of this alive,' said Erid as he looked on, terrified at the mere sight of the huge Malignant army.

'They must have known that we'd follow them here,' said Marcus, 'this must have been their plan all along. They wanted to draw us out into the open like this, as they know they can fight us better out in the open, and they knew this land was here. They're not stupid. Attacking the Capital would have been too tough for them, and killing in the open is what they do best.'

'We should fall back to Captain Slade,' said Lemy as he took a step backwards.

'No, Lemy,' said Hann gripping him by the neck-gap of his breastplate, 'we have our orders to hold the ruin, so we hold the ruin.'

'Hann,' said Marcus, 'Slade won't have nowhere near enough men to form a strong line against them; they'll surely quickly outflank and overwhelm them with their superior numbers.'

'Don't be so quick to lose faith, Marcus,' said Hann, 'we still outclass them in steel and armour, and man on man, soldier to soldier we should have the advantage.'

'I don't think they're going to give us that chance,' said Marcus.

'And I don't think that they know we're in here,' said Hann, 'they seem too distracted by Slade and the men. Quickly, get down, they'll surely pass through here in the advance towards Slade. Maybe we can take a few of them out quietly while they're passing through the ruin.'

'What do we do if we're spotted?' asked Marcus.

'I suppose we shall have to cross that bridge when we come to it,' said Hann.

Meanwhile, Slade was preparing for the upcoming battle. There was a gradual incline between Slade and the enemy, and they at least would have the advantage of the high ground even if their numbers could have been stronger in comparison.

'Aaron!' he shouted, 'how many?'

'The scouts count a few thousand strong Sir,' said Aaron.

'Have the men form up a line,' said Slade, 'we can't afford to have them outflank us. And place every man wielding a bow between every other man and have them take a step forward out from the line. We can take a few of the bastards out before they get to us and then sound the charge at the last second before they crash our ranks.'

'At once sir, very good sir,' said Aaron.

Slade did not have as many bowmen remaining as he had hoped, and the line did not stretch nearly as long as the length of the facing Malignant army.

However, Slade knew never to disband battle tactics, and that there was always a way to win a battle, even against unfavourable odds.

Although most of his men were battle worn and tired, Slade still had a few hundred good and diverse men left under his command, and he decided to wait for the

Malignants to make the first move.

Back at the farmhouse, Marcus and the others were hiding behind the low southern wall of the ruin.

'What are they waiting for?' whispered Marcus. 'Why aren't they attacking?'

'I don't know,' said Hann peering slightly over the wall, 'maybe they're counting our numbers.'

'There aren't many of us to count,' said Lemy sarcastically.

'It must be something,' said Hann to Marcus, 'you said yourself before that they never delay their attacks.'

Coincidentally, on Hann's word the Malignant army suddenly advanced.

'Quickly,' whispered Hann, 'spread out.'

Marcus and the men took up their respective positions in the ruin until eventually the Malignants were merely a stone's throw away from the farmhouse.

Marcus was positioned on the western wall of the ruin and the wall was just high enough that if a grown man crouched, he would be hidden from view from the other side.

Poor Hann remained at the southern wall, and Erid and Lemy took the remaining two walls.

Some Malignants made their way around the ruins and advanced towards Slade, but a few had hopped over the walls of the ruin to avoid going around.

The Malignants' guard was slightly down as they passed through the ruin, knowing they were still out of range of Slade's arrow fire.

Hann was crouching behind the southern wall as two Malignant Warriors vaulted over and carried on walking through the ruin.

Hann managed to get a hold of one of them and broke his neck from behind, then he dragged the body back and hid it behind the wall out of sight.

A few more vaulted the walls and before long there were over twenty Malignants within the ruin, with more still clearing the wall. Luckily, neither of them had yet seen Marcus or the others, even though one malignant almost vaulted the over wall and landed right on top of Hann.

Marcus was crouching and leaning up against the ruined wall, trying not to make eye contact with the Malignants as they passed through, clutching at the hilts of their jagged blades.

Erid had quietly adjusted his position so his back was now up against a pillar as a few Malignants crossed the northern wall on the other side.

However, Marcus realised he had made a grave mistake, only just realising that as Slade's army was positioned to the North West of the meadow, and the Malignants were approaching from the South East, the Malignants were not only vaulting the southern wall to cross over the north, they were also vaulting the eastern wall, and would surely pass across the western wall too.

Marcus slowly backed himself onto a pillar to avoid being seen, but it was too late.

He had caught the eye of a Malignant Warrior who

had seen movement from the corner of his eye and he immediately alerted his comrades in his foreign language.

'Shit,' breathed Marcus, 'Hann!'

The men all broke away from their cover and engaged the Malignants in combat.

Marcus and the men fought desperately as they weaved through the ruined pillars of the old farmhouse taking out whatever Malignants they could.

The Malignants immediately swarmed the ruin of the farm house once they realised what was happening inside, and Hann, Erid, Lemy and Marcus raced to the centre to cover each other's backs while giving each other enough space to move around.

Marcus dodged and avoided the Malignant's hacks, taking full advantage of the ruined pillars for cover as the enemy swung relentlessly and their blades collided with the stone.

He thrust his sword through the chest of a charging Malignant, but more and more warriors were swarming into the ruin as the four fought on desperately inside to defend it.

The attacking force of the Malignants grew thicker and thicker, and they now almost completely surrounded the ruin, and the chance of escaping looked impossible.

'This was a bad idea!' yelled Lemy, blocking a foe's attack with his shield.

'We should fall back to Slade!' shouted Erid.

'Hann!' Marcus screamed, 'take the men and fall back to Slade's ranks now!'

'Don't be ridiculous,' replied Hann as he forced his blade through a Malignant's neck, 'not without you.'

'We're going to die here if we don't move now!' said Marcus. 'Fall back to Slade, I'll be right behind you!'

'But you'll never make it!' cried Lemy.

'Go, now!' yelled Marcus at the top of his voice, and the three fought their way to the northern wall, towards the direction of Slade's ranks.

The Malignants swarmed the farmhouse even thicker than ever as the squad retreated, but soon Marcus stood alone at the centre of the ruin, trapped and fighting against dozens of advancing Malignant Warriors.

This was the end, Marcus knew it, but at least he could save the others. At least he had helped and had done everything he could do.

The Malignants disarmed and surrounded Marcus, toying with him as they cackled and pushed him around to one another like a play thing.

Marcus lay in the dust, concussed, winded, and coughing up blood as he tried to focus through his blurred vision. A large Malignant approached him through the cheering ranks of the enemy, wielding a sharpened blade. Marcus swallowed deeply as he finally accepted his fate and backed up against a stone pillar.

The warrior smiled with glee as he looked into Marcus's eyes.

Then he raised his blade high above his head.

Marcus clenched his eyes shut as the enemy brought his blade down onto him hard.

The sound of slashed flesh echoed throughout the Malignant ranks, and a thick stream of scarlet surged spectacularly before the eyes of the witnessing Malignants.

The blade-wielding Malignant thudded hard onto the dusty ground.

Marcus opened his eyes, and there before him stood Slade, facing the Malignants and ready to fight, gripping his longsword with both of his hands, his blade dripping with dark Malignant blood and his scarlet cape flowing off his back in the warm dry wind.

The Malignants charged at Slade shrieking and cursing, and Slade cut through each and every one of them like a hot knife through butter.

'Get up Marcus!' yelled Slade as he kicked an oncoming attacker to the chest.

Slade intimidated and struck fear into the warriors, and some of the Malignants now hesitated to attack him, despite their overwhelming numbers.

Marcus scrambled to his feet and reclaimed his sword as he hurried towards Slade to cover his back.

'Fight your way through towards the men, Marcus,' cried Slade, 'I'll follow you out!'

Marcus nodded, terrified, as they both desperately fought back towards the allied ranks. Marcus made a break for it as he vaulted the Northern wall and he landed on the ground on the other side. Hann and the others were still there waiting nearby.

'Marcus!' Hann shouted. He ran over and helped him up as the Malignants closed in. 'Where's Slade?'

The men waited for Slade to surface, but there was no sign of him.

'We have to go back for him,' said Marcus to Hann.

'No,' said Hann, 'come on, Aaron will have the command. Let's go!'

Suddenly, Marcus heard a roar and witnessed Slade leaping like a mighty gazelle out of the ruin through the Malignant ranks and onto the other side.

'Slade!' shouted Marcus.

'Go, run!' he said as he ran limping towards Marcus and the others.

The five ran back towards the allied ranks. Erid and Lemy arrived first, but Marcus and Hann were still a fair distance behind them, and Slade further still.

Marcus heard a growl behind him and he looked back as he ran to see Slade had fallen down.

'Slade!' he cried as he ran back to him.

'Marcus!' cried Hann. 'No!'

Marcus got to Slade as the Malignants closed in. He helped him to his feet and they both retreated towards the ranks with the help of Hann.

When Slade was within earshot he signalled to Aaron to commence the battle.

The archers nocked their arrows and drew their bows tight and let them loose into the advancing Malignant swarm.

The allied arrow fire did little to slow down the massive oncoming force of the Malignants, but just as

Slade, Marcus, and Hann had reached the safety of the line, the enormous approaching tide of black engulfed the second wave of arrows.

'Archers!' yelled Aaron at the soldiers, 'fire at will!'

The archer's quivers quickly emptied and the Malignant force reformed ready for the crash of the charge.

'Archers!' yelled Slade, 'draw your swords! No time for fancy speeches today. Sons of Termelanor, give them hell!'

Slade's army charged towards the Malignant advancement, swords and axes held high, all hungry for the clash.

Marcus was towards the left-hand side of the line when the men finally collided with the Malignants, and the bloody onslaught ensued for both attacking sides.

The battle was a bloodbath, with each and every free man of Termelanor fighting with sword and teeth as enemy and allies' blood alike splashed and drenched and stained all of the soldiers on the battlefield.

Already it was desperate for Slade and the men, and the Malignants quickly used their superior numbers to engulf them with a pincer-like flanking manoeuvre, like a giant black maw devouring its prey. Not even the most skilled warriors and officers defending the flanks could hold them back, and the line was soon pushed back.

The mass of the Malignant army now encircled the men, containing them in a thick ring of black.

Then when all seemed hopeless, Marcus heard Lieutenant Aaron bellowing a command from the ranks.

'Infantry,' he shouted, 'wedge formation!'

The allied soldiers suddenly warped as they fought back and folded in on themselves to form a triangular funnel, and they all pushed through together against the original attacking Malignant line.

The formation worked, at least for a short while, as the weight of the seemingly everlasting Malignant force compressed Marcus and the soldiers and they desperately tried to continue on with the fight.

Marcus spotted Slade nearby, and it seemed like he had given him a look that meant this was the end for all of them.

The men continued to fight on in the bloody, muddy, dusty carnage, and the allied forces gave one final push, but failed miserably.

Marcus looked around him as the bodies piled up beneath him, and faces familiar to him from Soulwind, Bridgewood and Goldstream lay lifeless in the blood-soaked mud.

The others fought on desperately for their lives with the last of their energy and strength; it was only a matter of time before they would be broken and slaughtered.

Marcus breathed heavily, gripping his sword as the pressure of the surrounding men pressed it up against his chest. He was trapped, and time seemed to have slowed down.

The screams of the battlefield fell deaf on his ears now, and all he could hear was his throbbing heartbeat. He looked around and awaited the inevitable.

Just then, Marcus heard something that rose above the

carnage of the battlefield, and above the deafening sound of his heartbeat.

It wasn't a scream or a yell; it pierced the ambience of the battlefield.

Marcus came around slightly as he heard it once again, louder this time, and far clearer.

The fighting slowed down and grinded to a halt, and enemy and ally alike now pondered the source of the sound.

The third time, the sound pierced across the battlefield as clear as crystal, and all of the soldiers and warriors on the battlefield darted their heads towards the North.

The sight made Marcus tremble with fear, delight, and disbelief.

A piercing silver trumpet sounded in the distance, even clearer than before.

The Capital had finally joined the fight.

Fast approaching the battlefield were hundreds of mounted armoured knights on horseback, hungrily charging towards the battlefield, lances pointing forwards, and behind them, hundreds of foot soldiers, sprinting quicker than hounds towards the meadow in smooth, shining silver armour.

It was none other than the Sterling Guard, the King's finest.

It seemed that the City and the Palace Guard had even arrived to join the fight; the whole city had been emptied to aid Slade and his men in battle.

The battlefield came to a complete and utter standstill, and the Malignant Warriors witnessed fearfully as the

Capital's army charged relentlessly towards their ranks, banners held high and spears held low, yelling a mighty war cry and blowing hard on their silver trumpets.

Marcus recalled what King Heath had mentioned in the throne room when he said he had the finest army in the Kingdom, and now he knew he was not lying. The sight was absolutely terrifying. He was just glad they were fighting on his side, and for a moment he almost pitied the fact that the Malignants had to face them.

The shining silver round shields of the Sterling Guard blinded all of the onlookers as the hot afternoon sun reflected off them, and the mere sight for the charging horses stunned the men, for horses were rare in Termelanor. They were scarce in the wild lands and the ones that were already wild were difficult to tame. It took centuries to raise them into war and battle-ready stallions.

As the cavalry charge finally collided and smashed against and clean through the Malignant ranks, each and every one of the Malignants turned and ran, knocking over and shoving past anything that stood in their way. Marcus was knocked face down into the dirt by a fleeing Malignant.

A soldier helped him back onto his feet.

'Don't leave us yet, Marcus of Soulwind,' said Slade, 'the battle isn't over. Forward men, trample them into the dirt!'

Marcus wished he could have given the final chase, but he stood there exhausted as he saw the cavalry and the sterling guard charging down the rest of the fleeing

Malignants to the last man.

Marcus and the men looked at each other as a refreshing breeze hit their sweaty, bloody faces. Marcus saw Lemy nearby limping and clutching his side.

'Lemy!' cried Marcus, rushing over to him, 'are you all right?'

'I think so,' said Lemy, short of breath and checking himself over. 'Do you suppose the others are all right?'

'I hope so,' said Marcus still gazing at the mighty riders and their stallions in the distance, slaughtering what was left of the Malignant horde. 'Do you think it's all over?'

'I don't know,' said Lemy. 'I pray so.'

'Have you seen any the others?' asked Marcus.

'Not since the battle started,' said Lemy. 'I got split up from Erid.'

'We should check on the wounded,' said Marcus.

Marcus and Lemy limped through the post-battlefield. The dead of both sides lay lifeless on the blood-stained ground. Countless Malignant Warriors, Slade's soldiers, and even some of the brave volunteers from Bridgewood and Goldstream littered the ground around them.

Marcus and Lemy paced forward, still looking down at the faces of the dead, then Lemy let out a blood-chilling cry.

'No!' cried Lemy, 'Hann!'

Lemy ran over to where the lifeless bloody body of Hann lay face down in the earth.

'No!' he cried again as he collapsed over and cried into

the body of his old friend and comrade.

Marcus stood behind Lemy, not used to comprehending such death and loss.

Cries erupted throughout the battlefield now as men lucky enough to hold onto their lives came across fallen friends and brothers.

Marcus spotted a man kneeling over a lifeless body nearby, a man wearing a scarlet cape.

Marcus limped over to Slade.

Slade was kneeling over the body of his First Lieutenant, Aaron.

'He was so young,' said Slade, 'but an intelligent and fine battle commander. He will be remembered.'

'Slade,' said Marcus, 'Hann, he, he's-.'

'I know,' said Slade bluntly.

Slade said nothing more as he remained at his deceased Lieutenant's side.

Marcus did nothing more over the next few passing moments, although it could have been hours, as he had lost all concept of time following the battle, suspended in a bubble of grief and death. He paced the length and breadth of the battlefield.

Some faces he recognised, both dead and alive, but he placed a face to the name of few. He witnessed two brothers that were reunited after the battle of Bridgewood sharing an embrace nearby as they cried at the mixed emotion and disbelief of seeing each other alive once again, and at the loss of their friends and both the horror and the miracle of the battle. Marcus gave a faint smile as amidst all of the carnage he looked upon a beautiful sight.

The surviving men were bloodied, but it seemed for now, that they had won.

Marcus turned and disappeared back in amongst the men to tend to the wounded and comfort the dying.

Chapter Twenty

The Aftermath

Marcus sat on the end of a very comfortable down bed, staring blankly at the floor, the very same bed he had found himself in following his retreat from Soulwind castle.

Marcus wished that the only difference was the fact there was now a fresh flower in the small glass vase on his bedside cabinet, however he now felt like a completely different person, and he was, for he imagined few could live through such trauma and still retain their innocence.

A few days following the battle, he had been checked over and treated by the nurse for minor injuries and wounds, which he had sustained from his many conflicts.

Everything and nothing raced through his mind, when suddenly he experienced a case of déjà vu, as a young nurse appeared in the doorway and showed Slade into the room. He sat next to Marcus on the bed.

'How are you feeling?' Slade asked.

'I don't know,' said Marcus, 'everything, sick and oblivious.'

'You fought well,' said Slade, 'to the very end, and I believe that neither of us would be here now if it wasn't for you.'

'That's not true,' said Marcus, 'it was you that saved me, back at the farmhouse.'

'It is true,' said Slade, 'my men fought bravely, but if you'd never warned us, the Capital would have crumbled.'

'I just did what I thought was right,' said Marcus, 'I'm no hero, Slade.'

'Young Marcus, modest to the last,' smiled Slade, 'what will you do now?'

'I don't know,' said Marcus, 'return home and help start rebuilding, I imagine. How are the others holding up?'

'Lemy is doing fine,' said Slade. 'He picked up a few minor wounds but he'll survive.'

'What of Erid?' asked Marcus.

'Erid was not amongst the dead,' said Slade. 'I've listed him on our military records as missing in action.'

'Not among the dead?' replied Marcus. 'How is that possible?'

'Many of the bodies were so mutilated from the battle that we couldn't identify them,' said Slade, 'it's quite possible that Erid was among those men.'

'Possibly,' said Marcus, thinking that Lemy could have identified Erid's dead body from his little finger if it came down to it.

'Anyway,' said Slade after a long pause, 'the King has called a gathering at the royal palace this afternoon and has requested everybody's attendance. I'll leave you in peace to prepare.'

Slade rose from the bed and walked out of the room before pausing by the door and peering back at Marcus.

'It's going to take a lot of time to rebuild,' said Slade, 'but we can do it if we all work together.'

Chapter Twenty-One

A Royal Ceremony

The throne room was full of people, and King Heath stood up from his Throne, and spoke in his usual booming voice. 'Men, women, brave warriors, and proud citizens of Termelanor, I have called you all here today to remember our fallen, and to recognise the brave feats of our heroes that stand here among us. Widowed wives and orphaned mothers, your husbands and sons fought bravely for each and every one of us and our freedom and their deaths were not in vain, and we have them to thank for the return of peace to our beloved Kingdom.'

The King continued his long speech to honour the brave and remember the fallen.

Marcus was stood in one of the front rows of the throne room next to Lemy and Slade and the many other brave soldiers who also fought in the battle, each donned in a decorative drape.

'How are you holding up Lemy,' whispered Marcus.

'I'll survive,' Lemy whispered back. 'How are you?'

'I'll be fine,' replied Marcus, 'is there still no word of Erid?'

'Sadly not,' said Lemy, 'I can't imagine what could have happened to him. He was my best friend.'

'What do you suppose happened to him?' said Marcus.

'I don't know,' said Lemy, 'maybe he went into hiding, into the wild. He's a good hunter, is Erid. He could survive on his own out there.'

'Why would he go into hiding?' said Marcus.

'You saw the way Wesley and the others looked at him in Goldstream,' said Lemy, 'it was blatant that he wanted to kill him as soon as all of this was over.'

'But why would Erid flee if he was innocent?' said Marcus, 'plus he's under Slade's protection.'

'How could he have been certain that Slade would survive the battle?' said Lemy, 'I don't think it was a risk he was willing to take, but I know he was innocent.'

'I'm so sorry Lemy,' said Marcus, 'and for Hann too.'

'I'm the only one left,' said Lemy, 'well, aside from you, Marcus,' he smiled.

Marcus smiled back as he felt warmth inside of him to be accepted by Lemy as one of his own.

The King finished his long speech and then he called up various men and awarded them with honours and medals for their feats of bravery during the battles.

Captain Slade was just receiving his sword of honour from the King when finally Marcus heard his name being called out.

'And finally, I'd like to call forward Marcus of Soulwind,' said the King.

Marcus nervously approached the King in front of his throne and bowed down before him.

'Marcus,' said King Heath, 'in the light of everything

that you have done for the Kingdom and people of Termelanor, I think everyone in this room would agree with me if I said that every free citizen owes you their lives. Therefore, I, King Heath of Termelanor, name you Sir Marcus the Swift, Hero of Soulwind, Protector of Termelanor and Battle Advisor to the king's army. And as a testament to your feats and bravery, I name this day your day, the day of Marcus the Swift, not only in Soulwind, but for all of Termelanor.'

'My King, I-' said Marcus.

'Enough of your modesty,' said the King.

Advisor Stern approached Marcus and forced a medal over his head.

'Marcus,' said Stern, 'as Royal Advisor I also present you with a rare gift.'

Marcus opened up a small polished walnut box to reveal a little ovular stone, slightly larger than an almond.

'That's the seed from a Spectre Tree, a very rare tree indeed,' said Advisor Stern. 'May it forever serve as a token of your status as Battle Advisor and a token of thanks from the royal palace.'

The meadows south of the Capital were also renamed The Crimson Meadows that day, as a sign of respect and as a memorial to the brave men who died there.

Marcus was hailed a hero, and every single man woman and child remained behind at the throne room to personally meet and thank him and to shake his hand. His arm ached even more than the entire sword swinging from the battles combined towards the end, but he didn't mind.

Chapter Twenty-Two

The Return Home

Marcus passed through the doors of the Capital one final time, and continued his long walk home at last to his beloved village of Soulwind, lugging a heavy pack over his shoulder, his eyes to the ground, thinking of all of the horror and excitement and adventure he had witnessed, while looking forward to his many days of peace.

Marcus had learned that shortly after the battle, King Heath sent taskforces consisting mainly of his Sterling Guard, to the remaining five villages to liberate them from any Malignant infestation and to free any enslaved prisoners. It seemed that a similar scenario had happened in each village to what had happened at Goldstream, and they were all now receiving aid.

Over the next few days, the remnants of the Malignant presence were hunted down and destroyed and it was not long before true peace finally returned to the Kingdom.

The men had learned that the Malignants had journeyed south from the volcano tribes of the north, but they never found out what they were looking for.

Marcus had not walked too far from the main gate when he heard the faint gallop of a horse's hooves approaching him from behind. He turned to see a rider coming towards him, none other than Captain Slade.

Slade stopped suddenly beside Marcus.

'Leaving already without saying goodbye, Marcus of Soulwind?' smiled Slade.

'I came to the barracks to find you before I made out, but you weren't there,' replied Marcus.

Slade climbed down from his horse and approached Marcus.

'So, what will you do after you return to Soulwind and help rebuild?' asked Slade.

'I don't know,' said Marcus, 'travel perhaps, see a bit of the world, maybe finally settle somewhere and start a family. Maybe not quite in that order.'

Slade smiled at Marcus.

'What about you?' asked Marcus.

'My fighting days are over,' replied Slade, 'I shall retire in good time, once all the affairs and arrangements are taken care of. Lemy will make a fine Captain of the Guard in my stead.'

'I'm sure he will,' smiled Marcus.

'Goodbye my old friend,' said Slade extending an arm to Marcus, 'I'm sure we'll see each other again someday, and thank you, for everything you've done for us.'

Marcus took Slade's arm and the two shared a long embrace. Slade gave Marcus one final tap on the back before they separated and Slade made his way back towards his horse.

'Oh, before you go,' said Marcus, 'I wanted you to have something.'

Marcus dropped his pack, and untied the cord around his neck, holding it out to Slade.

'What is it?' said Slade.

'It's a pendant,' said Marcus, 'I found it when I was a little boy. It's always been a bit of a good luck charm to me, but now I want you to have it.'

'Marcus, I can't accept that. You've had it too long, and it's sentimental.'

'You saved my life, Slade,' said Marcus, 'please take it. I want you to have it as a token of our friendship.'

'You've saved my life in more ways than you know,' smiled Slade, accepting the pendant. 'Thank you. You're a real hero, Marcus. I know neither of us would be standing here if it wasn't for you.'

'All the same,' said Marcus, 'I want you to have it, at least to remember me by.'

'Both your father and Raymond would be very proud of all that you've done, Marcus,' said Slade.

'Thank you, old friend,' said Marcus. 'I know we shall meet again someday.'

'I'm sure we will, my friend,' replied Slade as they shared one final embrace.

Slade mounted his horse and watched as Marcus disappeared into the distance.

Marcus returned to Soulwind and later visited every village in Termelanor, and even further afield before finally settling and starting a family in the Capital. He headed west one final time and was never seen again.

Slade retired as Captain of the Guard and settled with his family in the village of Soulwind as homage to his good friend Marcus after a long search looking for him.

Erid of Goldstream still remains on the Capital's military records as the only soldier listed as missing in action from The Battle of the Crimson Meadows.

Ninety-Eight Years Later

Book One - Part Two
THE ACCOUNTS OF CRUISE OF SOULWIND

Chapter One

Race Day

It was a relatively mild sunny morning, especially considering the fact that it was now nearing the middle of May, and a young lad named Cruise was ready to get up from a very restless night's sleep.

He had almost nearly forgotten beneath all of the excitement that he was trying to contain within himself, that today was also his eighteenth birthday.

For today was the day of The Great Festival.

This festival was famous for hosting a very long and arduous footrace around the border of his home village, and this year Cruise was finally old enough to compete.

He would train and push himself all year round to be the top athlete in the youngster's division, (which is a quarter of the length of the full track), and to which Cruise dominated almost every year.

His dream was to one day be as fast as the legendary Marcus the Swift, Cruise's hero, his role model, and also a brave warrior that once grew up, lived in, and both defended and freed Cruise's home village of Soulwind, and to whom both the race and the festival commemorates.

It was rumoured that the distance of the full race track measured roughly the same distance that Marcus had ran from Soulwind Castle to the Capital, wearing a full suit of heavy armour after surviving and escaping the famous Siege of Soulwind Castle.

The festival itself drew large crowds of people from all over the Kingdom, but the main event and attraction had always been the footrace, and over the years it had attracted all manner of athletes and challengers. Nothing excited Cruise more than the thought of running in that race, and this year it was his chance to prove to everybody that he had what it took to win.

A large fluffy black cat with bug-green eyes leaped off the wooden boards of the bedroom floor and onto Cruise's bare stomach, digging her claws in as she gripped her landing.

'Ouch, Cicada!' moaned Cruise as the cat leaped straight off of him and onto the windowsill before peering out of the window as if she had done nothing wrong, her head occasionally darting from left to right as she focused on something going on outside. 'Stupid cat.'

As Cruise flung his bed cover over to one side and sprang out of bed, he changed into his day clothes and got himself ready to head downstairs for breakfast.

Cruise was of average height with a strong, slim, slender build, looking almost scrawny and malnourished in certain areas of his body, especially around his protruding ribcage.

He had messy, dark, slightly matted hair in places and peculiar coloured eyes. They were not quite solely blue and not entirely grey either, but rather a fusion of the two, similar to gazing at a smooth stone pebble through a crystal flowing stream on a bright and clear summer's day, just like shiny and polished gemstones, with almost a tint of silver in the direct sunlight.

Although when darkness fell, his eyes would dilate to the extent that his pupils would engulf the irises almost entirely, and his eyes would become as black as the deepest and darkest cave.

Cruise swung open his bedroom door and trampled down the staircase and into the kitchen to find a surprise.

'Well, somebody is up early,' said a voice leaning over the kitchen surface, 'happy birthday, darling.'

It was his mother, Erika.

Erika was much shorter than Cruise. Her dark wavy hair stranded with a few lengths of grey, framed her pale white face and her two large shiny brown eyes.

She shuffled over to Cruise to give him a happy birthday hug.

'Thanks Mum,' replied Cruise, rubbing his eyes with a half smile as he plonked himself onto a chair and grabbed a nearby three-pronged wooden fork. 'You didn't make all of this just for me, did you?' He looked up, sounding slightly guilty.

The large oaken kitchen table was forced to the fringes with the most fantastic breakfast feast that Cruise had laid is eyes on in a good old while, if not ever.

There were both chicken and duck's eggs, boiled, poached, scrambled and fried. There was also wild boar sausage and salted streaky and back bacon, fresh brown farmhouse toast topped with thick layers of creamy churned butter, and even a variety of forest fruits and summer berries, a large chilled jug of pure squeezed apple juice from the orchard, and another filled with elderberry, both sweetened with honey from Sycamore Valley.

'Eat as much of it as you can,' smiled Erika, 'you'll need every ounce of your strength today, and it's also a special treat, since it's your birthday.'

Cruise knew his mother was right as always, but Cruise who surprisingly had a very unnaturally large appetite did not feel as hungry as he normally would at that time in the morning.

His nerves had been overwhelming him for the best part of the night, and he did not feel the need to eat, but Cruise knew his mother had put a lot of effort into making this birthday breakfast for him, and he did not want to hurt her feelings. Cruise also thought wrong of wasting food, therefore he tried his best to eat what he could, to satisfy his multiple culpabilities.

After managing about half a glass of apple juice, a few slices of toast and a couple of rashers of bacon, Cruise grabbed a handful of berries and got up from the table.

'Thanks Mum, that was delicious,' said Cruise with a mouthful of berries, as he pecked his mother on the cheek while she was washing the dishes in the kitchen basin. He walked towards the front door and forced his size nine feet into a pair of old worn soft-leather boots, 'I'll have the sausages cold for my supper later on tonight, if that's all right? I'm going to head to Red's place to see if he's woken up yet.'

'I think that the festival champion would deserve something a little more substantial than a couple of cold sausages for his supper, don't you?' smiled Erika. 'Oh, and just before you go, dear, make sure you go and find your father. He wanted to see you after you'd finished your breakfast. He should be out in the yard.'

'Okay Mum,' said Cruise as he left the front porch and yelled back, 'I'll see you at the festival!'

'Bye love!' she shouted as the door slammed behind him.

Cruise stepped outside into the warm morning sunshine. The smell of cut grass filled the air, and he found his father in the front yard mending a wooden cart wheel a short distance away from him.

Cruise's father looked a lot more like Cruise. He shared the same dark hair, although he was balding and it was not matted and peppered with grey. He also had similar features to Cruise, except for one striking difference; Cruise's father had dark brown eyes just like Cruise's mother, Erika.

'Good morning champ,' said his father, Rowan, as he placed down his wooden mallet, 'and happy birthday. Do you feel any older?'

'Thanks Dad,' smiled Cruise as he tried not to show how tired he was from having next to no sleep the night before.

'Are you feeling confident for today?' said Rowan, walking up to his son chuckling as he ruffled Cruise's already untidy, matted hair.

'As much as I'm going to, I guess,' he said, trying not

to act too nervously and vainly re-arranging his hair.

'That's my lad!' laughed Rowan. 'Wait here, I have a little something for you.'

'Oh Dad, we said we wouldn't this year,' said Cruise as Rowan scuttled off excitedly and disappeared into one of the out sheds.

Cruise's family were very poor, and they did not have much of anything, therefore Cruise never usually expected to receive anything on his birthday; in fact, the amount of food his mother had made him for breakfast just that morning would have usually been enough to feed the whole family for the week.

Cruise had heard his parents argue over the matter in the kitchen earlier that morning when they had both thought that he was upstairs sleeping. He had heard his mother say that it was a special occasion and they would have to get by. This was another of the many reasons that Cruise was reluctant to eat his breakfast that morning.

Deep down though, Cruise knew his parents secretly hoped he would one day win one of the festival races, even though they acted as if they supported him merely because he loved to run, as the prize money of one thousand gold Termellians would be more than enough to rescue his family out of poverty.

At eighteen, Cruise was now old enough to enlist in the army to earn a steady wage, if he wanted to, but his obsession with winning the race and the hefty prize money constantly played on his mind. But the sad truth was, mostly everyone who lived in the village of

Soulwind was poor.

Soulwind was once the wealthiest Greater Village in all of Termelanor and once boasted the title of Sub-Capital. At one time it was a prosperous mining village. Its rich silver mine and deep stone quarry were mined for decades upon decades, and the village itself traded extensively with the entire kingdom and beyond, but now, sadly, the mines had been depleted and the villagers that called Soulwind their home did what they could to get by.

Constructors and carpenters, handymen and blacksmiths, horse and cart drivers, inn keepers and farriers, were just a few of the many occupations the people of Soulwind now did for their work; a once proud and skilled people that were once looked up at by the other villages, now found themselves laughed at, mocked and looked down upon.

There was a time when the finest jewellers, architects, smiths, stone masons and miners and prospectors could be found in the village of Soulwind, back during the rule of King Norman. Both its large stone quarry and deep silver mine fuelled an age of wealth and prosperity for Soulwind.

Soulwind exhausted its raw materials prematurely, and as the quarry emptied, and the mines depleted, the miners had no work and ultimately the village struggled. This brought on an age of poverty for the Village.

Soulwind's Inn, The Shovel and Pick, was a popular watering hole for the thirsty workers after a long day in the mines and quarry, but even that struggled over the coming years.

Rowan returned from the shed clasping something carefully in both of his hands, which was concealed within a folded leather cloth.

'Here you are, son,' said Rowan as he proudly handed over the cloth.

'What is it?' asked Cruise as he took it off his father and gazed at him.

'Open it,' said Rowan eagerly.

Cruise unfolded the leather cloth, and within it he found a bright, marbled silver pendant attached to a thin length of leather cord. Cruise immediately recognised the pendant as the symbol of his hero, Marcus the Swift, the same symbol he remembered seeing him wearing in all of the books and statues.

Cruise looked up sarcastically at his father, as if he was expecting some sort of explanation.

'Cruise,' said Rowan, 'that pendant actually belonged to Marcus the Swift once, believe it or not, and it's not a cheap copy or replica as many might think. They say that pendant brought Marcus a lot of good luck, and it was even rumoured by some to give him his fabled speed, endurance and agility. It's been in our family for a few generations now.'

Cruise continued to stare at his father looking rather confused at the whole concept. 'Dad,' he said after a pause, 'don't tell me this is going to be like the year you gave me that old woodcutting axe and told me it once belonged to Mador the Barbarian? Please explain to me, how did the pendant of Marcus the Swift end up in our family?

Shouldn't it have stayed with Marcus? I'm sure I heard that he had children of his own, a lot of children.'

'Of course he had children of his own,' said Rowan, 'but that's the exciting thing, Cruise... Marcus gave it to one of our ancestors as a gesture of thanks and friendship after he saved his life at The Battle of the Crimson Meadows. You do remember me telling you stories just before bedtime when you were a child, about your Great-Great Grandfather, Grandpa Slade, don't you?'

'Oh yeah,' said Cruise, 'I remember now, after they'd both fought together to take back Soulwind Castle from those bad people and how they both took back the other villages from them and helped free the Kingdom?'

'Exactly,' said Rowan. 'your grandmother gave it to me when I was your age and now I'm giving it to you, and maybe one day, when you have children of your own, you can hand it down to one of them.'

Cruise gazed at the pendant deeply and thought about the history and the action that this pendant had seen, and he pondered the strange metal that it was crafted out of, whom was its maker, and where its origin lay, before finally tying it around his neck. The silver felt cool against his bare chest.

Cruise still remained partially sceptical at the whole concept that he had just been handed Marcus the Swift's pendant, and he kept an open mind that the pendant was a mere copy or a replica made by a blacksmith as a favour to Rowan to surprise Cruise on his birthday. After all, many of the folk tales regarding Marcus's pendant were rumoured to be hearsay.

'Thanks Dad,' said Cruise finally, 'I won't lose it.'

Rowan normally took things that Cruise usually said like that with a pinch of salt, but he knew Cruise would be extra careful when it came to this.

'It's all yours now,' said Rowan, 'take good care of it, and as I said, you may have a son or daughter of your own to pass it down to someday, and it might even bring you some good luck.'

'Thanks Dad,' said Cruise once more, 'I'm going to head to Red's place now and make sure that he's up ready for the race. I'll see you later?'

'Right you are son,' said Rowan, 'I'll see you at the festival.'

Cruise left his yard and made his way towards Red's home.

Red and Cruise had known each other ever since they were old enough to walk. Their families were quite close and today they would both be running in the race together, not just as friends, but also as rivals.

Red was often Cruise's training partner leading up towards the festival race, but this year Red was also old enough to run with the adults for the first time, and both of them would surely try their very best to win it, best friends or otherwise.

Red lived a few small fields away from Cruise, but Cruise normally took the old narrow dirt path that led behind his house and through a small old oak forest to get there.

Cruise arrived at Red's house to find him chopping firewood for his father's forge in his yard.

'Oh, so you're up then,' said Cruise.

'Looks that way, doesn't it?' said Red as he bent down and reached for another log from the wood pile and placed it on the chopping block. 'You're up early for a change,' he said as he brought down his axe hard and split the log in two, 'wet the bed again, did you? I was going to come and call for you once I'd finished up here. Are you ready for the race?'

'God no,' said Cruise as he shook his head and grabbed a spare hatchet from nearby to lean on, 'I didn't sleep a wink last night.'

'Oh man up will you, you pansy,' said Red as he split another log in half with a mighty swing of his axe.

They both caught each other's eye and gazed at each other for a while, trying to keep a straight face then suddenly they both smirked before bursting out laughing.

Red and Cruise were the complete opposites of each other.

Red was a few months older and a few inches taller than Cruise, and their features differed greatly. Red had rusty coloured, wiry hair, with green eyes and pale, pasty skin. He was also built a little lighter than Cruise for his height, but he had strong shoulders and looked a lot rougher. He had various scars over his body and almost constantly seemed to brandish a black eye or similar facial injury, and which he never disclosed how he had acquired, but despite their broad differences in appearance there were no two closer friends in the whole of the village.

Their mischievous childhood had earned them quite the reputation amongst the locals, with some, (or most to be more accurate,) of the folk describing mischievous as being a grave understatement.

'Are you just going to lean on that axe all day then or are you going to give me hand with these logs?' asked Red. 'It'll be good for you to warm up before the race, and we'll get this done a lot faster that way.'

'Hilarious,' said Cruise as he gave Red a sarcastic look.

'Loosen up!' laughed Red. 'You really thought that I'd forgotten, didn't you? Wait a second.'

Cruise smirked with excitement as he wondered what Red had got for him this year. They always bought each other birthday presents as Red was more like a brother to him than anyone, as well as his best friend. Most of the time it was more of a stupid contest as to whom could get the other the most ridiculous gift. One year, Cruise could recall Red getting him an old haggard goat from the nearby farm, which he had swapped with the farmer for a sack of kindling. *'What am I supposed to do with this?'* Cruise could remember asking Red at the time, to which Red quite bluntly replied, *'Stop being ungrateful before I knock you out.'*

Cruise named the old goat Frederick and kept him tied up in his front yard.

Frederick died shortly after of old age.

There were other times, however, where Cruise and Red would get each other a serious present – it all depended on their mood and financial situation at the time, but Red loved tea, to the point in which Cruise thought he had a serious addiction to the stuff, so Cruise would mostly buy Red a large sack of it every year, and sometimes he would get him a large jar of birch sap syrup from the neighbouring village, Birchwood Grove.

After disappearing into the house, Red returned bearing a crudely wrapped parcel.

'Here you go,' said Red, throwing Cruise the package.

'Thanks,' said Cruise as he caught it. 'What is it?'

'Open it and find out, you bat,' said Red as he leaned his back against the stone wall of his cottage.

Cruise tore open the package and inside he found two items.

The first was a slingshot, beautifully carved from of a single piece of solid oak, polished, and finished with a soft leather handle. It was very typical of Red to give Cruise such a birthday present that could potentially maim and cripple defenceless animals.

'You can kill rats with that,' said Red immediately on that thought.

The second item was a very nice pocket knife. Red's father, Ferlan, a big giant of a man, was the village blacksmith, so Red would use his forge from time to time.

'I made them both myself,' said Red proudly.

'You made both of these?' said Cruise sounding half surprised and half suspicious.

'Yes,' said Red, 'cheeky sod, it took me days.'

Cruise did not mean to come across as sounding ungrateful or disrespectful, but it was a shock to him to find that Red, whom usually was very rough and ready, had produced and crafted such fine items.

Cruise thanked Red and stowed the items in his pockets.

'Do you fancy a quick cup of tea before we head to the festival?' asked Red.

'No thanks, I don't want to fill up too much before the race,' replied Cruise.

'There's nothing like a cup of tea to hydrate and revitalise before a race!' said Red.

'I'll be fine,' smiled Cruise as he grasped the spare woodcutting hatchet from behind him and helped Red finish chopping the log pile.

Cruise thought of holding up the trophy in his victory as he brought up the axe ready to bring down for the final swing, and he hoped this warm up would aid him in achieving that lifelong dream, and not leave it in tatters like the log he had just split.

Chapter Two

Registration

After Cruise had finished chopping the log pile and once Red had made himself a swift cup of tea, they left Red's place and made their way towards the festival grounds to register before the race. Cruise could barely contain his excitement.

The morning was growing steadily warmer and there was not a single cloud in the sky.

'I hope it isn't going to be too hot today,' said Red, sounding rather worried.

Red disliked the heat.

The festival was always held in the same location each year, in the high field on the far side of the village to where both Cruise and Red lived. It was always a sight that made them both smile with great joy.

The huge pavilion tents that littered the field scraped the sky with their high bannered flagpoles. There were hundreds of different food, weapon, and toy stalls from traders from all around Termelanor, as far as the eye could see… game stalls, show stalls, and hundreds and thousands of people who had gathered from all over the Kingdom, all enjoying the sunshine and the clear blue skies.

Cruise could seldom recall a time when he would look at the main pavilion tent in the same way as he once did, following the year that he and Red decided to pick a side each and race each other from one end to the other while seeing who could undo the tent pegs the fastest, (much to the dismay of the people who were still inside it.)

It was no doubt a close race, judging by how evenly the tent had collapsed, but Red swears to this day that he won that contest, although Cruise begs to differ.

They argued that the 'next time' they would have a judge at the finishing line to settle any disagreements.

Red and Cruise both walked around the festival and took a look at the stalls before they headed over to the registration tent, as it was still too early to register, when suddenly Cruise's heart leapt as he caught a sight even more staggering than any in the entire festival; it was Amber.

Amber was a beautiful young lady who lived in Soulwind. She was about Cruise's age and had sweeping long raven hair right down to her lower back, and two perfect, clear, large and shiny sapphire coloured eyes.

Cruise had been interested in Amber for as long as he could remember. She would smile at him from time to time as he walked walk past her but his whole body would seize up and he forgot how to talk whenever she said hello to him.

Although they both lived in Soulwind, Cruise did not talk to her much as his nerves always got the better of him, and for this reason he actively tried to avoid her, usually regretting it shortly afterwards.

'Go over and talk to her,' said Red as he leant on an oak barrel munching on an apple.

'Nah,' said Cruise, turning to Red, 'have you paid for that?'

'Don't change the subject,' said Red, his mouth full and pointing. 'She just looked over at you, and I bet she's still doing it peripherally to see if you're looking back at her.'

'That's a big word for you,' said Cruise, 'and anyway, how can you possibly even tell that?'

'I just know, all right,' said Red. 'Look, look, at her pretending to pick things up from that stall, as if she has any interest in that reel of thread. She keeps playing with her hair, putting it behind her ear and-.'

'So?' said Cruise, 'what does that have to do with anything?'

'It means-oh shit, she's coming over,' said Red, turning to his side.

'What do I do?' said Cruise.

'Just talk to her. Calm yourself down,' said Red.

'What do I say?' said Cruise.

'Just pretend she's me,' said Red before swiftly double taking, 'actually, don't pretend she's me.'

Red loudly mentioned something about one of the stalls nearby then before Cruise knew it he was all alone, well, almost all alone.

'Hey Cruise,' said Amber with a pearly white bright smile, 'I heard that you're running in the race this year. Your parents were just speaking with mine.'

Amber's parents, Ash and Holly owned the village

inn, The Shovel and Pick.

Cruise tried to squeeze out a few words. He looked around for Red, but he was a fair distance away speaking with Rosie next to one of the cake stalls.

Rosie was a pretty young lady from the village with long fiery red bushy hair, and the only living thing that Cruise had never heard Red mention knocking out or disembowelling.

He had to say something back to her. He couldn't just stand there like an idiot.

'Yeah, it's the first year that I've been able to enter the adult race, and some of the competitors look pretty tough this year.'

'Oh well, I'm sure you'll do great,' said Amber, smiling widely. 'I'll be cheering for you.'

Cruise turned bright pink. It must have been bad because he caught a glimpse of Red looking over at him with a bewildered face.

'Thanks,' said Cruise nervously as he looked to the ground and scratched the back of his head distractingly.

'Well,' smiled Amber, 'good luck. I'll be sure to wait for you at the finishing line.'

As Amber went to leave she grabbed Cruise's shoulders and pecked him on the cheek, before hurrying off. Cruise turned around and caught a glimpse of her raven hair sweeping her lower back before she disappeared into the festival crowd.

Cruise stood there anchored to the spot as Red ran over to him.

'Don't die on me before the race,' said Red laughing.

'What just happened?' asked Cruise, touching his cheek.

Red shook his head, still laughing as he put Cruise in a headlock and they continued on towards the registration tent.

As Red and Cruise approached the registration tent, they heard a palaver in the nearby distance as crowds of people shoved past them to gather around a large, impressive looking coach drawn by six beastly-looking black stallions.

'It's the Agiles!' a woman shouted from the crowd.

'Is it really them?' yelled a man, as he shoved past Red and Cruise.

'Hey,' yelled Red at the man, 'watch it.'

'I hear that Zane is the favourite to win this year!' screamed a teenage girl.

'Well then I know who I'll be placing my bet on!' replied her father.

This was a sight all too familiar for Red and Cruise. The sight of the coach did little more to them than annoy them both and send Red on a jealous rant.

'Of course, it's the Agiles,' said Red flatly, 'one of them always bloody wins it, every year, without fail. Cheating bastards.'

'Don't worry about them now, Red,' said Cruise pretending not to be equally as bothered by the sight of the coach as Red was. 'Come on, let's go and register and try and stay focused, shall we?'

Cruise and Red approached the registration tent to sign up for the race after they had shoved past the rest of the excited villagers and fans.

The everlasting lines of competitors seemed to grow longer and longer each year, but the multiple registration tables made short work of the long queues.

Red and Cruise picked a line each and both approached a table together as the line quickly shortened.

'Name and village please?' said the lady behind the table.

'Cruise, from Soulwind.'

'Thank you, dear. Here's your race number, and good luck to you.'

Cruise turned around to go and wait nearby for Red to finish registering. He was clasping his race number in both hands, staring at it proudly as he walked when he bumped his head against a strangers' hard chest.

'I'm sorry I-,' said Cruise rubbing his head before he was cut short.

'Why don't you watch where you're walking, kid?' said the stranger aggressively.

Cruise looked up and immediately noticed the symbol of Marcus the Swift on the stranger's tunic. He raised his head and took a step back, and he found himself facing five strong and defined looking figures, all of them maybe a few years older than he was, all dressed in matching sky blue, white and silver-trimmed tunics that bore Marcus's symbol.

The Agiles arrived in Soulwind from the Capital each

year to compete in the race, and to this date an Agile had won almost every single race within the last eighty years, with only a few extreme exceptions.

And it was no small wonder, either.

As it happened, each and every one of them could trace their direct lineage of descent right back to Marcus the Swift himself, and each and every one of them had annoyingly inherited the legendary speed, stamina and endurance of Cruise's fabled hero.

At that moment, Red had caught up with Cruise.

'Hey, Cruise, I got number 33! What did you get? Cruise? Who are you talking to?' said Red, looking from side to side at The Agiles. Red knew exactly who they were, but he wasn't going to give them the satisfaction. Red strongly disliked The Agiles and always found it an unfair disadvantage that they had descended from Marcus the Swift.

'What do you mean, *who are you talking to?*' said the young man who Cruise had bumped into, sounding quite annoyed.

He was a tall, dark, muscular young man, taller than Red and Cruise. He was very handsome and had a strong, stubbled jaw line.

'Well, I wasn't talking to you, was I?' said Red.

'You'd better watch your mouth, kid,' he said angrily.

'Or what?' said Red.

'Do you want to find out?' said the man approaching Red.

'Don't Zane,' said the attractive blonde girl stood next

to him, while grabbing his arm. 'It's not worth getting disqualified from the race for.'

'You're right, Talia,' said Zane. 'You'd better watch yourself runt, I'll be looking out for you during the race.'

The Agiles shoved past Red and Cruise and approached a special registration stand with no line.

'What was that guy's problem?' said Cruise, still rubbing his forehead.

'You could swear they were royalty or something,' said Red, '*What do you mean, who are you talking to?* Did you hear him?'

'Forget them for now, Red,' said Cruise. 'Come on, we have an hour before the race starts. Let's have a little walk around and loosen up.'

The raw and pure anger of encountering the Agiles had evidently gotten to Red far more than usual as he spent the last hour venting over how ridiculous they all were, how they were all cheaters and how stupid their faces were, but Cruise thought of nothing more than the image of Amber's pale, flawless face and her perfect clear sapphire eyes peering up and her pearly white teeth smiling at him in the crowd as he was named the victor. He had to win this. Maybe then he would think that he would be good enough for her.

Chapter Three

At the Ready

The time had finally arrived for the contestants to approach and take their positions on the starting line, and as Red and Cruise hung back and warmed up, stretching out their limbs, Cruise came over with an overwhelming excitement and could not help himself from smiling broadly.

'Are you not nervous then?' asked Red, noticing Cruise smiling.

'Of course I am,' smiled Cruise as he stretched out his hamstrings, 'but I'm so excited at the same time, I can't help myself. Just look at all of these people, Red. How about you, aren't you nervous?'

'Nah,' lied Red, 'don't worry, I'll check back on you from time to time.'

'Oh, you wish, my friend,' smirked Cruise.

'All right then,' said Red, 'one bronze Termellian says I place higher than you do.'

'Oh, breaking the bank, aren't we?' said Cruise. 'Why don't we make it two if you're so confident?'

'You're on,' said Red as he shook Cruise's hand. 'Just promise not to cry when I'm taking your money from you.'

The starting line was, as always, jammed full of competitors; some who Cruise knew from the village, others strangers from neighbouring villages who he had never seen before. He couldn't recall ever being so excited.

Some of the runners from the neighbouring villages wore a little distinctive token or piece of clothing to indicate and to honour which village that they were from. A runner near to Cruise seemed to be from Bouldershore, as he was wearing an over shirt seemingly made out of a rope fishing net.

It was time for the runners to take up position behind the starting line. Cruise positioned himself next to Red upon the starting grid.

The grid positions were down to a first come first serve basis, although the front was always reserved for the Agiles. This was another unfair reason why Red hated them.

So this was it, the race that Cruise had been waiting and training for, and the day he had been looking forward to for as long as he could remember. He was going to win it. He had to.

Silence descended upon the grid as all eyes of the spectators were on the starting line. The spectator stands were full and the runners listened patiently for the starting horn.

There was a long silence and then the horn blasted and echoed across the field as the spectators cheered and the runners bolted off the starting line.

The race had commenced and Cruise was off to a good start. Red also had a strong first foot off the ground, but Cruise nearly stopped dead in his tracks when he witnessed the Agiles already in the distance.

They seemed to glide across the dusty path, making little impact on the hard ground, so smooth and cushioned yet so powerful and full of energy at the same time, and already Cruise could see they had an advantage over the other runners.

Cruise tried to ignore what he had just seen and concentrated on his own race. Considering what he had just saw, he wasn't doing too bad, and he had managed to get quite near to the front, even though the Agiles had long since disappeared into the lead. He even caught a glimpse of Red out the corner of his eye at one point.

The race continued on, and the pace did not change much for a fair chunk of the run.

Then something suddenly awoke inside of Cruise. He had to catch up with the Agiles, he just had to. What if they were already halfway through the race? He had to increase his speed. He had to pick up his pace.

He stopped thinking and shot off from the rest of the pack.

Red's eyes nearly bulged out of their sockets as he thought, *'That idiot! He's going to exhaust his energy before even half of the race is finished!'*

But Cruise didn't care, Agile or not, nobody was going to take his place as festival champion, and the honour of the title 'The Swift' just like his hero, Marcus. He didn't care that they shared blood with him; he believed that he was more like him than anyone, and that he somehow had a connection with him.

Cruise's training and increase in pace had paid off. He

could see the Agiles in the distance. They were far ahead, but nonetheless they were in sight, and he was determined to catch up to them. Hell, he was even determined to pass them and to beat them.

Cruise was catching up, until he noticed Zane glancing back and clocking onto him.

He noticed Zane smirk annoyingly as the Agiles effortlessly doubled their speed. Cruise could not believe it. This whole time they were merely jogging along, toying with the rest of the runners, as if they were out for a Sunday stroll.

How was it even possible? Cruise had nearly exhausted all of his energy, and these people had not yet warmed up or broken a single bead of sweat. He could not keep this up, but he had to try. He attempted to double his own speed to rival the Agiles'.

Cruise was concentrating so hard on the race that he had not noticed a good-sized rock protruding out of the race track right in front of him.

By the time he had seen it, it was too late to do anything about it. His big toe collided with it in a nasty sounding crunch and he flew through the air, head over heels, and landed square on his back on the dusty ground.

He let out a cry of pain. He tried to get up but the fall had done more damage than he had thought, and he had badly hurt his back. His toe felt broken and his ankle seemed to be sprained, plus he was covered in scuffs and scrapes.

He heard Zane laugh in the distance and Cruise yelled

out with a cry of rage.

That was it, his dream was over, and the Agiles were going to win the race again.

Just then, Red appeared out of nowhere alongside him. He must have not been too far behind Cruise.

'Cruise!' said Red. 'What happened?'

'Don't worry about me, Red!' said Cruise. 'You have to finish the race! Go on! Go! The Agiles aren't too far ahead!'

Red understood and continued the pursuit in Cruise's place.

Soon, all manner of competitors overtook Cruise giving him funny looks and asked him if he was all right as they passed him sprawled out in the middle of the race track. A friendly runner from Goldstream offered to help him to the side of the track as he continued on, leaving Cruise behind.

He couldn't just stay there. He could not win the race now, but he could at least try to finish it.

He got to his feet ignoring the horrible pain, and he limped and hobbled, continuing on his way, clutching at his side.

Chapter Four

Shattered Dreams

By the time Cruise had finally stumbled and fallen across the finishing line, the race was long over, and the winners had already claimed their rewards.

Cruise collapsed over the finishing line with a roar of pain.

Amber and his parents had been waiting by the finish line for Cruise and became anxious when there was no sign of him. Amber quickly rushed over to help him up off the ground.

'Cruise!' said his mother running up behind her. 'Oh my baby, are you all right? What happened? I was wondering where you were.'

'I'm fine, Mum,' lied Cruise. 'Who won?' more concerned about the outcome of the race.

'That Agile, Zane,' said Amber. 'He was well across the finish line before anybody else came close.'

'Damn it,' said Cruise. 'Where's Red? How did he do?'

'Well,' said Amber, 'I saw the race marshals take him away to the medical tent right after he crossed the finish line. He was cursing and shouting about something and he seemed to be bleeding quite badly. Rosie went in with him.'

'We should go and see if he's all right,' said Cruise as Amber helped him hobble towards the medical tent.

'Mother, father, I'll be fine,' said Cruise to his parents, as he signalled with his hand behind his back, urging them to leave him alone with Amber. They both got the hint and his mother smiled as she flapped her arms up and down with excitement.

Amber and Cruise had almost approached the medical tent, when an irritating voice piped up from behind him.

'Hard luck, loser,' laughed a voice. 'Did you have a nice trip?'

Cruise turned around to see the Agiles again, and Zane was holding a very large and impressive looking golden trophy. He was donned in an impressive ceremonial garment with Marcus's symbol on it, and a fine golden ceremonial blade at his side.

'Get lost,' said Amber, 'can't you see that he's hurt?'

'Oh, what's the matter?' said Zane. 'Are you upset because your boyfriend didn't win the race?'

'Hey, watch your mouth,' said Cruise, stepping forward.

'Or what, loser?' said Zane as he also took a step forward.

Cruise diverted his gaze to the ground. Zane was much bigger than he, and Cruise was worn out and injured from the race; besides, the festival was a very crowded place and Cruise knew better than to draw any unwanted attention.

'That's what I thought,' said Zane, looking Cruise up and down.

Cruise looked up for a moment and the pair of them met each other's gaze. Zane flinched slightly as he caught a glimpse of Cruise's eyes.

Their colour, and the way they dilated, he thought he was frightened for a split second. Why was he scared of them? His fear stayed with him for a while longer, as he stood there transfixed, staring into Cruise's grey-blue eyes, pretending not to be both amazed and frightened by them. Where had he seen them before? Had he seen them before? Why did they look so familiar? Zane then quickly shut his eyes and shook his head.

'Huh,' shrugged Zane as he composed himself. He took one last look at Cruise and Amber, scoffed, then turned and walked away followed by the others.

'That man,' said Amber through her clenched teeth.

'Forget about him, Amber,' said Cruise, not even realising what had just gone through Zane's head. 'Come on, let's get to the medical tent and find out what happened to Red.'

When Cruise and Amber arrived at the medical tent, Red was not a happy man. Medical pans scattered the ground and apparently it took three men to calm him down and restrain him.

'Red, what happened?' asked Cruise as he approached his bed.

'That bastard Zane tripped me up as I went to overtake him,' said Red.

'Whilst he was running?' asked Cruise. 'How did he do that?'

'I don't know,' said Red, 'but he did it with ease. It couldn't have been the first time he's done it. He must practice and train to cheat to win a race as well as having speed and good stamina handed to him.'

'What surprises me the most, Red, is that you managed to even challenge to overtake him. That's an incredible accomplishment,' said Cruise sounding very impressed. 'When you passed me on the ground, I had tripped too, but that was my fault. I should have been looking where I was going.'

'Clumsy sod,' joked Red.

'Well, come on, it's over now. What's done is done. Considering what happened, and who we were up against, we didn't do that bad,' said Cruise.

'Yeah, maybe we can lose again next year too,' said Red, 'but at least some good came out of today.'

'What's that?' asked Cruise.

'At least I won our bet,' smiled Red.

'Bastard,' laughed Cruise.

Chapter Five

The Stumble Home

Cruise and Red journeyed back to their respective homes, after they had been mildly patched up in the medical tent. Cruise was helping Red to walk with his arm over his shoulder.

'Well, that escalated quite quickly, didn't it?' Cruise chuckled.

'Yeah,' said Red flatly, 'another one for the long list.'

'I just can't believe it though,' said Cruise, 'all of that training we did, for nothing.'

'Don't think of it like that,' said Red, 'there's always next year, isn't there?'

'Well, yeah,' said Cruise, 'but even if we did train again for next year, wouldn't the Agiles just come back even faster and stronger than they were this year?'

'Good old optimistic Cruise,' laughed Red.

'Sorry,' said Cruise. 'It's just I thought that this was the year, that's all.'

'It was only our first year,' said Red, 'we didn't do that bad. Well, at least we finished.'

'Let's forget about it for now, Red,' said Cruise, 'let's just enjoy the rest of the festival.

'You're right,' said Red, 'we still have the champion's

ball to enjoy tonight.'

'I don't feel like going,' said Cruise, 'the thought of the smug look on Zane's face as he parades that trophy around the place, I don't think I could bear it.'

'Oh, come on,' said Red, 'if he does that, I'll ask him if I can see it for a minute and then throw it in that giant trifle they always have on the buffet table.'

Cruise laughed out loud.

'All right then,' he said, 'but only for a little bit, then I'm going home.'

'Who are you going to ask to go with you?' said Red. 'You can't go on your own or you'll look like even more of a loser than you normally do.'

'Oh damn,' said Cruise, 'I'd completely forgotten about that. Who should I ask?'

'What about Betsy who you took last year?' said Red.

'Oh god no,' said Cruise, 'that was only out of pity because my mum forced me to ask her.'

'You should ask Amber to go with you then,' said Red.

'Why?' asked Cruise slightly defensively. 'Who are you taking?'

'Rosie. I asked her earlier in the medical tent while you were with Amber,' said Red, 'I thought you would have asked her?'

'Oh no, brilliant, I didn't think about it at the time,' thought Cruise as they approached Red's house. 'Are you sure you don't need a hand with your injuries Red?'

'I'll be fine,' said Red.

Cruise helped Red into his house and then made his way slowly back down the old lane and to his own home.

Chapter Six

The Champion's Ball

Cruise had arrived home and strapped up his ankle, but strangely felt the pain ease ever so slightly. Maybe he was just imagining things and being his usual absent-minded self.

He was darting around the house preparing for the ball, trying to find suitable clothing to wear.

'Mum, where's my good tunic?' he shouted down the stairs.

'I had to clean it, dear,' she replied, 'it was caked in cat's hair.'

'Argh, Cicada!' he moaned, 'you stupid cat! What am I going to wear now?'

'Your father has a nice tunic you can borrow,' she said.

'Okay, DAD!' he shouted.

'Oh Cruise, I wish you'd stay in for the night and rest that ankle of yours. From what I heard from some of the spectators it was a pretty nasty fall,' said Cruise's mother.

'Mum, I'm fine,' said Cruise, 'you should have seen the mess on Red and he's still going. Can you imagine what he'd say if I didn't show up? He'd be calling me a pansy up until next year's festival!'

'I'll never understand you two boys,' she said. 'Have

you asked a nice girl to go with you tonight? I heard that Betsy has been asking about you.'

'No Betsy, this year I've already asked someone,' Cruise lied.

'Ohh, who's that dear?' she asked curiously, half knowing who he meant.

'Never mind,' said Cruise grumpily as he rummaged through a clothes drawer.

'You know I was speaking with Ash and Holly earlier, and they said Amber doesn't have a date yet.'

Cruise felt himself redden as he buried his face further into the clothing drawer.

'What about it?' he muttered.

'Well, I thought it'd be lovely if you both went together.'

'Oh Mum, give it a rest for now,' he said. 'Where are my good boots?'

'They're in the parlour dear, where they always are,' she said with a smirk on her face.

Cruise quickly finished dressing, trying his best to avoid any further Amber based conversation with his mother, before disappearing out of the front door once again and heading back to Red's house.

Red normally waited for Cruise at the end of the lane at the night of the champion's ball, but tonight he was not there.

Cruise waited for a while and before long Red appeared limping slightly, wearing a dark green tunic.

'You scrub up pretty well,' Cruise chuckled as Red came out to meet him.

'Shut up,' Red replied, 'you'd better not be trying to come on to me because you haven't got a date for the ball.'

'Hilarious Red,' said Cruise with a hint of depression, 'come on, let's go and get it over with.'

The pair of them walked back to the area of the festival and on to the large pavilion tent, which housed the Champion's Ball.

It was already heaving with people as they walked in through the front entrance.

'I'm going to find Rosie,' mumbled Red.

'Okay,' said Cruise, 'I'm going to see what they have to eat.'

Cruise walked right up to the feast buffet. His appetite had almost returned to normal now that the worry of the race was over, but the race itself was still fresh in his mind as he stared deeply into a very large platter of fruit on the buffet table, when a soft voice sounded from behind him.

'Deciding on the apple or the pear, are you?' said the voice, 'I must say it's a tough choice.'

Cruise shot immediately around to face a very beautiful young blonde woman smiling at him. It was Talia, one of the Agiles.

'Oh,' said Cruise, 'forgive me, I was just, deep in thought. I'm Cruise.' He said, quickly offering his hand.

'That's all right,' she smiled, taking his hand, 'I'm Talia. I'm sorry about that nasty fall. Are you all right now?'

'Oh yeah, I'm fine,' lied Cruise, 'and congratulations on your result. All of you ran a very good race and I was very impressed to see you all in action.'

'Thank you,' she replied, 'but it sort of comes naturally to us, you know? I admired your heart during the race. Very few people ever come close to challenging us. It was quite exciting.'

'I don't know what to say,' said Cruise, 'but you're all something else. I've never seen anything like it before in my life.'

'Well, you were quite impressive yourself, so don't ever doubt that. I actually felt kind of bad for you, but Zane would never have forgiven any of us if we'd stopped to help you out. He follows a really tight and strict plan while we race.'

'That's all right,' said Cruise, 'it wasn't your fault. I understand.'

'Well, there's always next year,' said Talia, 'don't give up all hope. I find it refreshing to face a new challenger.'

Cruise smiled.

'I'd better get back to the others,' said Talia, 'It was nice to meet you.'

'You too,' replied Cruise.

Cruise grabbed a few things off the buffet table then walked around to try and find Red.

Cruise was walking through the crowd munching on a large chicken leg and looking up at the spectacular tent roof when he knocked his back against somebody.

'Oh, sorry about that,' said Cruise as he turned around.

'That's fine,' smiled the young man in a polite manner.

Cruise took a better look at the young man and noticed he was wearing an Agile's tunic.

'You're an-?'

'Thomas.' said the man as he offered his hand.

'Cruise,' he replied after a short pause and he took Thomas's hand, 'I was just speaking with Talia, your… sister?'

'First cousin,' replied Thomas as he corrected Cruise. 'My mother and Talia's father are brother and sister. Humphrey, Oram, and Zane are our distant cousins on the other side, through our grandparents.'

'I see now,' said Cruise, 'you don't come across as, how can I say this without being too offensive, you don't come across as arrogant as the others, aside from Talia who I was just speaking to.'

'That's very kind of you to say,' smiled Thomas. 'No, Zane has always been the natural leader of the pack, ever since we were kids, and Humphrey and Oram are sort of his left and right-hand men. To be honest with you, I don't particularly enjoy any of this, but it seems that we've all been both gifted and cursed respectively, and we have a duty and a legacy to continue, in the name of our ancestor, Grampa Marcus.'

'I've never thought of it like that before,' said Cruise, 'that seems sort of sad. Why don't you speak to Zane about it?'

'I've tried,' said Thomas, 'but he insists that I'm being ridiculous. He knows nothing but this life and winning.

He sees me as a bit of a traitor to the bloodline when I speak of such things, so I tend to keep my thoughts to myself now and crack on with it to keep him happy.'

'What would you like to do?' asked Cruise, 'I mean, if you weren't doing this?'

'I'm not sure,' said Thomas as he looked up smiling as though thinking of the possibilities, 'I'd love to travel and see a bit of the world. We rarely leave the walls of the Capital aside from coming here.'

'As would I,' smiled Cruise, 'but my place is back here with my family for now, as I have to support them.'

'I'd better find the others,' said Thomas. 'It was nice to talk to you, Cruise.'

'Likewise, Thomas,' said Cruise as he shook his hand once again and dissolved into the crowd.

Cruise thought he had better go and try and find Red; he shouldn't leave him alone for so long.

He had not gotten far before he came across a sight that made his stomach twist and his heart nearly break into two.

It was Zane, grasping a large goblet of wine, whispering tenderly into Amber's ear as he ran his fingers through her long raven hair. She smiled and giggled lustfully as she stroked his broad chest.

Amber caught Cruise out of the corner of her eye as he slammed down his plate and turned and bolted back into the crowd of people.

Cruise ran outside to get some air as he tried to get over what he had just seen. He did not know whether to feel anger or sadness or confusion. He was just about to storm home when he heard a voice call out his name from behind.

'Cruise, wait.'

He turned to see Amber coming towards him as she exited the tent.

'Go back inside, Amber,' he said.

'Cruise,' said Amber, 'I know how that looked, but he came up to me.'

'I saw how it looked,' said Cruise flatly.

Just then, Zane appeared from the tent and approached Cruise and Amber. He looked at Cruise briefly before turning to Amber.

'Come on, Amber,' he said, 'let's go back inside.'

Amber said nothing as she looked from Cruise to Zane with a sorry look on her face.

'Just go Amber,' said Cruise. 'It's fine. Enjoy the rest of the party, I'm going home.'

Suddenly, a loud yell came from the direction of the tent, as Red stepped outside and noticed Zane.

'There you are!' shouted Red, 'I've been looking for you, you cheating bastard!'

Cruise had never seen Red so angry, and Cruise had once pushed him into the frozen lake at the bottom of the village during winter time. Red had cracked his head on the ice on the way in to the lake and was furious by the time he had managed to clamber out, soaking wet and freezing. The fuel was merely added to the fire when Red moaned and held the bleeding gash on his head and Cruise suggested that he *'put some ice on it,'* but this time, it was no laughing matter for Cruise.

'Like cheating, do you?' said Red as he approached Zane fuming, 'you saw that I was going to pass you, and you tripped me up. What was the matter, you couldn't take it that I was going to beat you?'

'So what if I did?' said Zane, now squaring up to Red. 'What are you going to do about it now, runt?'

Red was still suffering from his various injuries from the fall he had sustained when Zane had tripped him up during the race. Knowing this, Red stood there gripping his fists at his sides and grinding his teeth, looking down at the ground.

'That's what I thought,' said Zane as he turned around as the rest of the Agiles now appeared out of the tent, 'I don't waste my time with losers.'

Red snapped and leaped onto Zane's back as he let out a roar. Zane grabbed Red's arm and threw him onto the floor in front of him, just before Zane could throw down a punch. Red had rolled to the side and tripped Zane down onto the floor with him, and the two scuffled about on the ground.

Just as Zane was clambering onto Red to punch him in the face, Humphrey and Oram grabbed him from behind and lifted him off Red and Rosie and Cruise stopped Red from going after him once he was pulled off.

'You've done it now, runt,' said Zane, 'let me go you two!' he ordered.

The commotion was starting to draw a bit of attention now as people were stepping outside of the tent to see what all the noise was about.

'Zane, calm down,' said Talia stepping in front of him, 'you'll earn yourself a life ban from running in the festival if you're caught fighting at the champion's ball like a pair of wild animals!'

Zane looked at Talia then back at Red before closing his eyes and inhaling a deep breath.

'You're right, Talia,' said Zane. 'All right, runt, you want to fight me, do you? Tomorrow is the closing ceremony of the festival. What do you say we give the people of Termelanor a closing ceremony to remember? You and me, one on one, we'll fight in the arena, worthy of the warriors that this festival commemorates.'

'You're on,' said Red.

'You talk a good fight, runt,' said Zane, 'but tomorrow we'll truly find out if you can indeed back up your words.'

Zane turned with the rest of the Agiles as the disappeared back into the tent.

'Red,' said Cruise, 'you don't have to do this. You have nothing to prove to him, or to anybody, and besides, you're still injured and worn out from the race.'

'I have to do this Cruise,' said Red, 'you can't talk me out of this one.'

Chapter Seven

The Arena

The closing ceremony of the festival featured a day full of activity much like the rest of the festival.

As the festival winded down, plays and re-enactments of battles and history from the days of Marcus the Swift were shown in the fields and on the stages.

The centrepiece of these stages was the festival arena, which was erected each year out of mighty lengths of timber and used to show off the grandest shows and also the closing parade, and this year, it would be housed to also show the fight between the champion Zane and his challenger, Red, and the whole village was buzzing with excitement over it.

Cruise was waiting with Red in the preparation room of the festival arena.

'Have you decided how you're going to fight him?' asked Cruise.

'I'm not too sure yet,' said Red, 'I'm so angry that I can't even think straight.'

'You have to try and focus, Red,' said Cruise, 'you won't be able to fight him effectively with a mist clouding your vision.'

'You're right,' said Red, 'I'll try and calm myself down.'

'What about a sword? You always beat me one-on-one when we practice with those training blades which your father makes for the militia.'

'Maybe,' said Red, still not looking as if he had managed to calm himself down, 'I'll decide when I see him. Maybe I'll use a sharp spear.'

'You don't want to kill him,' said Cruise.

'Yes, I do,' said Red, 'at least it'll be less competition for us next year, and it'll serve the bastard right for cheating.'

A man suddenly appeared in the doorway.

'Challenger Red,' said the man, 'the festival champion will face you now.'

Cruise looked at Red once more.

'Red,' said Cruise, 'please don't do this, we can forget about it for another year, train together as hard as we ever have, every day, rain or shine, and beat him on the racetrack next year, together.'

'Come on pal,' said Red as he smiled at Cruise, 'let's go and get him.'

Red and Cruise both walked up the narrow walkway towards the centre of the arena. They could feel the rumble of the cheers from above as they came closer to the light of the opening.

As they came out into the open and held up their arms to shield their eyes from the bliding light of the day, they saw the hundreds of spectators cheering down at them.

At the centre of the arena, stood a large, square, fenced off wooden and rope pen, and inside, stood Zane, tall, strong, and intimidating.

Red nervously approached the pen and clambered inside between the rope to face Zane. Cruise waited and leaned eagerly outside on the fence.

A man then came between the two young warriors and spoke loud enough so every spectator in the arena could hear him. Cruise could see the rest of the Agiles on the other side of the pen behind the fence on Zane's side.

'You'll now both choose your weapon of choice for the match,' said the man, 'you may mutually decide on the weapon of choice, and also the armour. This will be a one-on-one match. The winner is victorious if the loser exits the pen, yields, or of course, is killed during the course of the fight. Are there any questions?' asked the man.

Both men said nothing as they stared each other down, and Cruise wondered which weapon both the warriors would choose. Would Red choose a sword? Or would he choose a spear? Red normally dominated Cruise in both sword and stick fighting and he was quite naturally talented as well, as he would practice a lot. Although it would all depend on how good Zane was also, which neither of them could know, but he knew Red wouldn't decide to wear any armour. He knew him well enough that he liked to remain light on his feet. Finally, after a long silence, Red was the first to speak out.

'Why don't we keep this simple,' he said to Zane, 'we both use no weapons, fists only.'

'Have it your way, runt,' said Zane, 'it makes no difference to me.'

'It has been decided!' spoke out the man loudly,

'the challenger will face the festival champion, Zane the Swift, in a fist fight for your entertainment right here in the festival arena! Both of you, please now retire to your respective corners to prepare for a moment. The match will commence when both fighters are ready.'

Red walked back over to Cruise as he stretched out and warmed himself up ready for the fight.

'How are you feeling?' Cruise asked Red, sounding concerned.

'Good,' replied Red, as he focused on Zane the whole time and stretched out his limbs.

Cruise had never seen this side to Red before and he was deeply worried for him.

The man signalled for both fighters to return to the centre of the ring after some time preparing.

'Red,' said Cruise, 'be careful.'

Red approached the centre of the ring and stopped a few metres shy of Zane.

The signal was given by the man, and the match commenced.

Red circled Zane lightly, dancing on his feet with his fists raised up protecting his head. Zane stood in the centre with his arms down, rotating on the spot and constantly facing Red.

Suddenly, Red engaged Zane like a raging bull and swung wildly at him with his fists, and Zane just smiled and effortlessly dodged every single one, arms still held at his side.

It was obvious to Cruise to see that the race had hardly

tired Zane, but Red was still very much worn out from it, and his injuries from the fall were blatantly affecting his performance. Cruise had tried to strap Red up well enough to support his injuries back in the preparation room, and he assured him that he would remain in his corner.

Zane was older, larger, and more powerful than Red, but Red was surprisingly strong and tough for his size and age, and the years he had spent working his father's forge had hardened him considerably, to the point that Cruise thought that he was almost as tough as the iron he was shaping.

Zane now fought back, although slightly mockingly, and unsurprisingly to Cruise, Red had taken many of Zane's blows, and he was equally impressed with Zane's chin when a few of Red's blows had landed on him.

Cruise had caught a few of Red's punches in the past during one of the rare occasions that they had argued or from going too far whilst they were play fighting, and they were not pleasant to receive to say the very least.

It seemed Red was gaining the upper hand over Zane, as he gradually chipped away at Zane's head and body with quick jabs and hooks as he danced and dodged to avoid and counter any of the oncoming punches.

At one point during the fight Zane had thrown Red into one of the corners of the pen and unloaded a flurry of punches at him, but somehow Red managed to dodge every single one and escaped the corner. It was as if Zane was fighting a ghost.

The crowd cheered loudly for Red as he was definitely

getting the better of Zane for the majority of the fight, and he was certainly landing more punches than Zane, but Cruise recognized that Zane was still holding back.

'That's good, Red!' Cruise yelled, 'keep sharp, and don't let your guard down!'

All of a sudden, Zane caught one shiner of a right hook from Red to his jaw, and Cruise saw something click in Zane's eyes.

'Enough of this child's play,' said Zane out aloud.

Before Cruise could do anything, and just as quickly as it had all started, Zane unloaded a mighty uppercut directly onto the tip of Red's nose, which sent him flying halfway across the pen.

Red was dead before he hit the ground.

Cruise stood frozen for a few seconds, staring at the lifeless body of his best friend. He then vaulted the fence and ran towards Red's body.

'Red?' he said as he shook his friend's flaccid, lifeless corpse, 'Red, come on, get up.'

There was no response.

'Red, you never give up on anything, now come on,' said Cruise as he continued to shake his friend's body, 'wake up.' He cradled Red's body and cried out uncontrollably, 'wake up…' But it was over, the light had long since left Red's eyes.

'Red…' he continued, 'Red… wake up…'

Silence filled the arena, as spectators rose from their seats to get a better look at what had just happened.

Zane stepped forward towards the two.

'Oh,' he smiled, 'did I kill him? What a shame.'

A shroud of rage engulfed Cruise.

'You bastard!' bellowed Cruise, as he ran towards Zane, only to be gripped by him and thrown across the pen with a single shove.

'I won't let you get away with this,' wheezed Cruise, 'trust me, I'll make you pay for what you've done.'

'He knew what he was letting himself in for,' stated Zane as he pointed down at Red's lifeless body, 'the old warriors of this Kingdom gave their lives for its freedom, and now he has the honour of joining those fabled heroes of old, as he had the honour to fight me in front of all of these spectators.'

'Honour?' said Cruise. 'What about what you did to him during the race? Do you call that honour too?'

'Either way,' said Zane, 'I call it winning.'

Cruise gritted his teeth as Zane continued to talk.

'I'll return to the Capital a hero,' he gloated then he turned to face Cruise, 'and you'll think twice before showing up at next year's race, if you know what's good for you. Goodbye loser.'

Zane exited the arena and left Cruise in the pen with his thoughts, and Red's lifeless body.

Chapter Eight

A Red Day

It was raining, and the day after the closing ceremony. Almost everyone who had come to Soulwind for the festival had returned to their home villages.

Cruise sat in his room at the end of his bed, alone, looking down blankly at his floorboards and clutching the birthday presents Red had made for him only a couple of days previously. His cat Cicada rubbed up against his legs, purring away.

'Good puss,' he said as he stroked her back.

There came a light rap on his bedroom door, and his mother entered the room.

'Are you ready, dear?'

'Yes Mum,' he replied feebly as he sat up from his bed and followed her out.

Cruise and both his mother and father made their way over to the graveyard, where they would see Red off before he was put to rest.

When they arrived at the graveyard, few people were there to meet them.

Cruise's father Rowan embraced Red's father, Ferlan, in an attempt to comfort him as he broke down in his arms, his giant shovels of hands buried in his face, as Erika escorted Cruise towards Red's grave.

Cruise looked down at the hole in the ground which held Red's coffin. Shoddily built out of old timber, not but a wooden grave-marker to pin point his place of his rest.

Anger overcame him once more as he thought this was such a sad ending for his best friend.

Sadness soon overcame his anger as Cruise looked around at the few who had come to bid Red his last farewell. He looked around at his family, and at the villagers, all poor and helpless.

One by one the villagers passed Red's grave to pay their last respects.

Cruise knelt down in front of the grave and gripped some of the earth in his hand, trying to hold back the tears as they ran down his face.

'Come on now Cruise,' he thought to himself, *'Red wouldn't want you to cry. He would be calling you a pansy if he was still alive.'* Cruise smiled a little at the thought of it.

He had lost his best friend. Red meant everything to him, and now he was gone, and Cruise was all alone.

Rowan approached Cruise from behind and placed his hand upon his shoulder.

'I promise you I'll win the race for you next year Red,' said Cruise out loud, not caring who heard him, 'Agiles or not, I promise you I'm going to win. Even if it kills me, I'll win that race for you. I hope you're watching and can hear me up there, Red. I'll train twice as hard, for both of us; and you'll still be with me in spirit Red, I know you will.'

Erika now approached Cruise on his other side as the

rain got a little heavier and soaked his dark matted hair, and the smell of damp earth filling his nostrils.

'Come on, sweetie,' said Erika as she helped Cruise up.

One by one, the villagers departed the graveyard as they all returned to their homes.

'I think I'll stay here for a while,' said Cruise to his mother.

'All right dear,' she replied, 'don't be too late, will you?'

'Okay Mum,' he said as Erika and Rowan left him in the pouring rain on his knees at the foot of Red's grave.

Chapter Nine

Landon's Proposal

A few days following Red's funeral, Cruise sat on a fallen oak tree down by the lake.

Cruise often came here to think, or if he needed time alone. He also spent a lot of time here with Red. There was a stone statue of Marcus the Swift nearby, leaning on his great sword and wearing his helmet.

Cruise missed Red so much already. Who would he train with now, in the build up to next year's race? Even running in the race wouldn't be the same without him there.

Cruise got up from the oak tree and walked towards the edge of the lake.

He peered down at his reflection and then reached into the water to retrieve a smooth, flat stone before skimming stones on the clear, mirrored surface of the lake.

He and Red would often challenge each other at skimming, or to who could throw a stone the furthest out into the lake. Red would normally win.

He recalled a time when they were wading far out in the lake looking for suitable flat stones for skimming, when they came across a golden nugget by accident that must have washed down from Goldstream, a big surprise for both them. Their families sold it and split the profit between them.

Alas, Cruise no longer had that. He had nobody to share anything with, nobody to spend his time with. He had never felt more alone.

Cruise heard footsteps approaching from behind him on the pebbles, as he continued to lob stones into the lake.

'Cruise,' spoke out a soft voice.

'What is it, Amber?' he said flatly, still looking in the direction of the lake and tossing in stones.

'I knew you'd be here,' she said, 'I just wanted to say, I'm so sorry about what happened to Red.'

'It's okay,' he said, 'it's not your fault.'

'Cruise, please talk to me,' cried Amber, 'look at me!'

'What do you want, Amber?' snapped Cruise as he threw a stone into the lake and turned to face her. 'What is it that you want from me?'

'I just wanted to talk to you,' she said.

'Well, we are talking,' he replied flatly.

'It's just,' she continued, 'what happened at the ball, I-'

'You don't have to explain yourself, Amber,' said Cruise. 'I know what I saw.'

'Cruise, he means nothing to me,' said Amber, 'I don't even know him.'

'You seemed pretty close to him at the ball,' said Cruise.

'Cruise,' said Amber, 'it was just, I'd had some wine and…'

'And what?' shouted Cruise. 'He's the festival champion? Is that what you were going to say? Why don't you just come out and say it, Amber? Is that all you wanted? Well, I'm sorry that I'm such a let-down to you, and I couldn't win that trophy.'

'Is that what this is about?' she replied. 'Is that why you're angry at me? I told you it didn't mean anything.'

'Just go, Amber,' said Cruise, 'just leave me alone.'

'Cruise, please,' she said as she took a step closer.

'I said go away!' yelled Cruise at the top of his voice and it echoed across the lake.

Amber held her chest and swallowed her sadness.

'Okay,' she whined, 'I'm so sorry again, Cruise, for everything.'

Amber slowly backed away and turned to walk off, the tears still seeping down her cheeks, and she disappeared down the nearby forest path.

Cruise exhaled loudly as he went back to sit on the oak tree. He sat there for a while with his hands in his face. He reached into his boot pocket and pulled out the pen knife Red had made him for his birthday. He ran his fingers along its fine crafted handle and then he did the same to the slingshot, which Red had also carved for him.

Cruise raised his head and stared at the nearby statue of Marcus when a sudden rage and hatred came over him. He stomped over to the lake and grabbed a handful of pebbles, then angrily fired stones at Marcus's statue with his slingshot through gritted teeth, unable to control himself.

He fired volley after volley fast and furiously without

aiming until a stone finally hit Marcus's statue square in the middle of the chest of his breastplate.

Cruise felt a forceful shock in his own chest, which knocked him back several feet and onto the ground.

He curiously and fearfully grasped the pendant around his neck while looking up at Marcus's statue, imagining his eyes peering towards him from behind the shadowy slit in his helmet. Just as he was wondering what had happened to him, he heard footsteps approach him from behind and once again a voice spoke out to him.

'It looks like you could still use some practice with that,' said the voice.

Cruise darted around to face a heavy, middle aged man who he did not recognise.

'Who are you?' said Cruise sharply. 'What do you want?'

'Well actually, I'm here to meet someone,' said the man.

'Well, on your way, old man,' snapped Cruise, 'there's no one else here but me.'

As Cruise got up from the ground and dusted himself off, he walked away from the man if not just to get some distance from him, when he heard the man speak after him once more.

'That was quite a race you ran,' he said as he bent over and picked up a pebble, 'up until that impressive tumble, of course.'

Cruise stopped in his tracks and turned to face the man, taking a closer look at him.

Cruise put the man roughly in his late forties, although he could have easily been in his early fifties; it was difficult to say as he looked weathered and had strong hairy arms. He wore a thick tatty hooded cloak and gripped a tall clothed walking stick, and he was very heavily built, with greying brown hair tied back into a short ponytail, and friendly mutton chop facial hair framed his face.

'Who are you?' asked Cruise, trying, but blatantly failing to hide his curiosity.

'My name is Landon,' said the man. 'I live not too far from here, on the fringe of The Crimson Meadows, although I seldom make my way out this far.'

Cruise had heard his mother and father speak of Landon the Hermit when he was a little boy, but no one in Soulwind saw much of him, or knew that much about him either. All that he knew was that he owned a small holding and lived in a hut alone on the fringe of the crimson meadows, and he mostly kept to himself. Some parents would tell their children that if they did not behave, Landon the Hermit would take them away to his hut.

'You're Landon the Hermit?' asked Cruise.

'Hermit?' said Landon.

'Sorry,' said Cruise, 'I didn't mean to insult you.'

'No that's all right,' chuckled Landon, 'I suppose I don't get out as much as I once did.'

Cruise smiled at how lightly Landon took being called a Hermit.

'So, young lad,' said Landon leaning on his stick, 'tell me something... will you be competing in the race again next year?'

'Well, I'd thought about it,' said Cruise, 'I was going to run it again for my friend, as I promised that I'd win it for him. Maybe I could then afford to get him a decent gravestone. Then I thought, what's the point? What's the point if the Agiles are just going to come back next year even faster and stronger than this year?'

'I saw a spirit in you during that race lad,' said Landon, 'and that isn't the same spirit that I'm hearing from you now.'

'Look,' said Cruise bluntly, 'those bastards killed my best friend, and crushed my only dream, and more, all in the space of one day. What exactly are you getting at from this conversation? What is it that you want from me?'

'To cut it quite straight, lad,' said Landon, 'you have a lot of potential, and more importantly, a spirit and heart that I don't see in many athletes that run that race, and I was thinking I'd extend you an offer.'

'What kind of offer?' Cruise asked suspiciously.

'Well,' said Landon, 'I was wondering if you'd be interested in letting me train you.'

'Train me?' said Cruise sarcastically looking Landon up and down. 'What could you possibly teach me that I don't already know.'

'You need guidance lad,' said Landon, 'and I have that wisdom and knowledge to offer you, providing you're willing to apply it.'

'You don't look like much of an athlete,' said Cruise, still looking Landon up and down.

'Trust me,' he said, 'I know a thing or two. I used to do a bit of running myself back in the day, believe it or not.' He chuckled as he grasped his belly fat with both hands.

'Thanks for the offer, old man,' said Cruise, 'but I think I'll pass. It was nice talking to you, I guess. Goodbye.'

Cruise walked away from Landon and the lake and directed himself back towards the forest path.

'Don't be so rash, lad,' said Landon, 'I could turn you into a champion!'

'If I want tips on how to be an old hermit, I'll call for you, but for now leave me alone and excuse me, as I need to get home to my parents.'

'I wish you'd reconsider,' said Landon as he followed Cruise hastily up the path and grabbed his arm.

'Get off me!' said Cruise, shrugging Landon off. 'I said I'm not interested! Leave me alone, you fat old man!'

Cruise sped off angrily and disappeared down the forest path.

'Look, if you'd only just let me train you!' shouted Landon as Cruise disappeared out of sight.

'Go away!' he faintly heard as Cruise continued to run through the forest.

Chapter Ten

Change of Heart

Cruise continued to jog along the forest path back towards his home, his mind still a soup of emotions and his anger still looming over him. As Cruise came closer to his home, he had a sudden gut feeling that something wasn't right. He picked up the pace a little as he approached his yard.

Cruise arrived at the entrance of his home and came across a devastating sight.

The whole yard was strewn with broken carts, some set alight, and his father lay on the ground, badly beaten up and bloodied with Erika kneeling over him bawling and trying to wake him. Erika spotted Cruise and she continued to panic as she ran towards him.

'Cruise!' she cried. 'Cruise! Where have you been?'

'Father!' cried Cruise as he ran towards her. 'What happened, Mum?'

'Three men came!' she cried, trembling. 'They asked your father where you were and when he wouldn't answer them they beat him and trashed the yard. Cruise, they trashed the carts that your father was mending, our livelihood. How can we afford to replace them?' she continued as she trembled and cried out uncontrollably.

'Oh Mum,' he said, holding her as they both rushed over to Rowan's lifeless and bloodied body.

Cruise skidded down to his knees alongside his unconscious father.

'Do something, Cruise,' said Erika, still shaking. 'Do something!' she continued as Cruise knelt over his father and placed his hands on his shoulders and shook him.

'He's still breathing,' said Cruise. 'Landon…' whispered Cruise before speaking louder the second time. 'Landon! That old hermit, Mum. He must have taken the forest path back to his hut. He wouldn't have gotten too far from here. He's quite old and he was on foot. Go after him, now!'

Erika hurried off and left Cruise in the yard to care for his unconscious father.

'Come on, Dad,' said Cruise holding his father's hand, 'you'll be all right.'

Rowan feebly groaned in pain as he slightly writhed his head. He was in and out of consciousness and still breathing, but he was badly bloodied and beaten.

Cruise overlooked his father for what seemed like hours when Erika suddenly called out from behind him, with Landon rushing up behind her.

'Move over lad,' said Landon to Cruise as he shoved him over and checked Rowan over.

'Cruise,' said Landon, 'help me get your father inside. Erika, could you boil me some water?'

The pair moved Rowan into the cottage and made a space in the living area as they lay Rowan down on the sofa. Landon continued to eye Rowan up and down as he muttered to himself, trying to get a response from Rowan.

'Cruise,' said Landon, 'fetch me a rag or some cloth and a salt pile. Erika, that bowl of hot water, when you're ready, please.'

Landon seemed so cool, calm and collected as Cruise and Erika rushed about to gather the required items.

Cruise returned with a handful of old clean cloth and a small salt bowl from the larder and handed them to Landon.

'Thanks lad,' said Landon, grabbing the salt pile and the rags, 'you can step outside and give me and your father some space, lad. I'll call you if I need you for anything. I have your mother here to help me if I need it.'

Cruise stepped out of the kitchen and into the next room as instructed, where he sat down on a wooden chair and waited patiently. He felt mixed emotions once more and he got up and paced around, unsettled.

Sometime later, Landon came out of the living area and shut the door behind him. Cruise looked at him eagerly waiting for an answer.

'Your father will be fine, lad,' Landon smiled and nodded faintly, 'he's been badly beaten but he needs plenty of rest. Your mother is taking good care of him.'

'Zane did this,' said Cruise angrily.

'You don't know that, lad,' said Landon, 'and besides, the Agiles must be halfway back to the Capital by now.'

'Who else would do it?' asked Cruise, 'he's trying to get the message across to me so that I don't turn up for the race next year. I heard what he said to me in the arena.'

'Now, lad,' said Landon, 'I think you just need to-'

'I've changed my mind, Landon,' said Cruise as he interrupted Landon's sentence, 'I want to come and train with you.'

'I thought you'd decided not to run the race next year?' said Landon.

'I was in two minds and I had mixed emotions, but now this is unacceptable, no, unforgiveable. I'm not going to let Zane get away with this. I'm going to give it everything I've got even if it kills me, and then next year I'm going to show those bastards who the real champion is.'

'Your father needs you here, Cruise,' said Landon, 'you have to stay with him.'

'You said he was going to be fine, didn't you?' said Cruise, 'and that my mother is here to look after him.'

'Your father can't work like this, Cruise,' said Landon, 'at least not for a few months. You have to stay here and support your mother.'

'It'll be one less mouth to feed without me here,' stated Cruise, 'and I'll be a lot more help to them in the long run if I train to win the race. If not to beat the Agiles, then at the very least to win the prize money for my parents. They can survive a year without me. They have plenty of friends in town to draw upon for support.'

'You know,' said Landon, 'I'd still allow you to visit and check up on them from time to time, if you do come back with me to start your training.'

'Thank you,' said Cruise, 'and even though I'm not on speaking terms with Amber, her parents, Holly and Ash are both good people and are very close friends with my parents, so I know that they'll take good care of Mum and Dad while I'm away.'

'You know Cruise,' said Landon, 'there's no haste for you to come right away, and you're welcome to join me for your training after your father makes a full recovery, or at the very least wait until morning before you make your decision.'

'No Landon,' said Cruise, 'my mind is made up. Every day counts now. I have to start my training as soon as possible. I'll go and pack my things and we can leave first thing.'

'All right, lad,' said Landon, 'well, if your mind is honestly made up, I'll still agree to train you, however I still I think you should tell your mother first.'

'I'll tell her just before I leave,' said Cruise. 'She'll only worry, otherwise. I'd better go and start packing my things.'

'Right you are,' said Landon, 'I'll just go and check up on your father and see if your mother is managing all right.'

'Thank you, Landon,' said Cruise, 'I won't be long.'

Landon watched as Cruise disappeared up the stairs, hoping he was not wrong with his gut feeling about him.

Chapter Eleven

Preparation to Leave

Cruise was busy in his room, stuffing old sacks with spare clothes and anything else he thought he might need to take with him for his stay with Landon, when he heard a rap on his bedroom door.

'How are you getting on, lad?' asked Landon.

'I'm almost done,' he replied, 'come in.'

'Your father's doing all right, lad,' said Landon as he entered Cruise's room. 'Your poor mother said she'd stay up all night with him. I urged her to get some rest but she wouldn't leave his side.'

'That sounds like my mother,' said Cruise, 'always so strong.'

'Are you just about done?' asked Landon.

'Almost,' said Cruise, looking around his room, 'not that I had much to bring in the first place.'

'Make sure you bring enough footwear,' Landon advised, 'that's the most important thing, and plenty of comfortable light, loose fitting clothing.'

'I should be fine,' said Cruise finishing up and hoisting a sack over his shoulder. 'Bye Cicada, I'm going to miss you, you stupid cat. Take care of Mum and Dad while I'm gone, won't you?'

'What's that?' said Landon as he pointed.

'That's my cat, Cicada,' said Cruise.

'No, not your cat,' he said, a hint of excitement passing his voice, 'that?'

'What, Landon?' said Cruise.

'That,' Landon repeated again, 'that lump of iron in the corner.'

'Oh, that old thing,' said Cruise, 'it's just a door stop.'

'A door stop?' said Landon, sounding perplexed, 'that must be the very best quality iron ore that I've ever laid my eyes on. Where did you get it?' he said as he walked over to it and picked it up, holding it up and observing it.

'I found it years ago,' said Cruise, 'in the fields just south of The Crimson Meadows. I was with Red at the time. We were stick fighting near the stream when suddenly there was a loud explosion and we saw a bright flash of light in the sky. A ball of fire appeared from behind the clouds and then it collided with the ground with a huge blast in the distance. At first, we thought it was a dragon or something, you know, from the fairytales? Red and I ran towards the direction of the explosion where the fireball had landed. It left a huge crater in the ground, and in the middle of the crater was that lump of iron. It looked really hot when we first saw it, far too hot to touch. It looked like a piece of metal that had just come out of a furnace and hotter! So we returned that evening and by then it had cooled down at least enough to pick it up with Ferlan's enormous blacksmiths gloves. I got to keep it because I won the coin toss, and it's been here in my room ever since. We had to take turns carrying it because it was so heavy, and for something that heavy to fall from the sky, we couldn't believe it. Neither of us had ever seen anything like it.

'I didn't want to say anything unless I was absolutely sure,' said Landon now breathing quite quickly and heavily, 'but now I know that it must be true. I've heard rumours about this stuff.' He continued, gradually getting more excited, rolling the smooth chunk of metal about in his palms. 'Some of the common folk call it 'Sky Metal,' or less commonly 'Star Metal' among some blacksmiths and as I've read in some books, although the actual name for it is unknown. It's extremely rare, and I've only ever read about it in the old smithing books from the Capital's library, and heard about it in stories of legend, but I never thought I'd get to see any in my lifetime, It doesn't tend to fall commonly in these lands.'

Cruise listened attentively as Landon continued to speak, admiring his passion and expressiveness as he gawked at the lump of metal as if he was in love with a beautiful woman.

'The metal is normally very dense and heavy for its size, as a rule,' Landon continued, 'a sign of good quality. But when worked with correctly, it can produce weapons and armour which are extremely light and tough, lighter and tougher than the finest steel, and can forge a blade rumored to hold its edge, if worked with correctly.'

'Take it if you want,' said Cruise casually, 'I can get a rock or something as a new doorstop, or a wooden wedge would do just fine.'

'No, no, don't be so ridiculous,' said Landon as he composed himself, 'I couldn't ask that of you. This is far too special. It belongs with you, so you keep it here.'

'All right,' said Cruise, 'I think I'm all ready. I'll go and break the news to my mum.'

'Okay, lad,' said Landon, 'I'll be waiting for you in the yard when you're ready.'

'Bye Cicada,' said Cruise, as his fluffy black cat sat on his bed, purring and staring at him with her bug-green eyes, 'you stupid cat.'

Cruise took one last around his bedroom as he left Cicada sniffing at the alien scent of Landon that he had left behind on the sky metal.

Chapter Twelve

Proposal Accepted

Cruise trampled down the staircase and plonked his luggage in the hallway and then he walked into the living area to find his mother dabbing his father's head with a cold damp cloth.

'Cruise,' she said as she shuffled up to him and gave him a hug.

'Mum, I-.'

'You must be hungry,' she interrupted, 'let me go and fetch you something to eat darling.'

'Mum,' said Cruise sternly.

'What is it dear?' she said as she smiled faintly.

'This isn't an easy decision for me to make while Dad is like this but-.'

'What are you trying to say, sweetie?' she said with a worried look on her face.

'I…' he hesitated, 'Landon has offered to train me, Mum. Train me up for next year's race.'

'Why, that's great news dear,' smiled his mother.

'Which means, I won't be here,' said Cruise, 'to help you look after Dad, to help support the family while Dad can't mend the carts, but I have to do it Mum, I have to. If I win the prize money it'll be more than enough to help us, and I have to beat the Agiles for what they did to Red, for what they did to Dad. They won't scare me out of running the race next year. I'm going to train hard with Landon and win it for you, for Dad, and for Red. Ash and Holly will look after you and Landon said I could still visit and check up on you from time to time. And don't worry Mum, if those men come back to hurt you, I'll kill them.'

Erika said nothing as she walked back over to her only son.

'My little Cruise,' smiled Erika proudly as she patted his chest and held his shoulders tight, 'all grown up, and so fast, I can hardly believe it. I'm so proud of you, dear. I'll manage just fine here, sweetie. You go and train with Landon, and don't you worry about us. Landon said your father will be just fine. He just needs plenty of rest, and we'll manage all right,' she said still smiling.

'Mum,' said Cruise, 'before I go, I wanted to give you this; it's all the money I've been saving in my room. It's not much, but it should tick you and Dad over for a while, at least long enough until Dad gets better. I won't need it when I'm staying with Landon.'

'I can't accept that,' said Erika.

'Mum, please,' he insisted as he placed the small leather coin purse into her hand and shut it tight around it for her.

'All right,' she nodded, a tear running down her cheek, 'thank you, dear.'

Erika kissed Cruise quickly on the cheek and he walked over to his father's side.

'Take good care of him,' said Cruise as he knelt down and kissed his father softly on the forehead, 'we're leaving right away. Every second is precious now. I love you both and I'll try to visit you both really soon.'

'All right,' she said understandably, 'goodbye for now dear. Your father and I love you very much and know we're both very proud of you, no matter what happens.'

'Goodbye Mum,' said Cruise as he kissed his mother on the head and gave her a hug, a little tear in his eye, 'you can always sell the cat if you're hard up for some cash,' he joked.

'Don't act like you don't love that cat,' his mother chuckled.

'Bye for now Mum,' he said as he smiled faintly and left the room. He looked back at his mother as he shut the door behind him.

Cruise gathered up his things in the hallway and made his way out to the yard, where Landon was waiting for him, puffing on a small wooden tobacco pipe.

'Are you sure you wouldn't rather stay and help your mother clean some of this mess up?' said Landon looking at the strewn carts. 'This yard is in a pretty bad way.'

'Every minute counts now, Landon,' said Cruise. 'My family will be all right. They have many good friends in the village to look after them, and I'll be back to check up on them soon enough. Time is the key now.'

'All right lad,' smiled Landon with a hint of adventure in his eye, 'let's get going.'

Cruise left the carnage of the yard behind him for his

long stay with Landon, in the hope that when he returned here in a year's time, he would be a champion.

Chapter Thirteen

Landon's Holding

After a couple of hours walking and lugging his heavy pack of belongings, and as Cruise followed Landon over the brow of a hill, Landon stopped and pointed in the distance. 'There it is lad,' said Landon, 'my home.'

Landon lived in a secluded location of what seemed like the middle of nowhere, acres upon acres of fenced fields and land, until he noticed one particular detail, which he was all too familiar with.

'Wait, I know where we are,' said Cruise, 'the race course passes right by here.'

'That's right lad,' smiled Landon, 'in fact it wasn't too far from here that you took your nasty fall.'

'Now the location of your home explains how you had such a good view,' said Cruise.

'Follow me,' said Landon, 'just a little while longer.'

Cruise followed Landon through his yard and past his various outhouses.

They passed an outdoor forge and finally came to a large round wooden and stone hut.

'Here we are,' said Landon.

'You live here?' said Cruise sounding confused, 'in this hut? It seems a bit small.'

'It isn't much,' said Landon, 'but it's home, and it's all that I need. Come on, I'll show you to your room so you can unpack your things.'

Cruise followed Landon into his hut.

The hut looked slightly larger on the inside than it did on the outside. There was a small kitchen area on the left just through the front door and at the back there was a cosy living area with a warm fire. Large wooden beams held up the structure's roof, peppered with woodworm.

There were two doors on the right of the living area, and Landon led Cruise through the first door on the right.

'This is where you'll be staying,' said Landon, 'you can leave your things on the floor for now and unpack later if you'd prefer. Would you like a cup of tea?'

'That would be nice, thank you,' said Cruise, looking around at what would be his home for the next year.

It was a very basic room, filled with only a few wooden shelves, a small wooden bedside cabinet, and a basic single bed. Much like the rest of the hut, it looked bare, but cosy.

'All right,' said Landon, 'I'll put the kettle on.'

'When do I start training?' asked Cruise.

'Get settled in first, lad,' said Landon, 'we start training first thing in the morning. Rest is just as important as training, and you've had a busy couple of days.'

'All right,' said Cruise as he followed Landon into the kitchen area.

'Take a seat,' he said as he moved a large cast iron kettle to the fireplace.

Cruise took a better look around the room, as he sunk into a snug armchair close to the log fire.

Various oddments hung from the ceiling of thc hut, including dry herbs, pots, pans, ladles and even hanging pheasants and rabbits curing on lengths of cord.

'How long have you lived here for, Landon?' Cruise asked as Landon was preparing the tea.

'Oh, about a decade now,' said Landon.

'Why don't people see you around much?' Cruise asked, 'I mean, you're aware of what people call you?'

'Landon the Hermit!' chuckled Landon, 'it honestly doesn't bother me, lad. I'm happy enough here on my own, I guess,' he said as he took two old chipped mugs from the cupboard.

'I didn't mean to offend you again,' said Cruise, 'no one really cares you know, it's just, well, you know.'

'Different,' said Landon as he poured hot water into the mugs.

'Yeah,' said Cruise.

'Here you go,' said Landon, handing Cruise a mug.

Cruise thanked Landon, and they both sat in front of the fire in the living area mostly in silence. They drank their tea until Landon fell asleep in his armchair.

Cruise retired to his room and got into bed. He lay awake for a while, thinking of the last few days, until he finally fell asleep, ready to awaken on his new day of adventure.

Chapter Fourteen

The First Steps

Cruise slept for hours undisturbed, until suddenly he was awoken by a loud racket.

'Up lad!' yelled Landon at the top of his voice as he banged together a pair of large black cast iron pans. 'Today is a good day for training! Get up, it's time for breakfast!'

'Oh Landon,' moaned Cruise as he rolled over in his bed and covered his head with a pillow, 'it's not even the crack of dawn.'

'The early bird gets the worm!' continued Landon. 'Get up, lazy bones!'

'I doubt even the worms are up yet,' muttered Cruise.

'I'll have less of that talk!' said Landon as he yanked the blanket off of Cruise and hit him on the head with it. 'Up, breakfast time!'

'All right, all right,' moaned Cruise as he rolled out of bed and dragged his feet into the kitchen. He pulled up a stool to the breakfast table and rubbed his eyes as he sniffed and cleared his throat.

Landon, now wearing what looked like a worn looking blacksmith's apron, placed a bucket-sized mug of water in front of Cruise along with a basin-sized bowl, full to the brim with an unappealing looking pile of gloop.

'What on earth is this?' said Cruise as he slopped the paste up and down with his wooden spoon.

'It's porridge, lad,' said Landon, 'the breakfast of champions!'

'There's no milk?' said Cruise.

'Milk is full of fat, lad,' stated Landon, 'which slows you down. That's made with water! Now eat up quickly before it gets cold.'

Cruise immediately regretted accepting this training offer, as he force-fed the porridge down his throat while holding back his wretches.

'You'll finish that bowl every morning,' said Landon, 'you'll need every ounce of your strength if you're going to win this race. Once you're finished, come and find me outside.' Then he disappeared out into the yard.

Cruise finished eating his porridge and downed his water then he threw on some old clothes and went outside to find Landon.

He wandered around the yard trying to find him. He had probably got halfway across the yard when he heard a door fling open in one of the out sheds.

Cruise turned around and saw Landon grasping onto a pile of very heavy looking metal objects, which from a distance, almost looked like a suit of armour.

'Here you go lad,' said Landon as he plonked the pile of metal onto the floor in front of him.

'What are those for?' asked Cruise.

'This,' said Landon proudly, 'is weighted training armour that I made and designed myself.'

Cruise bent down and struggled to pick up a single piece of it.

'That one there's a vambrace,' said Landon, 'it goes on your forearm.'

'What?' said Cruise, sounding shocked, looking down at the pile as he realised what Landon had just said. 'You want me to wear these? The whole set must weigh as much as I do, if not more!'

'As I was saying, I made and adapted it especially myself,' said Landon ignoring Cruise's last statement, 'when I was younger and I did a bit of training myself I used to wear something similar, and don't worry, once you've grown used to the full weight from wearing the suit, eventually you'll be able to run in it. You see, the thick cow hide leather lining on the inside prevents the metal plate from rubbing and digging into your skin while you run,' Landon stated.

'You want me to run in this?' said Cruise. 'You must be joking, right? I'd be lucky if I could even stand in that yet alone run in it.'

Landon blanked Cruise and continued to talk.

'Now for the first part of your training,' said Landon, clearing his throat, 'just put the armour on, move around in it, and get used to the weight. Once you've done that, come and find me. In the meantime, you're free to explore my grounds. I'd suggest walking over to the end of the yard and back first of all to get used to the weight, and don't even think about removing any part of it. I'll know if you do, and besides, you'll only be cheating yourself if you did.

Lunch is served at midday, every day. I'll leave it out for you on the kitchen table so you can have it whenever you're ready, and dinner is at sun down.'

And with that, Landon disappeared back into his shed and left Cruise alone with the pile of weighted training armour.

Cruise looked down at the pile.

There were five pieces in total, a very heavy looking iron breast plate, two iron shin guards, and two iron vambraces, all lined with thick cow hide and leather straps and hinges to hold them in place onto their respective limbs.

Cruise wondered in which order to put all of this on, before reaching the conclusion that it would be a struggle either way.

First of all, Cruise strapped on his shin guards, which immediately cemented him in place. Next, he put on the first vambrace with some effort, which made it extremely difficult to put on the second. Finally, he lifted the heavy plate body over his head then tightened the straps. He immediately felt unnaturally top-heavy.

Cruise stood in the yard like an iron statue before he attempted to take his first step. His leg alone felt like it weighed a ton. With all of his might, he strained himself forward, only managing a single step, and already he was breathing heavily.

'*This is crazy,*' thought Cruise as he hoisted his other leg forward with extreme effort, now breaking out into a sweat.

It had taken Cruise almost an hour to reach the other

end of the yard, when he heard Landon yell from his hut.

'I wouldn't stray much further if you want to make it back in here in time for dinner!' shouted Landon, sounding quite amused at the sight of Cruise having a difficult time.

'Sarcastic old bastard,' muttered Cruise under his breath, as he panned around to face and lunge towards the hut, flinging his arms forward for momentum and to help counteract the tremendous weight.

After a long struggle, and now completely out of breath and soaked with sweat, his legs wobbling with weakness, Cruise finally arrived inside the hut, a little after midday.

Landon was nowhere to be seen but there was a large clay plate left out on the table, presumably his lunch.

On the plate there was probably around half a pound of sloppy wet boiled cabbage, two large raw carrots and a couple of cold sausages along with yet another bucket-sized cup of water.

'Landon?' Cruise called out.

There was no reply.

Cruise wolfed down the meal and then went back out into the yard as he munched on the last carrot.

'*Where is Landon?*' he thought to himself. Never mind, he needed to get used to the weight, so that's what he was going to do. The sooner he got used to the weight, the sooner he could run in it, and then the real training could commence, he hoped.

Cruise decided to circle the yard as many times as he could before sundown. He optimistically aimed for ten.

The sun was setting pretty quickly now and Cruise did not know how much strength he had left in him as the effort increased with each step and he panted heavier and heavier.

He was starving, and his whole body was shaking with exhaustion, plus he was absolutely drenched in sweat, as the sun had been beating down on him all afternoon.

'Dinner time, lad!' he heard Landon's voice call out from the direction of the hut.

His vision was blurry now and the sunlight was fading fast. He turned and made for the hut.

As Cruise finally stumbled into the hut a little after sundown, Landon was there to meet him.

'How was your first day, champ?' said Landon.

Cruise threw a dirty look in Landon's direction and said nothing as he struggled to catch his breath.

'You can take off the armour for now and leave it by the door,' said Landon, 'put it back on first thing in the morning after you've eaten your breakfast, and you may only take it off again the last thing in the evening before dinnertime. I've prepared a bath for you out the back. Go and clean yourself up then you can come back inside for your dinner.'

Cruise, still struggling for breath, got out of his armour and piled it near the door of the hut in the corner of the kitchen. It was the best feeling he had ever experienced.

He wobbled out to the back to find his bath, a cold barrel of spring water just outside the hut. He welcomed it as he climbed in and felt the strain of his day partially leave his body. He soaked off inside the barrel for five to ten minutes until his hunger got the better of him, then he got out, dried off and changed, and made his way back into the kitchen.

Landon had prepared dinner. The menu for the evening was rabbit haunch and boiled root vegetables with the standard bucket of water.

Cruise pretty much inhaled his meal, sucking the rabbit bones dry, before withdrawing back to his room and collapsing on his bed. He passed out and fell asleep as soon as his head touched the pillow.

Chapter Fifteen

The Training Continues

Cruise tossed and turned during the early hours of the morning and he suddenly awoke from a very bad nightmare. He did not quite remember what he was dreaming about, so he sat up awake in his bed, remembering where he was. All he remembered was shouting for Red and his father as he woke up, his face pouring with sweat.

Cruise groaned as his body already ached awfully from the previous days training and he already dreaded the next day if he felt like this in the morning. He quickly fell back asleep and had no more nightmares for the rest of that night, a cosy warmth engulfing him as he slept.

Cruise was awoken yet again the following morning at the crack of dawn by Landon's racket, and he dragged himself out of bed and shuffled into the kitchen for his dreaded breakfast.

He was three spoonfuls into his large basin of porridge when he suddenly dropped his spoon into the bowl, and a splatter of gloop splashed on his face.

'What's wrong, lad?' asked Landon.

'N-nothing,' he replied sounding quite confused as he slowly picked his spoon back up.

'Muscle ache from yesterday playing up is it? said Landon. 'Don't worry, that's perfectly normal. It'll get better with time.'

'Well, no,' said Cruise still sounding confused, 'that's the thing… I'm not aching at all.'

'Well, that's a new one to me!' laughed Landon, almost sounding like he didn't quite believe him.

Cruise finished his porridge, still thinking about his aches, or rather the lack of them, and he approached his armour pile and put it on once again.

The training repeated itself much the same over the next two or three weeks as Cruise got used to moving about in the heavy armour, slightly improving day by day.

At the end of the third week Cruise was so used to the armour, that he was moving about in it as naturally as he would have been in his own skin, and sometimes he forgot he was even wearing it.

He had explored a good stretch of Landon's holding and the surrounding land, and he often rushed and scurried around effortlessly, vaulting over fences to get from field to field.

As he was making his way back to the hut for his lunch, he noticed something near to the fence in the field next to the yard which he had never noticed before. It was a rather large and scruffy looking horse, wild-looking, but no doubt hardy.

Cruise walked closer to the horse to get a better look at it. The horse was very weathered and it was difficult to guess its age just from looking beyond its condition, not so much that it wasn't well looked after. It looked happy enough in its own little world, he supposed.

Cruise walked up to the gigantic steed and reached out to scratch it behind its ear.

'Hello boy,' said Cruise as he gave the horse had a good scratch, 'do you like that?'

The horse lowered its head as though it was enjoying it, and then suddenly it turned and clamped down and bit Cruise hard on the tender part on the inside of his arm, just below his armpit.

'Argh!' cried Cruise, 'Bastard!'

'I see you've met Locust,' said Landon as he appeared from behind Cruise, cleaning a pair of blacksmith tongs with a dirty rag.

'He bit me!' said Cruise as he attempted to lunge towards the beast, but Landon held him back.

'A-ah, cool down lad,' said Landon, 'I should have warned you he's a little nervous around strangers.'

Cruise massaged his bicep with his thumb.

'That's going to bruise,' said Cruise, 'where did you get a horse from Landon? They're really rare around here, and they're seldom found outside of the Capital.'

'A local farmer a few fields away from here was having a little problem,' said Landon, 'a lot of his crop was going missing and it seemed that old Locust here was the root of the problem. It was his lucky day as I just happened to pass by as the farmer was about to execute the poor beast. I offered the farmer payment in lieu of his lost crop and took the horse off his hands. I have more than enough grass here in my fields to feed the hungry beast, and sure enough he does a good job keeping on top of it. Locust seemed a precise and fitting name for the old boy,' said Landon as he patted Locust on his side.

'Where do you suppose he came from?' asked Cruise as he stepped a little closer to Locust.

'I'm not sure,' said Landon, 'he could be the offspring of some of the horses that got their riders killed in The Battle of the Crimson Meadows, or maybe just a wandering stray. Your guess is as good as mine.'

'He's huge,' said Cruise.

'Yes, he's a mighty beast all right, and equally as stubborn,' said Landon, patting Locust's side again as the horse chewed on a mouthful of straw, a slight dopey look on his face as he eyed up both Landon and Cruise.

'Do you ever ride him?' Cruise asked.

'Oh lord no,' laughed Landon, 'I tried to once, but as much as he seems to trust me, he bucked me straight off and I haven't tried since. That was years ago and I'm not getting any younger, or lighter as you can see,' said Landon, again grasping his bulging tub of belly fat.

'I fell off a horse once too,' said Cruise, 'I hit the ground hard and I dislocated my shoulder, and I haven't been on once since either. It wasn't as big as Locust. It was one of those small horses used to pull carts. Red, on the other hand, was such a naturally gifted rider, he made it look easy. I'm sure he could have tamed Locust if he'd wanted to.'

'You really miss him,' said Landon, 'don't you, lad?'

'I do,' Cruise nodded, 'he was always better than me, at everything, but I'll never forget him.'

There was silence as Cruise tried to hold back a tear and looked away from Landon so he wouldn't notice.

'Anyway,' said Landon, 'on that note lad, it looks like you're ready to progress your training.'

'Really?' said Cruise, cheering up slightly.

'Well, look at yourself,' said Landon, 'you've been walking around effortlessly in that weighted armour for days now. Do you think you could try running in it?'

'That completely slipped my mind,' said Cruise, 'as ridiculous as it sounds, I'd almost forgotten I was wearing it.'

'I knew you were special lad,' chuckled Landon proudly as he placed an arm around Cruise, 'we'll start first thing in the morning. Come on, let's go and grab something to eat.'

Cruise clattered back to the hut, smiling as he put a heavy, armoured arm on Landon's shoulder, smiling at his current progress and the thought of what would next be in store for his training.

Chapter Sixteen

Steady Progression

The sun rose once again over Landon's holding, and Cruise was breakfasted and dressed eagerly and awaiting his trainer's guidance in the yard in the bright and warm morning sunshine.

He was wondering what the next stage in his training would entail as Landon approached him.

'All right, lad, follow me,' said Landon, 'the next part is pretty straight forward, and I'm sure you'll agree that this stage of your training will make perfect sense.'

Landon guided Cruise to the other side of his hut, and before he knew it, Cruise was looking down the long dusty and empty stretch of the festival racecourse.

'It shouldn't come as a surprise to you what the next part of your training is, lad,' said Landon, 'I want you to run the length of the course, from this spot, once a day, every day, in full armour.'

Cruise said nothing as he stared into the distance, and towards the location where, roughly, somewhere, he took his nasty fall during the race.

'You'll have a natural advantage over the other competitors if you run the course daily,' said Landon, 'and now is the time and place to make your mistakes if you're going to make them. Fall if you must, rise and continue if you can, but the more often you run it, the more you'll grow accustomed to it. You will get a feel of the track, learn the nature of the track, and then, when the race day comes, running it will be second nature to you. Straight forward enough, right? Do you have any questions?'

'No, I don't think so,' said Cruise as he continued to look up and down the track.

'Good,' said Landon, 'you know yourself how difficult it is, but do it in your armour every day and then you'll feel like a feather when you run it for real. I'll leave food and water out for you in the kitchen as usual. Don't worry, just come in and fetch it when you're ready. So long as you run the track at least once a day you can carry on with what you have doing up until now for the rest of the afternoon. Continue exploring and moving about the grounds in your armour, alright?'

'Alright, Landon,' said Cruise.

'All right, lad, there's no time to lose, off you go,' said Landon. 'I'll leave an hourglass out for you to know if you're improving or not, but have a few practice runs first to warm up and get a feel of it.'

Cruise stretched out then made his way around the track slowly, breaking into a light jog. It was easier than he thought now that he had gotten used to the weight of the armour. It just felt like a normal training run that he would have normally done during the build-up for the race.

It was strange starting the race course from a different starting point, but ultimately it was the same track and exactly the same length.

He was nearing the area where he took his tumble but he did not notice any obvious rock that could have been responsible.

He was more aware of the course surroundings now he was not concentrating so hard on the Agiles, and he felt as though he had a clearer mind, which he realised was a far more intelligent way to run a race for obvious reasons, as he was not clouded by a red mist.

He enjoyed the light jog around the course and he felt good. He enjoyed the sunshine, the birds singing in the trees and the scent of the wildflowers, but in a split second, something came over him.

A sudden urge appeared out of nowhere.

He was not here to enjoy, he thought, he was here to train, and train hard. He remembered the promise he made to Red, '*Even if it kills me, I'll win that race for you.*' He focused hard in his mind and then picked up the pace into a steady run, pounding the hard dusty track.

As he ran, he thought about Red, he thought about his father, about Zane and about Amber, about the prize money and how he desperately needed it to help his family.

The cocktail of thoughts and emotions raced through his mind quicker than he could run.

He felt good, and strong, but there was still a doubt at the back of his mind.

What if, in the end, it wasn't enough? All of this effort, and all of this training.

What if the Agiles were training just as hard as he was right now, or even harder?

No, he couldn't risk it.

His mind instantly switched and he quickly flipped back to his angry state, pounding the race track as hard and as fast as he could run.

He did not know how long he had been running for and had completely switched off from his surroundings and lost all concept of time. All that was driving him was his maddening anger, and his desire to run and win.

Cruise did not realise he had already nearly ran the entire length of the track, and Landon was waiting for him at the finishing line waiting for him, smiling widely.

'Excellent time Cruise,' shouted Landon proudly, 'and a good pace. Now come on in for something to eat. Cruise wait, stop!'

Cruise was so shrouded that he did not even notice Landon standing at the finishing line. He did not notice that he had already completed a full lap of the race track; he just kept on running, right past Landon, and onto his second lap of the course.

'Shit,' said Landon, 'that boy is going to kill himself!'

Cruise kept going, not letting up the pace or his determination, his anger still blinding him from all of his surroundings.

Cruise was now nearing the end of his second lap, but this time Landon was ready for him.

As Cruise charged towards the finish line, like a relentless iron juggernaut, Landon braced himself and tackled him to the ground hard, and they both struggled as Cruise swiped and kicked out like a wounded zebra.

'Let me go!' screamed Cruise, as he flailed around on the dusty ground.

'Don't be so foolish, lad!' said Landon, struggling to control him, 'you're going to end up passing out from exhaustion running like that in this heat and carrying that weight. You'll kill yourself if you carry on!'

Cruise continued to thrash about like a wild animal.

'What on earth has gotten into you, lad?' said Landon, 'snap out of it!'

After several more minutes of wrestling about on the ground, Cruise finally stopped and lay still, panting on his back, his eyes shut.

'Phew,' Landon sighed, 'you're pretty strong lad, even with that armour on and after running two whole laps of the course. I couldn't have controlled you for much longer. What the hell are you made of?'

Cruise still lay there panting, until he opened his eyes and lifted himself slightly off the ground. He came around and returned to his old self again.

'I'm so sorry, Landon,' he panted, 'I don't know what came over me. I was just so focused on getting better.'

'That's okay, lad,' said Landon, still breathing heavily and helping Cruise to his feet, 'come on, you must be dying of thirst.'

The pair stumbled back into the hut, where they both remained for the rest of the evening. They spoke little that night, both too exhausted and embarrassed by the whole experience.

Cruise turned in for an early night as Landon sat up

all night in his armchair smoking his pipe and staring into the fireplace, wondering what had fuelled him.

Chapter Seventeen

Re-assessment

Over breakfast, it was Landon who broke the awkward silence between the two.

'Lad,' said Landon clearing his throat, 'what would you say if we both agreed to put that little, shall we say, episode, from yesterday behind us.'

Cruise put down his spoon and looked up at Landon. He swallowed a mouthful of porridge and replied.

'Yes,' he nodded and agreed, 'I think that would be a good idea.'

'I don't know what came over you,' said Landon, 'but having said that, it was impressive to witness what you did, to say the least. Everything from the distance that you covered and the speed that you did it in, and the strength you showed at the end of it. However, having said that, it was damn right irresponsible on your part and you could have gotten yourself killed or seriously injured. How would you plan on running the race and helping your family if you were out of commission? It's no good cramming a year's worth of training into a single day, it just can't be done, and it isn't good for you. You're only human when it comes down to it.'

'I understand,' said Cruise, 'it won't happen again, Landon.'

'Not while I'm training you, it won't,' said Landon, 'I won't get to live to see my next birthday this Harvest if you keep putting me through this sort of stress. I'm not as young as I once was, you know. And think about your poor mother and father, they're depending on you, Cruise. Don't let your anger overwhelm you. You have to focus your emotions and not let them get the better of you.'

'I will Landon,' said Cruise, 'I promise I will from now on.'

'All right,' exhaled Landon, 'I've had another think and I've decided that for now a little change in your training will do you some good, something to simulate your mind a little bit instead of mindless droning about and running around all day. It's not healthy for a lad your age. I tell you what, take the day out for today, and I'll prepare some fresh methods for you by tomorrow. You can go into Soulwind or visit your family, but keep that armour on, do you hear me?'

'Thank you, Landon,' smiled Cruise broadly, 'I will.'

It had been almost a month since he last saw his parents, although he knew they were doing just fine from what Landon had heard. He could not wait to see their faces again.

'Try and be back before sundown,' said Landon, 'I'll leave some dinner out for you.'

'Thanks Lands!' said Cruise as he wolfed down the rest of his porridge, downed his water and put on his armour. 'I'll see you later!'

'See you later, lad,' said Landon.

This was the longest that Cruise had ever gone without seeing his parents and he couldn't contain his excitement at seeing them again. He knew his father would be feeling a lot better now after over three weeks of rest.

He hurried along the forest path to his home, passing the sights which he had always taken for granted growing up in such a beautiful village. He inhaled the sweet smell of the bluebells which carpeted the forest floor as he walked swiftly beneath the canopy of the forest.

Cruise finally arrived back at his yard. It was no longer strewn with broken carts and looked exactly how he had always remembered it, which meant his father must have been up and about again.

He ran to the front door and called out for his parents as he rapped on the front door.

'Mum?' he shouted as he entered his home. 'Dad?'

Erika poked her head around the corner of the kitchen door, immediately overjoyed with happiness and excitement at the sight of her son.

'Oh, Cruise!' she cried, 'is it really you, pumpkin?' She approached him to hug and kiss him.

'Yes, it's me, Mum,' he smiled. 'How are you? Where's Dad? How is he?'

'Your father is doing just fine, honey,' said Erika, 'he's just resting upstairs but he has been slowly getting well enough to carry on with his work. That man is so stubborn!'

'I'm so glad to hear that,' he said, 'how have you been managing?'

'Oh, we've been just fine,' she said, 'Ash and Holly

have been wonderfully supportive and so have the rest of the village. We're on the mend, but enough about us here. Tell me about you dear… how's your training going, and what are you wearing? It looks so heavy! Here, come in and let me help you take it off.'

'I can't take it off, Mum,' said Cruise, 'it's weighted training armour. Landon said I have to keep it on all day, but it's really helping me, and the training is going great. Landon has given me the day off to come and see you guys. I can't believe it has been nearly a month since I last saw you. I've missed you both so much.'

'I know dear, we've both missed you too,' said Erika, 'it shouldn't be long before your father wakes up. He normally gets up around this time for a little something to eat.'

'Have you had any more trouble, Mum?' said Cruise. 'Has anybody been back here?'

'No dear,' said Erika, 'everything has been just fine so don't you worry. The village militia are fully aware of what happened and are patrolling the area most nights. We haven't had any more trouble.'

'Well, that's a relief to hear,' said Cruise.

'How about I make you something to eat?' she said, 'you must be famished?'

'Thanks, Mum,' he said as he followed her into the kitchen. 'How's Cicada doing?'

'Oh, she's doing just fine sweetheart,' said Erika as she clutched the kettle from the fireplace with both hands and poured some tea, 'she keeps on bringing dead field mice into the house and leaving them at the foot of your bed. I think she's missing you.'

'Stupid cat,' he chuckled as he took a seat.

'She's not the only person who has been missing you, mind,' said Erika, eyeing Cruise.

'What are you talking about?' said Cruise.

'Amber has been around a few times asking after you. Are you both all right, dear?'

'Oh Mum,' said Cruise, 'I don't want to talk about girls right now. I'm trying to focus on my training.'

'Okay, sweetheart,' she said, 'but you should at least go and visit Ash and Holly at The Shovel and Pick when you can. And have you had a chance to re-visit Red's grave since the day of the funeral?'

'Not yet,' said Cruise, 'I was thinking of going later before heading back to Landon's place.'

'Well, I've put some fresh flowers on there for you, dear,' said Erika handing him a hot cup of tea.

'Thanks Mum,' said Cruise. He tried to suppress a smile as he tried to picture the look on Red's face if he were ever to hand him a bouquet of flowers.

Cruise heard some movement from upstairs then heard footsteps slowly coming down, creaking the wooden steps.

'Dad!' said Cruise, getting up from his seat in the kitchen and almost spilling his tea. He ran into the hallway and there stood his father at the foot of the stairs. 'Dad!' he shouted again as he lunged forward to give him a huge embrace.

'Steady, son,' chuckled his father feebly.

'Are you all right?' said Cruise looking his father up and down.

'I'm just fine, son,' he smiled, 'it's good to see you, and why are you wearing that armour? Did you change your mind about training and decided to enlist in the army?'

'It's good to see you too Dad,' smiled Cruise, 'and I'll explain the armour to you later. Come and have a seat in the kitchen, Mum has just made tea.'

Rowan was still covered in fading cuts and bruises, but he looked a lot better. He walked with a slight limp as they went into the kitchen together.

'So tell me,' said Rowan, as he sat back in his armchair and Erika handed him a cup of tea, 'how's your training going?'

'Really great so far,' said Cruise, 'I feel a lot stronger already, and it's only been a month. Imagine how I'll feel like after a year! That trophy is as good as mine.'

'That's my boy,' he smiled proudly, 'don't' get too over confident though. Make sure you stay focused.'

Cruise conversed with his parents for hours as they all caught up with the goings on in Soulwind and the extent and the involvement of Cruise's training so far. But as much as he wanted to stay, it would soon be time for him to leave if he was going to have enough time to visit Red's grave before he returned to Landon's hut by sundown.

Rowan and Erika saw Cruise out to the front door and they said their farewells for the time being.

'It was lovely to see you, dear,' said Erika as she hugged

and kissed him goodbye, 'you'll come and visit us again soon, won't you?'

'I will Mum,' said Cruise, 'whenever I can.'

'Goodbye for now, son,' said Rowan as he gave Cruise a hug.

'Father,' said Cruise, 'could I please speak to you alone for a minute before I go?'

'Of course you can,' said Rowan, looking at Cruise and then at Erika.

'Oh I see,' said Erika, 'you need a little man to man time with your father. Take care, sweetheart, I'll see you again soon.'

'Goodbye, Mum,' said Cruise, before he turned again to his father.

Cruise and Rowan walked a short distance away from the house when Cruise turned to face his father.

'What is it, son?' said Rowan.

'Dad,' said Cruise, 'did you ever experience anything strange when you were wearing the pendant before you gave it to me? Did you ever feel anything strange or out of the ordinary was happening to you?'

'What do you mean?' said his father, looking confused.

'Did you feel that... well... something you couldn't explain was happening sometimes?' said Cruise.

'Well son, to be honest with you, I couldn't tell you,' said Rowan.

'Why?' asked Cruise.

'Because I never wore the thing, son,' said Rowan. 'As

soon as your grandmother gave it to me, I kept it wrapped up and safe in a wooden box underneath my bed, and then when I moved here and married your mother and had you, I kept it in the very same box out in the shed. Why do you ask, son?'

'Well, it was just,' said Cruise, thinking, 'it's nothing, father. I guess it's just all in my head. Are you sure you'll both still be fine here and manage all right until the next time I visit?'

'Yes son, we've been doing just fine,' said Rowan, 'please stop worrying about us. You need to focus on your training now. I'm on the mend and I'll soon be back to full strength and up and about repairing carts again.'

'Okay,' said Cruise, 'I'd better get going. I'll see you soon, and I love you.'

'I love you too, son,' said Rowan as they shared one final long embrace, and he watched his son disappear out of sight and down the woodland path once more.

Cruise detoured from his journey back to Landon's slightly so he could stop to visit Red's grave.

He thought way back to their childhood and remembered everything they had been through together, and all the times Red had stood up for him. He never had a chance to properly repay him, but now he could. He was determined to win that prize money, and to get him a decent gravestone to replace the shoddy wooden grave marker.

'Hey Red,' said Cruise, 'it's been quite a while now, hasn't it? How are you getting on? My training isn't going too bad. I'm not sure if you knew, but that old hermit, Landon, offered to train me, and he knows some pretty good methods to be fair to the old guy. Anyway, I just wanted to update you. I'll see you again really soon, and I miss you every day, and I'll win this race for you, I promise.'

Cruise remained with Red until the sun set, and he spoke long with him before returning late that evening to Landon's hut.

Landon had long since turned in to sleep by the time Cruise returned, but there was a covered plate left out on the table for him, with cold venison sausage and boiled cabbage again.

He took off his armour and polished the plate then turned in for the night, awaiting the next morning's training.

His head hit the pillow that night, but he lay awake for a while, over thinking anything and everything that entered his mind. What if he wasn't good enough? What if in the end all of this wasn't enough? Cruise eventually drifted into a deep slumber, his thoughts of doubt still whizzing away and knocking against the inside of his skull.

Chapter Eighteen

A Clean Slate

Cruise awoke surprisingly early just before Landon's wakeup call that morning, and he felt the rising sun hit his face through the bedroom window. The day off yesterday must have done him a world of good.

He could hear Landon in the kitchen, moseying about and clattering plates and pans, accompanied by the usual smell of porridge.

'Morning Lands,' said Cruise as he strolled into the kitchen and dragged out a chair to sit on.

'Will you please stop calling me that?' snarled Landon.

'Not so long as it keeps annoying you,' said Cruise, 'what's for breakfast?

'Chocolate cake,' said Landon bluntly as he carried on with what he was doing.

'Oh lovely, my favourite,' said Cruise sarcastically, 'and a cold mug of beer to wash it down, I hope?'

'Correct lad,' said Landon as he plonked a large basin of porridge in front of him.

'Thanks,' said Cruise half hoping that Landon wasn't joking about the chocolate cake.

'So, how did yesterday go?' said Landon, 'how are your folks keeping?'

'Very well thank you,' said Cruise.

'Did you visit your friend too?' asked Landon.

'I did,' said Cruise sadly, 'I just thought I'd fill him in and let him know what was going on, you know?'

'I'm sure he's watching over you lad,' said Landon, 'so, are you ready to continue your training?'

'Of course,' said Cruise, 'what did you have in mind?'

Landon and Cruise both finished their breakfasts, and Cruise yet again put on his weighted training armour.

Cruise followed Landon into the yard and they walked towards the fenced field adjacent to his hut.

Cruise clearly did not notice it last night in the fading light, but it seemed that Landon had been busy converting a section of his field into some sort of training area for him.

'What do you think, lad?' said Landon proudly.

'I like it,' said Cruise, 'what's it all for though, exactly?'

'I'm still working on it, and it's not quite finished yet,' said Landon, 'but over here you have a hurdle course that should help build up your leg muscles and your explosive power, and over here I've laid these cartwheels with the spokes removed for you to step in and out of, which should help with your agility. I'm still thinking of extras to add to it. You can train here every afternoon once you've completed one, that's ONE lap of the race course every morning, and I do mean that this time.'

'Understood, Landon,' said Cruise.

'Right you are, then,' said Landon, 'hop to it. I'll meet you back here after lunch.'

As the days got dryer and hotter, Cruise struggled on as the summer days beat down on hard on him.

The training did not get any easier. He would run the race course faster and faster each day than before, training with Landon in the field area in the afternoon.

Landon's training was ruthless, but he was fed, watered and rested well. However, Cruise never gave up. He took everything Landon threw at him, and more, never losing his motivation. Soon the agility and the hurdle area had expanded as Landon built and added extras onto the training course. He added a balancing log and an archery range, which Landon said would improve his focus and his concentration.

Miles and miles he pounded, and hours and hours he trained his strength, his agility his balance and also his spirit, but still, nothing broke him. He felt himself growing stronger, faster and healthier day by day, and the peak of summer quickly arrived. And just as quickly the summer ended, and still the training grew harder. Cruise's spirit remained unbroken.

Chapter Nineteen

Harvest

Autumn arrived all of a sudden and the nights drew in and grew steadily cooler. The leaves of the oak trees transformed from green to vivid orange and deep red and littered the yard of the holding.

'Autumn certainly has crept up on us quickly this year around,' said Landon looking out of his kitchen window cleaning a mug in a basin of water, 'it seems that we've had a short summer… either that or the concentration of your training has made it seem like time has gone quicker than normal. You can go ahead and take the day off today. Why don't you show your face at the harvest festival? It will give me the day off to have a little peace and quiet and a chance to relax.'

'Oh, that reminds me, here you go, Landon,' said Cruise, as he lifted up a wrapped parcel from beneath the table and it thudded onto the table.

'What's that?' asked Landon.

'A present,' said Cruise, 'you mentioned before that your birthday was on Harvest, didn't you?'

'Lad, I…' said Landon, 'you shouldn't have gotten me anything.'

'It's nothing really,' said Cruise, 'I didn't have very much to give you, but I hope you like it all the same.'

Landon opened the parcel and his eyes bulged wide open. Cruise almost though they were going to fall out of their sockets and into his porridge.

'The Sky Metal.' he said.

'I knew you'd like it,' smiled Cruise.

'Cruise,' said Landon,' I told you before, that you can't give me this.'

'Please,' said Cruise, 'I was using it as nothing more than a doorstop in my bedroom and I saw how you reacted to it when you first saw it. It belongs with you.'

'I, I don't know what to say,' said Landon. 'Thank you, lad.'

'You're very welcome,' smiled Cruise warmly. 'It's the very least I could do for you after everything you've done for me.'

After breakfast, Cruise dressed in the smartest clothes he had with him and got ready for the harvest festival.

It would be a welcome break from his training, and he would see his family and old friends from the village again whom he had not seen in months.

The Harvest Festival was always a big event in Soulwind. It was similar to the Festival of Marcus the Swift, although it was rare for the other villages to be there, and the villagers would make a whole day and a night out of it, celebrating the end of the harvest year.

The day was always filled with all sorts of events and activities, including the giant pumpkin competition, where after the winner was decided, they would carve them all out into giant lanterns to ward off the evil spirits of

Darkshade, and the flesh was used to make pumpkin pie and spiced soup.

The children would bob for apples in large wooden basins, and all manner of comfort food stalls would line the fields as the days and the nights grew bitterly cold. And, of course, there was the harvest masquerade ball in the evening.

'Why don't you come along too, Landon?' asked Cruise as he pulled on his boots.

'Oh no,' said Landon, 'I don't do so well with big crowds. I always love a day to relax and do my own thing on my birthday. You go ahead and have fun, and you can leave the armour behind for today.'

'Okay, thanks,' said Cruise, 'I'll bring you back a toffee apple.'

'None of that sugary stuff, lad,' said Landon, 'oh heck, it's only one day, you go and enjoy yourself.'

'I was only joking,' said Cruise as he left the door of the hut, 'see you later, Lands!'

'Stop calling me that,' he shouted after him, 'and no drinking!'

It was always tradition at some point during the harvest festival for Cruise's family to meet at The Shovel and Pick to gather with friends from the village for a social drink.

Cruise thought of avoiding this tradition this year, after everything he had been through with Amber, although he owed it to the fact that Ash and Holly had been so supportive of his mother and father after their tough time, so he decided to go along.

Cruise arrived at The Shovel and Pick and walked in through the front door where already it was already bustling with villagers.

"Ello there Cruise,' said a short, cheerful man from behind the bar, 'pint o' Dragonslayer?'

'No thank you, Ash,' said Cruise as he approached the bar, 'I'm deep in training.'

'I heard. I'll make that half a tankard of sewer rat then,' Ash winked and chuckled.

'If you insist then, Ash,' said Cruise, 'I'll have half a pint of Ruby Arrow, please.'

Ash poured the ale like a flow of molten rose gold into a pewter tankard and handed it over the bar to Cruise. 'It's on the house,' he said.

'Thank you, Ash,' said Cruise as he peered around the inn for his parents.

Thirsty farmers and villagers of Soulwind all gathered around wooden tables as they ate, drank and spoke merrily.

Cruise spotted his parents nearby speaking with Holly; there was never any wonder to Cruise where Amber got her looks from.

Cruise approached his parents and gave them both a long embrace, and thanked Holly for her support. Ash came over after a while, and they all conversed and laughed happily together.

There was a bard sat in the corner of the inn strumming on his lute.

His name was Garrett, and every year he would sing a particular song; Cruise's favourite.

Marcus the Swift,
He ran twenty miles!
In a full suit of armour,
To warn them at sunrise.

To the King he brought tidings,
That fell on deaf ears,
And brave Marcus the forthright,
Plead with his fears.

Then Marcus the Brave,
And the King's army too,
Marched right back to Soulwind,
To face them once more.

Marcus the Cunning,
He knew of a way,
He sneaked in the castle,
And helped save the day.

The battle was won,
And the enemy broken,
And Marcus the Legend,
Won't be forgotten.

Into the west he vanished,
Where 'unto this day,
Nobody knows,
Where he may lay.

Has anyone seen,
O! Marcus the Swift?

The song always made Cruise think deeply about the fate of Marcus the Swift, but the memory did not last too long this year, as Marcus now reminded him of the Agiles.

After the song, Marcus turned to Ash.

'So, where's Amber?' said Cruise, 'how is she keeping?'

'I haven't seen her all day,' said Ash, 'I was hoping for a hand behind the bar this year but she made no mention that she was coming. She's normally here by now.'

'I don't know what she's told you, Ash,' said Cruise.

'I'm not getting involved,' said Ash, 'but I'm sure you kids will work it out. I'm sure she'll show her face at the harvest masquerade ball later, though. Are you going to head over too, Cruise?'

'I'm not sure yet,' said Cruise, 'I really shouldn't stay out too late. My training continues in the morning and Landon my trainer can get pretty grumpy when I don't do as he says.'

'I understand,' said Ash. 'It sounds like you're taking the race very seriously this year, I'll have a wager on you come the race, for sure. You look very strong.'

'Thanks Ash,' said Cruise, 'I won't let the village down, and thank you again for taking care of Mum and Dad while I've been away. I won't forget it.'

'Not at all, young man,' said Ash, 'another drink before you go?'

'No thank you, I really shouldn't,' said Cruise, 'I think I ought to get going.'

Cruise said his farewells to everyone at the inn then made his way slowly back to Landon's place.

Maybe ten minutes wouldn't hurt to show my face at the ball,' thought Cruise. He couldn't help it. He just had to see Amber, her slender figure, her flawless face, her beautiful sapphire eyes, he just had to see her.

Cruise diverted back to his home and hurried up the stairs into his bedroom.

His cat Cicada meowed when he walked into the room and stood up on his bed with her tail in the air.

'Hey puss,' said Cruise, 'sorry, I can't stay too long.'

Cruise rummaged through the drawers of his cupboard and fished out an old frog mask.

He made it to the ball, and there he saw Amber and Zane, each in a cat and a hawk mask.

Cruise smiled to himself. It wasn't a smile of joy or happiness. He smiled because he didn't care anymore. He was glad he saw the sight. For some reason all thoughts of her had emptied from his head. He felt fine and tossed his mask on the floor eager to get back to his training, only one thing invading his mind space now.

Cruise returned to Landon's with an even stronger

will to train than ever. He would show everyone, but the truth was he still feared Zane. He was scared of both what he would do to him and to his family if he entered the race again next year. But he wasn't going to be bullied out of it, not a chance.

Chapter Twenty

Keen Focus

Cruise did not see much of Landon over the following few weeks. He was busy beating away in his forge, and Cruise wondered what he was up to.

Meanwhile, Cruise went about his training as usual.

Whenever he had a spare minute or two he would practice with his slingshot to entertain and challenge himself. He was getting a lot better.

However, he quickly grew bored of the repetitive training and lack of guidance at Landon's absence, and he decided to make things a little more exciting for himself.

He rummaged around in one of Landon's out sheds and found a length of rope, and he suddenly thought of a good idea. If Landon wasn't going to train with him, he would train with Locust.

Cruise crept up behind Locust as he was grazing nearby, and he managed to lightly loop and carefully tie the rope around his head and neck.

'Okay, boy,' said Cruise, 'let's see how strong you really are.'

Cruise suddenly pulled on the rope and pulled Locust towards him.

Locust neighed loudly as he lifted himself on his back

legs and pulled back against Cruise. Cruise was yanked hard by Locust and he landed hard on his front on a hard patch of dusty ground.

At this moment Landon appeared from out of the forge and approached Cruise in the nearby field.

'I thought I heard a ruckus,' said Landon, 'what are you doing with my horse?'

'I'm bored,' said Cruise, 'what exactly are you doing in there?'

'Never you mind what I'm doing,' said Landon, 'why aren't you training?'

'I've done my run today and I've gone through the training area like a million times. When are you going to add something new to it? I'm losing my mind with boredom.'

'If I promise to add extra things onto your training area will you promise to keep training hard and stop loafing around?' said Landon.

'Yes Landon,' said Cruise, 'I promise.'

'The youth of today…' said Landon. 'I'd be lucky if I had half of this stuff growing up.'

Over the weeks of autumn, Landon slowly added to the training course to keep Cruise entertained.

Altogether, he added a balancing log, and an agility course complete with swinging hay sacks.

Not much changed for the rest of the autumn. The damp rains came and the remaining red, orange and yellow leaves turned a golden brown and fell from the branches and onto the damp ground, revealing the skeletal frames of the naked oak trees, haunting the holding, as red squirrels buried their winter stock of acorns, and Cruise grew stronger and faster day by day.

Chapter Twenty-One

Winter Falls Upon the Valley

As the nights drew in and became even colder and autumn had long come to an end, the days of the training shortened for Cruise as daylight now became scarce and the first frost had hardened the ground.

'Here, put these on,' said Landon, approaching Cruise and dumping a fresh pile of weighted training armour at his feet one morning.

Landon now steadily increased the intensity of Cruise's training as the days grew shorter.

'In case you were wondering, this is why I've been so absent over the last few weeks,' said Landon, pointing down at the pile, 'I've been smithing additional pieces of weighted armour at the forge for you to wear. A new heavy weighted helmet, and a weighted back pack, and additional weight to the old versions vambraces and leg weights. With the days getting shorter you need to intensify your training and make the most of the short hours of daylight that you have.'

'Oh great,' said Cruise, 'that's the next few weeks written off then as I struggle to get used to the new weight again.'

'No,' said Landon, 'no more luxuries, no more getting used to the weight. Stick it on and get on with your lap.'

Landon's training grew harsher, and Cruise struggled through with the run in his new armour that cold and frosty morning.

Right after he was done with his lap, Cruise was forced straight into doing circuits at the agility course. Now weighing even more than ever and on top of the bitter cold weather, Cruise struggled on, and Landon watched nearby chanting cruel motivation.

As Cruise was finishing off another circuit of the agility course, he caught his foot on the end of a cart wheel and tripped and fell on hard frozen ground right in front of Landon.

A couple of dying daisies jeered up at him from their smug, frosty-green face, and he growled as he ripped them out of the earth.

'Get up,' said Landon, 'and do it again.'

'No.' said Cruise.

'What did you say to me?' said Landon, 'I said, get up and do it again!'

'I said no!' yelled Cruise.

'Don't you talk back to me!' said Landon.

Cruise rose quickly and picked up a nearby training stick and swung it at Landon's face.

Landon glared at Cruise angrily then picked up another right next to him.

Cruise swung again and Landon parried the strike.

'You're pretty good with that,' said Landon as he parried another angry strike from Cruise, 'who taught you?'

'I'd stop talking old man, and concentrate,' replied Cruise.

'Oh, you've done it now lad,' smiled Landon as the fighting intensified.

Cruise got cocky as he turned up the heat on his attacks and left himself open before Landon pegged Cruise's leg with his stick and he fell flat on his back.

'Not bad lad,' chuckled Landon, 'but not good enough.'

'I could have taken you if I wasn't worn out and wearing this junk pile.'

'Taken by an old man,' said Landon. 'I can teach you how to use that properly, if you'd like.'

'Could you?' said Cruise, getting up from the ground.

'I'll set up some sparring dummies and a pen to the course,' said Landon, 'I'll teach you for an hour a day, but only if you've been good.

Cruise smiled at the thought of learning how to properly fight. He had always messed around with Red, but he knew Landon would show him how to properly handle himself.

Chapter Twenty-Two

Long Nights

Cruise and Landon sat around the fireplace one evening enjoying a hot cup of tea.

Cruise watched as the flames danced and the sparks flew high above the fireplace, telling their own story.

'With the nights drawing in and getting colder and darker every day now lad, there's only so much training you can squeeze into a day, even with your new weighted armour,' said Landon.

'So why don't we just add more weight to it?' asked Cruise.

'If I made that thing any heavier lad, I'd be using Locust to pull you out of the ground,' said Landon, 'so we're going to take this opportunity to work on probably the only muscle that you don't seem to use as much as the others.'

'Oh hilarious,' said Cruise, 'are you a jester now as well as a hermit?'

'Less of that,' Landon snapped impatiently, 'now every evening just after sundown I think it'd be a good idea for you to study in detail the layout of the course.'

'Landon, that sounds incredibly dull,' said Cruise.

'Well, seeing as it was the course itself that caused

your defeat last time, I think it'd be a bright idea for you to respect it and walk it through at least once by torchlight, and remember every lump and bump in your mind until it's second nature to you. Sketch them down if you need to, to help you remember the details. I want you to be borderline obsessed with it. I want you to eat it, sleep it, breathe it and live it. Do you understand me? I want you to remember every corner, every dip, every incline, until you know it like the back of your hand. Not only will it make you respect the course, but it'll drastically reduce your chance of stumbling again if you know it inside out, and with some luck it should shave a few minutes off your best time. That's the idea, anyway, and the advantage of walking the course by torchlight is that every bit of the uneven surface will show up better than it would in the daylight, as it will cast a shadow on the larger stones and rocks.'

Cruise rolled his eyes into the back of his head trying to overcome the thought of the boredom that this additional training would bring, but he knew Landon had a point. At least he would only have to walk it once, but he dreaded studying the sketches every night before bed.

Chapter Twenty-Three

Grey Matter

Cruise was hesitant to leave the hut that evening, but Landon insisted, lit him a torch and kicked him out of the front door.

Cruise dragged himself towards the start of the race track shrugging like a teenager at the thought of the walk that lay ahead of him.

Cruise began and he memorized every lump and bump in his head that he would sketch later on. He wasn't expecting to remember every single one, but it was more like a memory game if anything, and he felt like it was doing his brain some good as the rusty cogs jumpstarted in his head.

Cruise approached roughly the spot where he had tripped during the race.

Landon must have been watching not far away from here when it had happened.

Already Cruise was becoming more aware at self-enhancing his perception skills and it made more and more sense to him by the minute as to why Landon wanted him to do this. His senses would naturally heighten if he kept an eye on the race course as he ran.

The track was roughly twenty miles long, which included various inclines, declines, and both muddy and grassy areas. It was a lot for Cruise to remember, but he normally had quite a good memory and he would be sure to sketch down the major details as soon as he got back.

When Cruise finished his walk, he returned to the hut and sketched while everything was still fresh in his head. He did not remember falling asleep, but he had never felt more mentally and physically drained.

Chapter Twenty-Four

A Curious Discovery

Cruise was bored again after his morning run and he was exploring Landon's holding as usual when he suddenly came over all peckish. His body was crying out for calories as the weather grew colder and Landon would not let him eat anything else bar his rabbit food and sloppy wet cabbage, worrying that he may put on excess weight. The winter was no excuse in Landon's opinion to put on an extra layer of fat.

Cruise decided to wander around Landon's out sheds to see if he could discover a hidden larder – he could literally murder a wedge of brie.

Cruise walked into a shed, but all he saw was junk and tools.

In the next one there were barrels full of various things. Surely, he would finally find food in the next one.

There was a little rundown shed right at the back, looking rather sorry for itself, and it was padlocked.

There must be something good in there then, he thought as he searched until he found a small key underneath a rock near to the door.

He unlocked the shed and entered; it was a small and rundown shed, with not much light in it.

When his eyes adapted to the dark, he found himself

looking upon a strange sight.

The shed's walls were covered from floor to ceiling with various pin-ups and sketches, cuttings, pictures, clippings, drawings and notes, so thick he could not see any of the shed wall.

Upon closer inspection, Cruise discovered that the cuttings were from all of past festival races, and photos of all of the champions who had won it.

'*What is all of this?*' said Cruise to himself, delving deeper into the eerie shed, approaching a wall and taking down a cutting for a closer look.

As he took down a sketched drawing of a past champion, he heard a footstep behind him in the doorway.

'This was locked for a reason,' said a gruff voice.

'Landon,' breathed Cruise, 'what is all of this?'

'Never you mind,' said Landon, sounding unamused, 'get out.'

Cruise looked back down at the picture.

'Give me that,' said Landon, going to grab the sketch out of Cruise's hand.

'Is this you, Landon?' said Cruise, taking a closer look at the picture, noticing a young athlete smiling widely and proudly holding the festival trophy, donned in the all too familiar champions garb.

'What part of 'get out' don't you understand?' said Landon looking slightly embarrassed.

'You were festival champion, Landon?' said Cruise, looking up at his trainer, bright eyed, and amazed. 'How come you never told me?'

'All right lad,' Landon sighed, admitting defeat, 'yes, that's me, and yes, I was festival champion many years ago.'

Cruise continued to listen attentively, as though waiting for Landon to continue his story.

'What's that look for, lad?' said Landon, 'that's all there is to it.'

'Come on, Landon,' said Cruise, crossing his hands and begging like a toddler who was after a new toy from his parents, 'please, you have to tell me now.'

Landon exhaled loudly and still looked uneasy.

'Why are you so sheepish about it all?' said Cruise, 'it's fantastic!'

'I just don't like talking about it much, all right?' said Landon.

'Why not?'

'I have my reasons,' said Landon, 'now would you please get out of my shed?'

'All right, all right,' said Cruise, sounding annoyed at having missed out on what he thought would have been an explanation of a lifetime. 'Boring old man,' he said as he threw the cutting onto the ground, barged past Landon and slammed the door of the shed behind him.

Landon picked up the cutting from the ground and sighed.

'Cruise, come back here,' he said, 'all right, yes, I was the festival champion one year. What more is there to say?'

'What more is there to say?' replied Cruise coming

back into the shed, 'you were festival champion, Landon. Why do you hide from such a fantastic achievement?'

'Well, to be honest with you, I felt like I didn't deserve that trophy.'

'Why not? Please don't tell me you cheated, Landon?'

'No, no, it was nothing like that,' said Landon, looking at his young self in the photo, 'I won it fair and square.'

'Then why didn't you deserve it?' said Cruise. 'You look so happy in the photo.'

'I would have thought that's obvious, isn't it?' said Landon. 'Think about it lad, a young blacksmith from the Capital, nothing special going for him, no defining attributes, enters the festival race one year and then wins it with no problem?'

Cruise gazed blankly at Landon, wondering what part he was missing from this puzzle.

'There were no Agiles active on the racing scene during the year I won it, lad,' said Landon. 'Did I really have to spell it out for you? I never had the opportunity to race one, and it was always held against me by the people.'

'I still think it's an achievement,' said Cruise.

'Undeserving, they shouted,' he said, 'easy,' he continued, 'not a real challenge. I've heard it all being yelled at me. I expected to return to the Capital a hero, but instead I was shunned by everyone I knew. Do you get it now, lad? Landon the Hermit? I did it to get away from it all.'

'It's all right, Landon,' said Cruise, 'honestly, it is.'

'You don't understand, lad,' said Landon, 'to be

mocked by not just the people, but by your family and your friends, who all said I didn't deserve it; that's the part that hurt the most, that's why I keep everything hidden in here. It got to the point where I agreed with each and every one of them.'

'Don't be so stupid, Landon,' said Cruise approaching the cabinet at the rear of the shed, 'look at all this stuff. Look at your trophy, Landon.'

Cruise took the trophy out of its display case and handed it to Landon.

'Remember the feeling you had when you first held it? Do you remember how it felt?'

Landon stroked the trophy and looked at himself through the tarnished metal, a tear trickling down his face.

'Were there really no Agiles around the year you won the race, Landon?'

'The previous year's champion, Bernard, had just announced his retirement,' said Landon, 'and the fresh up-and-coming Agile, Oscar, was only seventeen the year I won. I never had a chance to race him, but now you have that chance!' said Landon, turning to Cruise. 'Do you understand now? Only you can give me that, a chance for me to see it in my lifetime… an Agile defeated at the hands of a villager, and to show that it indeed can be done. I may not have my youth anymore, but you do, Cruise, and there isn't just one Agile to beat this year, there are five of the bastards. I'll die a happy man if I knew for sure that same the training that made me win the race that year when there were no Agiles, will be enough for you to win this year's race when there are five, and it would show everyone how wrong they were about me.'

'I won't let you down, Landon,' said Cruise, 'you know I won't, and now I have another reason to win.'

'Thank you, lad,' smiled Landon, 'thank you for understanding.'

'I still can't believe it, though,' said Cruise, 'Landon the Swift!'

'I was always humble in my victory, lad,' said Landon, 'despite what the people said. But the truth of the matter is that since that day I've always felt empty and disappointed in myself, so I hid away and went into exile, and buried my past from the rest of the world. I know this shed comes across as creepy and borderlines the obsessive, but I couldn't help myself. I developed an unhealthy obsession with the Agiles. I was intrigued with what made them all tick, why were they all so naturally talented? So every year I studied them… the way they ran, their strengths, their weaknesses if they had any, and I kept everything hidden away in here.'

Cruise stopped for a second, looking around the shed, then he turned to face his trainer with a hopeful look in his eye.

'Do you have anything on the five that are running this year, Landon?' asked Cruise.

'I do,' said Landon, 'why do you ask?'

'Teach me about them, Landon,' said Cruise, 'with all due respect, I'm pouring all of my learning into an inanimate strip of dirt, and in here you have a fountain of information about my real rivals. Please teach me everything you have on them.'

'All right lad,' said Landon, 'you know about it now so there's no use hiding it from you any longer, and you're right, it'll be a more useful, worthwhile and stimulating subject for you than pouring over sketches of the racetrack for hours on end. Come on, help me with these stacks of paper.'

Cruise helped Landon to empty the shed of all of its paperwork, notes, and sketches and took them all into a more spacious room nearer to the hut.

Chapter Twenty-Five

Decoding the Agiles

Cruise sat down in a chair in front of a table with a quill and a piece of parchment like a school child at his desk.

'We should start by studying your average runner from every village to give you a better background on the runners you'll be competing against,' said Landon, 'We'll go through their strengths and the main things that you need to look out for, but in all honesty the only racers you need to be concerned with are the Agiles. But knowledge is power, and you'll learn about them all and respect them none the less.'

'All right,' said Cruise, 'let's do it.'

'Now, let's start with what we already know; the runners from Soulwind,' said Landon, 'A pretty obvious starting point seeing as you fit into that category. What can you tell me about them that you already know?'

'That one is a loser and the other one's dead?' said Cruise.

'Take this seriously now, lad,' said Landon, 'now as a rule, Soulwind's runners are generally all-rounders in their field, and their speed and endurance are consistent throughout the race, however, as you know this doesn't guarantee a race win.'

Cruise started jotting down notes.

'Your Bridgewood neighbours have naturally stronger arms and good core strength,' said Landon, 'and they tend to be dominant off the starting line, but decline as the race goes on, so you don't need to worry about them so much, but don't rule them out entirely. Now as for the Goldstreamers, they're very sturdy runners, but again, they don't pose much of a threat for the rest of the race. Greystone Ridge, excellent fitness, and leg power, and these runners are used to very low levels of oxygen, having living all year on those high peaked mountains, so they're at natural advantage at lower altitudes. Sycamore Valley runners tend to have good agility, as a result of living in such a dense wooded area of Termelanor. Bouldershore, much like Goldstream, have strong arms from rowing their boats and bringing in full nets of fish day in and day out. They tend to be dominant at the start and the end of race, but struggle in the middle. Eastvale are very similar to Greystone Ridge... they're used to slightly higher altitudes and hills, and they have good fitness and leg strength. Birchwood Grove runners tend to have higher levels of energy, from their rich diet of birch sap.'

'This is a lot to remember,' said Cruise, frantically taking notes, 'can you slow down a bit? And how do you spell *Sycamore*?'

'It doesn't matter,' said Landon, 'as I said, the only runners that you really need to be concerned with are the Capital's runners, and more specifically, the Agiles.'

'No shi-' said Cruise.

'Watch your language!' snapped Landon, cutting

across him, 'now annually, they're generally the dominant runners, strong all round, and they boast blood relation to Marcus the Swift. You have been born into an unfortunate time, Cruise, for as you know, you have five of them to contend with. Also, I've found if you managed to run the race in a quicker time than Zane won it last year, it doesn't guarantee your win, as the Agiles have only ever ran as fast as they need to be. Their full potential has so far remained unseen, as they've never have had an outsider to prove a challenge to them.'

'So, what can I do then?' asked Cruise, 'if they've only ever been as fast as they need to be, they could still potentially be faster than me no matter how hard I train and no matter what my best time is?'

'Highly possible,' said Landon, 'but you'll train to the bone and give them a hell of a run, so let's take a more detailed look at your competition, shall we?'

'All right,' said Cruise, 'shoot.'

'First off, the lovely Talia,' said Landon, 'sweet and elegant, she's light, she's nimble yet she's sturdy and don't underestimate her just because she's a girl. She's just as talented as the rest of them.'

'Got it,' said Cruise.

'Thomas,' said Landon, 'probably the truest to Marcus's bloodline, personality and looks-wise, but just like Talia, he's highly naturally talented, but he has one flaw... he lacks heart, which will never make him a true champion while the others are around. Oram comes across as a bit of a bone-head, but he's a very powerful and passionate runner, and Humphrey is sharp and crafty. Watch yourself around these last two.'

'I know who's coming next,' said Cruise.

'That nasty piece of work, Zane,' nodded Landon, 'he's by far the best I've ever seen in my lifetime, and realistically, if you end up rivalling the Agiles by the time the race comes, ultimately, he's the one you're going to have to beat.'

Landon spoke for a long time and he told Cruise everything he knew about the Agiles. Cruise took down notes until his hand was numb, but he felt now he had a better insight on whom he was challenging, and it made him even hungrier to beat them.

Chapter Twenty-Six

The Vultures Attack the Holding

Cruise was going over what he had learned about the runners the night before in his head as he lay in bed that morning. He was drifting in and out of sleep and having a rather nice lay in, and he was having an interesting broken dream about Amber, and then for some reason about Talia. But his lovely dream was interrupted by a flock of crows cawing at his window. He sat up in bed and he heard a bit of a ruckus coming from outside the hut, and faint shouting in the distance, then Landon suddenly burst into his bedroom.

'Get up lad,' said Landon, 'we have some trouble.'

'What's wrong?' said Cruise, 'what's making that noise?'

'There's no time to explain,' said Landon, 'get dressed, now, and forget about the armour.'

Cruise and Landon burst out of the hut and looked across the holding. The squawks and the crowing grew louder, but it wasn't a murder of crows as Cruise had first thought.

Landon sped into his forge and returned with two sharp steel long swords. He threw one towards Cruise and he caught it by the handle.

'Landon,' said Cruise, 'would you please tell me what's going on?'

'Vultures lad,' said Landon, 'they've come to raid my supplies.'

'Vultures?' said Cruise, sounding confused.

'Time to put that practice into play, lad,' said Landon, 'here they come.'

Just as Cruise was wondering exactly what a Vulture was, he saw a large group of people approaching the holding, cawing, crowing and taunting as they did.

The large group of Vultures were dressed in shoddy black-feathered leather rags and beaked masks, similar to the plague doctors in the storybooks that his father read him as a child.

'Who are they?' said Cruise, trembling slightly.

'They're a bandit group that target small holdings and farmsteads just before winter sets in,' said Landon, 'they target them for their supplies, but they haven't attacked for a few years now. I used to have a couple of hounds here to protect me and to help me defend the holding. They must have discovered that I no longer have them. There's quite a large group of them this year.'

The Vultures approached ever closer, wearing a mixture of armour and wielding terrifying looking weapons, all looking ready to kill.

'Get ready to fight, lad,' said Landon advancing the Vultures, 'and cut Locust free. Horse meat will be like fillet steak to them. At least he can make a run for it. I'll try and hold them off. Do the best you can to keep them away from the hut and the out sheds.'

Cruise heeded Landon's words and made straight for Locust. When he reached the horse, he felt a panic in the beast before he hewed the rope in two with his sword and cut him free.

'Run boy,' he said as he struck Locust on the backside hard with an open palm, 'get out of here, quickly boy.'

Cruise turned and saw Landon in the distance fighting one of the Vultures while the rest of the pack were quickly encroaching on his location, with a few straying wide and heading towards the hut and the out sheds.

Cruise started to run back to the hut when he heard a screeching behind him. A Vulture had broken off from the pack and was sprinting towards Cruise.

Cruise held out his blade and the Vulture swung wildly for him, continuing to screech and crow.

Cruise parried the Vultures' blade and slashed the Vulture across her chest, felling her in an instant.

Cruise felt very mobile without his weighted training armour on. He was lucky in a sense that the Vultures chose to attack this early in the morning, because if they had left it any later Cruise would have been like a sitting duck wearing lead boots to them.

Cruise continued with the fight as a second Vulture challenged him, while keeping an eye on Landon.

Landon was now engulfed by several Vultures, but he was still holding his own.

A few of the Vultures had now made it to the out

sheds, and were raiding whatever they could, as more and more of them flocked into the holding.

It was hopeless; Cruise could not fight his way towards the hut, and the Vulture he was fighting was persistent and would not let him pass.

Even more Vultures were now engulfing Landon and he was becoming overwhelmed in the distance.

Cruise's blood froze in his veins as he witnessed a Vulture shank Landon through his flank, and he let out a mighty howl.

'Landon!' cried Cruise, and the Vulture that was fighting him barged him onto the ground.

Cruise held his blade out in front of him ready to protect himself as the Vulture prepared to bring down his blade upon him, when the Vulture was suddenly knocked down by Locust, who had returned and had backed onto his hind legs and hoofed the Vulture over onto the ground, dazing him.

Cruise rose then forced his sword into the fallen Vulture and raced over to Landon, who was still putting up a fight despite just being stabbed.

Cruise sprinted hard and with all of his might lunged at the Vultures, killing two very quickly.

Cruise fought off the last of the group, and Landon fell down onto one knee.

Cruise showed a formidable display of sword combat but it was still three against one, and the rest of the Vultures were busy ransacking Landon's hut and out sheds.

'Lad,' wheezed Landon, 'the supplies.'

Cruise struggled desperately to quickly take care of his enemies so he could defend the sheds, but alas, he was only one man, he could not be everywhere at once, and he felt now with the Vultures were merely distracting him and keeping him busy so their comrades could empty the sheds and retreat.

Cruise heard an ear deafening caw from the direction of the hut and the three he was fighting replied with several quick screeches in quick succession.

The Vultures retreated, some carrying sacks of food, others with whatever they could carry, including supplies, provisions, tools and trinkets.

'Come back here!' yelled Cruise, chasing after the fleeing Vultures.

'Leave them, lad,' Landon struggled, 'let them go, or you'll get yourself killed.'

'Locust!' shouted Cruise in a red mist as he ran back to the gigantic horse and quickly mounted him. 'Come on boy, come on, yah!'

Cruise was engulfed by a radiating heat as he straddled the unsaddled Locust and grasped his filthy unkempt mane. He felt unconsciously at one with the beast.

Locust bolted forward and Cruise raised his sword high as he charged his mount towards the fleeing bandits.

He trampled one down into the dirt, and then he cut one down and then another, and the shrieking raiders dropped what they were carrying.

Cruise chased the Vultures as far as the creek, and the Vultures retreated across it as Locust came to a sudden halt and neighed and whined as he stamped the ground.

The Vultures waded across and made it to the other side and retreated across the plain with their rewards in their clutches.

'You bastards!' he panted, 'don't you dare come back here or I'll kill you all!'

The Vultures were soon out of sight, but they had gotten what they had come for.

'Landon...' said Cruise as he galloped Locust back to the holding to find Landon lying where he had left him.

Cruise dismounted Locust and hastened to his fallen master's side.

'Landon,' said Cruise, shaking him. He was unconscious, but still breathing and blood was seeping out from his wound. Luckily, he wasn't bleeding too heavily considering the size of the wound.

He attempted to lead Locust over so that he could try to get Landon onto the horse, but Locust dug in his heels and had reverted back to his old stubborn self.

'Come on Landon,' said Cruise as he attempted to bring him round and get him onto his feet, but Landon was a great lump of a man and he could not budge him.

Cruise went around behind him and tried to drag him back to the hut by holding him underneath his armpits. He managed to move him a few feet, but now red-faced and straining he couldn't shift him anymore.

Cruise spotted a small wooden cart in the distance of the yard. If he could get Landon onto that he could probably manage to pull him back to the hut.

Cruise rushed over to the cart and back over to Landon. 'Come on you lump,' said Cruise, 'help me out here.'

Cruise heaved Landon, but he would not budge.

He tried again to no avail.

On the third attempt he yelled and lifted him with all of his might. Cruise lifted Landon off the ground and onto the back of the cart.

Wondering where he had got his strength from and panting for breath, Cruise grasped the handles of the cart and lugged it back to the front door of the hut.

He dragged Landon off the cart and into the hut and set him down on his seat in the kitchen area.

Cruise cleaned his wound and dressed it and then lay Landon down to rest. Cruise went back and forth to survey the loss and damage that the Vultures had caused, while checking up on Landon every now and then.

Cruise retrieved what he could from the fallen Vultures, before piling up the bodies and burning them in an empty field; he hoped that would serve as a warning to any other bandits or raiders who planned on doing the same as the Vultures. He then assessed the larders and how much food they had left. Not much.

Cruise put his training on hold and spent the next few weeks taking care of Landon. He kept him watered and changed the dressing on his wound.

He didn't sleep much, still haunted by the Vultures, as the snow began to fall.

Chapter Twenty-Seven

Supply Run

Cruise stood anxiously and peered out through the kitchen window of Landon's hut. The snow continued to fall thick on the frozen ground of the holding and large lazy flakes floated past the window.

'There's no sign of this stopping,' said Cruise to the still unconscious Landon, 'it's coming down really thick now and at this rate there won't be enough food to see us through the winter.'

What am I going to do? he thought to himself. It was looking more and more probable that he would have to go out in this weather and head into the village to restock on supplies for the winter, but he felt lost without his trainer's guidance.

Cruise looked out of the window again and stared at the snow falling. If he didn't go and get some supplies soon they definitely wouldn't make it through the winter. He had to decide on what to do soon, or he would eventually lose his strength through lack of calories, and then he would be of no use to Landon.

Cruise approached Landon and kneeled at his side. It seemed as though he was coming down with a fever. He checked Landon's wound. It was starting to smell bad, and if he did not get him some medicine soon, the wound would certainly fester.

Cruise rummaged about in Landon's cupboards and fished out an old large pestle and mortar. He had to make him something for his fever and wound, at least until he could get him some proper medicine.

He didn't have a clue when it came to medicine, apart from what he had picked up from his parents. He looked up at the herbs that were hanging and drying off on the hut's ceiling beams.

Feverfew, he knew what that was. He grabbed a handful and threw it into the mortar.

What else did Landon have here? He looked from side to side at the dozens of various hanging dried herbs.

Peppermint and spearmint, they would have to do, and into the mortar they went. Cruise struggled to identify the remaining drying herbs, so he grabbed a little bit of everything and threw them into the mix. He also threw in some garlic cloves, along with a huge chunk of honeycomb and a large ginger root. He started to smash up the mixture and the pungent smell immediately hit his nostrils.

'Oh!' said Cruise, flinching, 'I hope you have a strong stomach, Landon. If this stuff doesn't cure you, it may very well wake you up.'

Cruise forced the thick paste down Landon's throat and after massaging his neck he swallowed it all. Then Cruise wiped the remnants of the bowl clean with a fresh wound dressing and placed it over Landon's wound.

'Hopefully that should hold you off until I get back,' said Cruise, 'I'm going to head into the village now. I have to get us some supplies, and you desperately need some medicine. I won't be too long, I promise.'

Cruise dressed as warm as he could and left the hut with an empty sack.

The weather was getting colder still, and rifts formed as the wind picked up and the snow fell heavier.

Cruise pressed on through the snow, heading towards the village of Soulwind.

Time was of the essence now – if he did not get Landon the medicine he needed he would surely die, and if he did not make it back in time, he would certainly get lost in the storm.

He made it as far as the forest path, and the skeletons of the oak trees provided a little cover from the snow, but the visibility was steadily growing worse.

If it continued like this, he would not even make it into Soulwind. He had to divert his route. He decided to head to his parents' house instead. He did not want to worry them or deprive them of their own winter supplies, but he was desperate, and his hands already felt like ice.

He navigated the forest path, estimating the direction to his home, when he noticed the outline of his cottage.

Cruise burst into his home, shivering, and he threw up on the hallway floor. His mother came out of the kitchen when she heard the commotion.

'Cruise,' she said, 'oh my, Cruise, what are you doing out in this dreadful weather?'

'It's Landon, Mum,' said Cruise, 'bandits attacked the holding, and stole all of our supplies. Landon was wounded during the attack and now he's very sick. I think their blades must have been coated in some sort of poison or something and he's coming down with a fever and he has a nasty wound. I hate to ask this of you, Mum, but do you have any supplies to spare us and any medicine? I tried to make it into town but the storm is too thick. I barely made it here.'

'Of course we do, dear,' said Erika, 'your father restocked the larder last week. Let me fill up that sack up for you.'

'Thank you, Mum,' said Cruise, 'where is Dad anyway?'

'He went over to Ferlan's to get some extra firewood, when he noticed that the weather was getting worse,' said Erika, 'he's not long left.'

Cruise welcomed the warmth of the nearby hearth and the feeling slowly returned to his hands. Cruise dried out his wet clothes above the fireplace and warmed himself for a short time until he felt he could continue his journey back to the holding.

'Here you are, dear,' said Erika, handing Cruise a full sack of supplies, 'you will stay a while at least, won't you, son? At least long enough for the weather to clear up a little?'

'I don't think that it's going to, Mum,' said Cruise, 'and I have to get back to Landon as soon as I can with these supplies and the medicine. I'd better get going right away. Thanks for the supplies and I'm sorry that I couldn't stay longer. Make sure you stay warm.'

'I understand dear,' said Erika, 'don't you worry, both your father and I will be fine.'

'Thanks again, Mum,' said Cruise. 'I love you.'

'I love you too, son,' said Erika. 'Be careful out there.'

Cruise journeyed back, the snow coming down thicker by the minute, so he could not see even a few feet ahead of him. Maybe his mother was right... maybe he should head back, spend the night at his place, and wait for the storm to die down before continuing his journey in the morning.

No, Landon was depending on him, he needed those supplies.

This was the worst storm he had ever experienced.

He was shivering all over now, and his whole body was wet and numb.

Suddenly, his whole body warmed up faintly, and his joints felt looser. The adrenaline must have kicked in.

His pack was heavy, and the storm was gradually worsening.

He was lost.

He had now even lost his general direction.

He decided he would rest.

Just for a moment.

Just for a little while.

Just, until he regained his strength again.

Just a little snooze...

Just a little sleep...

Chapter Twenty-Eight

Awakening

Cruise awoke to the sound of a kettle whistling faintly in his ringing ears, and through his blurred vision he noticed a large figure standing over him.

'Landon?' said Cruise in a weak voice.

'Well I'll be damned, Cruise,' said Landon, 'you're awake. I could have sworn on my last silver coin that if the cold hadn't taken you, then the fever certainly would have, and I thought for sure that the frostbite would have claimed your limbs even if you had somehow managed to pull through but look at you. What exactly are you made of lad?'

'How long have I been out?' asked Cruise.

'About three weeks,' said Landon, 'I found you in the front yard, buried underneath about a foot of snow. I was surprised to find you still breathing, lad. You were colder and more rigid than an icicle. If it wasn't for the top of the supply sack sticking out of the snow I never would have found you. I brought you straight inside and put you in front of the fire but you kept mumbling something that I didn't understand, something about going into the west. The medicine that you brought back just about saved my life. You then passed out and the fever set in. You had early onset of frostbite on nearly every single one of your limbs, but look at you, sitting up on your bedding like you've just got up for your breakfast.'

'I wish I was dead if it means eating any more of your porridge,' said Cruise, 'three weeks? That paste I made you must have done you some good then if you were well enough to wake up and try and find me, and I'm one lucky devil by the sounds of it,' said Cruise as he looked at his hands, flexing and checking out his fingers for any evidence of frostbite. 'Is the worst of the storm over?'

'Most of it,' said Landon, 'the worst of it has passed. You're lucky that you made it back to me, and you're so lucky that I found you when I did, otherwise you'd have probably still been frozen out there somewhere and I'd be rotting in here. Here, drink this. Get some fluid into you.'

'Thanks,' said Cruise, accepting the cup of water. He felt the cool liquid flowing down his throat.

'You've lost a lot of weight, lad,' said Landon, 'you need to concentrate on getting back to a healthy weight before you even consider continuing your training.'

Cruise looked down at himself and saw that Landon was right. He looked gaunt and his skin was pale, his ribs protruding once more.

'This has been an unfortunate setback,' said Landon, 'we may not have enough time now to prepare you for the race.'

'Then we train twice as hard,' insisted Cruise, 'we'll do whatever it takes. Do we have enough supplies to last us through the rest of the winter?'

'We should do,' said Landon, 'I'll be able to head out

and get anything else if we need it now though, with the worst of the storm over. I'm sorry you had to go through all of that.'

'It's not your fault,' said Cruise, 'you would have died if I hadn't gone out to fetch supplies and your medicine.'

'The Vultures would have killed me if you weren't there to protect me,' said Landon, 'I owe you a lot, lad.'

'Don't mention it,' said Cruise, 'but come on Landon, I have to get back into training as soon as possible. The cold weather will make my training tougher, which will surely put me at an advantage against the Agiles?'

'Torturing you body in this weather is neither training nor an advantage,' said Landon, 'so you'll do as you're told, and concentrate on getting your strength back and getting plenty of rest.'

'All right,' said Cruise, 'hey… Landon?'

'What is it, lad?'

'I'm glad you're all right,' Cruise smiled.

Cruise spent the coming weeks mainly resting, sleeping, eating, and recovering his strength, but deep down, Landon worried that it wouldn't be enough.

Chapter Twenty-Nine

A Welcoming Spring

Spring had finally arrived and the heads of the sprouting daffodils and the snowdrops poked through the receding snow, as the first of the morning dew specked the young budding saplings.

It had been a long and harsh winter, and Cruise had lost a lot of weight, and was greatly weakened by his fever, but he was now up and moving again, and recovering his strength day by day.

It was looking more and more desperate as only a short amount of time remained now before the lead up to the race, and there was a drastic and obvious decline in Cruise's appearance and strength. Things were looking bleak.

But Cruise persisted with his training as well as he could.

Landon had recommended that Cruise run in next year's race instead, but Cruise wouldn't have any of it.

Cruise did what he could and recovered as much of his strength as possible while doing his best to carry on with his training.

He continued running his laps, and he was even wearing his weighted training armour once again.

The sun finally melted the remaining frost on the

ground and the steam evaporated off the thawing ground like a boiling kettle.

The snow and ice all melted and the earth became soft once more after the harshest winter in over a hundred years.

The days were mild and getting lighter by the day, and Cruise did what he could to recover back to full strength.

But apprehension and doubt had already slipped into his mind. Perhaps this was not his year, perhaps something or someone was telling him he was not ready.

Chapter Thirty

Pre-Race Nerves

'I wanted you to have something, lad,' said Landon, 'it's a day early, but I was meaning to give this to you for your birthday. I just couldn't wait to see your face when you opened it any longer.'

Landon handed Cruise a long item wrapped in a piece of cloth.

Cruise unravelled the cloth and his eyes widened and his mouth dropped open as he held a beautiful strapped leather handle and scabbard with an embossed image of a flaming rock on it.

'It's a sword…' said Cruise looking up at Landon with awe.

'I made it,' said Landon, 'for you.'

'Thank you, Landon,' said Cruise as he smiled down at it.

'I made it from the sky metal you gave me,' said Landon.

'Landon,' said Cruise, sounding a little guilty and disappointed as he looked back up, 'I gave that to you, for your birthday.'

'It was a privilege to work with that metal, lad,' said Landon, 'you gave me that much, and that's more than anyone has ever given me, and you fought so well against the Vultures and have saved my life more than once. I wanted to say thank you, so the end product is yours to keep.'

'Landon,' said Cruise, 'I don't know what to say. Thank you so much.'

'Be careful with it, as it's a very tough and sharp sword,' said Landon, 'tougher and sharper than any steel.'

Cruise unsheathed the sword; it was a little longer than a short sword, and it had a shiny, silver and marbled blade, harder and finer than the finest iron or steel smithed sword. It had distinctive patterns of banding and mottling reminiscent of flowing water.

'Blades forged from sky metal are reputed to be resistant to shattering,' said Landon, 'and will forever hold a resilient edge.'

Then Cruise noticed something quite obvious and he was surprised he hadn't noticed it sooner – the blade had a similar marbled pattern to his pendant. Was the pendant also crafted from sky metal? Surely not. He fumbled beneath his tunic and fished the pendant out, staring between both the pendant and the sword.

'What is it, lad?' said Landon, wondering what Cruise was doing.

'Look,' said Cruise as he showed Landon the pendant, 'do you think that this pendant is made from sky metal just like the sword?'

'Let's take a look at it,' said Landon as Cruise took off and handed Landon the pendant.

Landon looked at the pendant carefully and fumbled it around in his hands. Squinted at it attentively, he held it up to the sunlight and took turns looking between it and the sword.

'It seems you could be right, lad,' said Landon, 'although the metal seems brighter than the sword, if anything. Where did you get this?'

'My dad gave it to me,' said Cruise, 'it was a birthday present last year. It's been handed down through my family for a few generations, and he said it once belonged to Marcus the Swift.'

'That's rather peculiar,' said Landon, 'I've never heard or seen anything like this. I'll have to do some more digging to see if there are any references to it in my blacksmith books. Take good care of it, lad,' said Landon, handing Cruise back the pendant.

'Things have happened to me, Landon,' Cruise suddenly spouted.

'What do you mean?' said Landon.

'Since I've had the pendant, I mean.'

'What sort of things?'

'I thought I was just imagining it all at first,' said Cruise, 'but the more I think of it, the less likely it seems that it was all just a coincidence. The lack of aches the day after the all that intense training, the healing, the sudden bursts of energy and strength, the heightened senses. Did you seriously think that anybody else could have survived being buried under a foot of snow for that length of time, Landon? I'm telling you, it's something to do with this pendant. I always feel engulfed by a strange warmth, which stems from it just before something like that is about to happen to me.'

'Have you told anyone else about this?' said Landon.

'I tried to tell my father once,' said Cruise, 'but it turns out he never wore the pendant, so I kept it to myself to save myself from sounding like a madman.'

'Well,' smiled Landon, 'what the Agiles don't know, can't hurt them.'

'What do you mean?' said Cruise.

'Well, if this thing can give you an edge in the race, then it's best to keep it to yourself, don't you think?'

'I don't know,' said Cruise, 'the more I think about it, the more it feels like cheating.'

'They already have an advantage over you with their unnaturally heightened speed and endurance,' said Landon, 'and if that truly is the pendant of Marcus the Swift, you must keep it a secret from them, especially from Zane. If he learns about it, he'll surely try to take it from you. He'll believe it belongs with them as a family heirloom, no matter how fairly you got your hands on it.'

'You're right, Landon,' said Cruise, 'I'll keep it quiet.'

'Maybe it'll come through for you in the race,' said Landon, 'you need all the help you can get now after that lengthy setback. I hope you like your birthday present, lad; your very own shard from a fallen star.'

'Shard,' said Cruise, 'shard,' he repeated, 'I like that. That's a good name for it.'

Landon smiled.

'I wish Red was still here,' said Cruise, 'it won't be the same running the race without him this year, and he would have loved to learn from you as a blacksmith.'

'He'll be with you tomorrow lad,' said Landon, 'in some ways, he never left you.'

Chapter Thirty-One

A Parting Gift

Much like the previous year, Cruise attempted a good night's sleep the night before the race, but he did not sleep a wink. Tomorrow would be race day once again, and doubt had already entered his mind.

He arose that morning after what would have been the last night he would spend in Landon's hut.

'So,' said Landon preparing the breakfast as normal, 'today is the day.'

'I can't believe it's finally here,' said Cruise.

'Are you sure you still want to do this, lad?' said Landon, 'you're nowhere near the peak you were at just before you fell ill, and there's always next year.'

'No Landon,' said Cruise, 'I have to do this. I can't wait another year.'

'You still look a little underweight,' said Landon, 'and slightly gaunt, so are you absolutely sure?'

'I'm entirely sure,' said Cruise, 'I'm not waiting another year. I'm ready.'

'I thought that might have been your answer,' said Landon, 'well, you're almost ready, lad,' and he handed Cruise two large parcels.

'Landon, you've already given me a birthday present,'

said Cruise, 'I can't accept anything else from you.'

'These aren't birthday presents,' said Landon, 'well, they are, sort of, but they're just a little something for you, for today.'

Cruise ripped open the larger of the two packages first.

It was a brand-new pair of leather running boots.

'Landon, you shouldn't have,' said Cruise.

'I felt like your old pair needed replacing,' said Landon, 'those old worn things wouldn't have done you many favours during the race.'

'They're beautiful,' said Cruise, 'thank you.'

'And most importantly they're very hard wearing,' said Landon, 'they're both light and comfortable. Now, open your other one.'

Cruise ripped open the last parcel.

It was a beautiful scarlet tunic, trimmed with blacks and golds.

'Landon…' said Cruise, not sure what to say.

'The sigil on the back shows that you're a runner from Soulwind,' said Landon, 'and the small sigil on the front on your chest indicates that you were trained under me.'

'I love it,' said Cruise, 'I'll wear it with pride.'

'The pleasure was all mine, lad,' said Landon, 'try it on and see if it fits you.'

'It's perfect,' said Cruise after he pulled it over his head.

'Scarlet is definitely your colour,' said Landon.

'If I go and pack my things now,' said Cruise, 'could

you bring them along to the festival and mind them for me, please? I can take them straight home after the race then to save me coming back to the hut for them later.'

'All right, lad, no problem,' said Landon, 'but hurry up, as we need to get you over to the registration tent. You don't want to be late and miss it.'

'Thanks Landon,' said Cruise, 'I'll be quick.'

Chapter Thirty-Two

At the Ready Once Again

Cruise and Landon arrived at the festival and Cruise couldn't believe a year had passed so quickly.

He spotted Zane and the Agiles arriving in their coach in the distance, and he turned red and frowned with anger.

'Keep it together, lad,' said Landon, 'don't lose your focus.'

'You're right Landon,' said Cruise, 'I'll try.'

Cruise hurried over to the registration tent and quickly signed up for the race before he headed back over to Landon, who was carrying Cruise's belongings in a large sack.

'So, this is it lad, I'll go and wait over for you by the starting line, then,' said Landon, 'I'm sure your parents should be around here somewhere, too. I'll see if I can find them, and I'll see you when you cross the finish line, lad. Best of luck.'

'Thank you, Landon,' said Cruise, 'I'll see you at the end.'

Cruise headed alone to the starting line, where he could see the Agiles warming up at the front of the grid. Amber was there seeing Zane off and wishing him good luck, kissing him lustfully.

Cruise huffed and continued to stretch out his limbs, with no one to talk to this year, and no one to share the experience with, and wondering how things went so wrong with Amber.

The announcer instructed the runners to take up their positions on the starting grid, and before he knew it he was in the exact same position he had been a year before, with exactly the same dream and goal, but the reasons could not have been more different.

In no time at all, the starting horn suddenly blasted, and the participants all bolted. Cruise nearly stumbled over himself as his overwhelming acceleration speed surprised him and caught him off-guard. He still wasn't entirely used to himself without wearing his weighted training armour.

He quickly recovered and steadied himself out and before he knew it he was leading the pack of the runners.

Well, almost leading the pack... much like the year before he saw the Agiles quickly lead the race and disappear into the distance, and doubt overcame him once again, but he constantly reminded himself why he was running this year. He had to catch up with them. He would catch up with them.

After a while longer and when he had left the large cluster of the runners from the other villages far behind him, Cruise did not see a single runner over the next couple of miles. No one was behind him and he could not see a soul ahead of him either.

At least he had gotten further than he did last year, he thought, as he passed the point where he tripped, but he had not journeyed too far past that point when suddenly he saw two small figures running in the distance.

As he got closer, he noticed it was indeed two of the Agiles; Thomas and Talia, running side by side.

He picked up his pace and passed them easily enough, nodding as he passed. They both nodded back, Talia even smiled at him.

Soon, he saw another two figures up ahead, one slightly taller with longer brown hair, the other stockier with a slight receding hairline: it was Humphrey and Oram. He grew worried when he realized that there was no one else around him, and he remembered what Landon had told him about them during his studies.

He carefully attempted to overtake the pair, when suddenly he was grabbed by Oram's strong hairy arm, and they both held Cruise down and started to beat him.

'So, you got past the other two, did you?' said Humphrey punching Cruise in the face, 'well, we'll make sure you don't get past us.'

Cruise noticed there was a high ledge up ahead and that the pair were dragging him towards it, but before they could get him anywhere near it, Cruise stepped on Oram's big toe and punched Humphrey hard in the gut, winding him.

The pair quickly recovered and were about to grab onto Cruise once again when all of a sudden Talia and Thomas appeared out of nowhere and grabbed onto the pair from behind, holding onto them tightly as they dragged them back, and away from Cruise.

'You traitors,' said Humprey, 'you both wait until Zane hears about this.'

'This isn't why we race, Humphrey,' said Thomas, 'this goes against everything our name stands for, and you're both a disgrace to our heritage if you agree that acting like this is acceptable, Grampa Marcus would be rolling in his grave. Run for it, Cruise.'

Cruise couldn't believe it… two of the Agiles had stepped in to help him out. His faith was suddenly restored in the descendants of his hero as he sprinted away from the quartet and continued with the race, but he knew there was still one more challenge left to face.

Cruise ran for miles, and soon he saw a lone figure running ahead. Surely, Zane!

He picked up his pace until he caught up with him.

'So, you got past them, did you?' said Zane, 'well I'm telling you now that you aren't going to get past me.'

Zane barged into Cruise, and he stumbled, tripped, and fell to the ground hard.

A strong heat emanated out of Cruise's pendant, and he leapt up from the ground and sprinted hard. He immediately caught back up with Zane who could not believe his eyes.

Cruise's body now felt like it weighed nothing. He was lighter than a feather, and more agile than a shark.

Cruise smiled at Zane as he passed him and sped on, continuing with the race as if nothing had happened.

Zane grew angry as Cruise effortlessly led the race, and Cruise couldn't believe it himself, but there was still a long way to go.

Before long, Zane caught up with him again.

'If you think I'm going to let you to win this, loser,' said Zane, 'then you have another think coming.'

'Oh, hey Zane, I didn't see you there,' said Cruise, 'how did my backside look to you from behind there? Any good?'

Zane and Cruise were now neck to neck, but Cruise started to feel himself deteriorate. He was short of breath, his chest was tight, and his heart thudding hard in his head and ears.

Cruise spotted the finish line ahead, and Zane was ahead of him now.

He felt him inching away, and the finish line felt unreachable.

He was so close, he couldn't be beaten now. He clenched his eyes shut and sprinted forward with all his remaining speed and energy, engulfed by the now all too familiar warmth of the pendant. He would keep running as hard and as fast and for as long as he could, even if it killed him.

Chapter Thirty-Three

The Final Push

Cruise collapsed with exhaustion, his teeth clenched, his eyes still shut tight, feeling as though he was suspended in time.

He looked back to see he had crossed the finish line, and then he heard the announcer's voice.

'Ladies and gentlemen, boys and girls, we have a winner! I am pleased to announce, your festival champion for the year is Cruise, from Soulwind! And let's also hear it for our runner up and last year's champion, Zane from the Capital!'

The crowd went wild, and Cruise looked around as confetti flew all around him and the spectators cheered louder than any year he could remember. A group of supporters ran up to him and held him high as the festival music celebrated his victory.

He was pouring with sweat, and his whole body was shaking and wobbling, but he had done it, he had finally done it... after all of that training, after years of fanaticising, he was finally the festival champion.

'Thank you, Landon. I did it, Red, I did it for you.'

Cruise was put down but the crowd and the supporters all continued to cheer and congratulate him. He was donned in the festival champion's garb and handed the golden trophy.

But then a commotion came from behind the large crowd.

It was Zane, gripping the gilded festival champion's blade in his clenched fist, his eyes psychotic.

'You cheater!' yelled Zane, frothing at the mouth as he forced and pushed his way through the crowd, grasping the sword at his side. The spectators immediately backed off, gasping. 'You damned cheater. How could you have?'

'I beat you fair and square, Zane,' said Cruise, but without warning Zane charged at Cruise and hacked and swung for him with the festival sword.

Cruise dodged the swipes and shuffled back as Zane continued to advance towards him. Then in a moment, a large figure came between the pair of them.

Landon was standing in front of him, still holding Cruise's large, heavy sack of belongings.

'That's enough now, lad,' Landon said to Zane, 'now why don't you put down the sword?'

'Why don't you back off, old man?' said Zane, 'before you get hurt.'

'Hand over the blade,' repeated Landon, 'there's a good lad. Nobody needs to get hurt today.'

'Step aside old man,' he said again, 'this blade belongs to the Agiles, as does that trophy!'

'It belongs with the festival champion,' said Landon, 'and you're not the festival champion.'

Zane charged towards Landon in his anger, and Cruise

didn't notice that Landon was hiding Shard underneath his sack of belongings. Landon dropped the sack, strewing Cruise's belongings, and he quickly unsheathed Shard. However, just as he had unsheathed it, Zane lunged forward and forced the festival blade through Landon's chest.

Zane smiled cruelly, his eyes still psychotic, as Landon coughed up his own blood before Zane finally kicked Landon to the cold hard earth, stone dead, right at Cruise's feet.

Cruise stood there and watched the light leave Landon's stone-grey eyes.

He trembled.

Zane had not only killed Red the year before, but he had now killed Landon too. Zane was much bigger and stronger than Cruise and the race did not seem to have had any effect on his physical condition, but Cruise still felt exhausted.

An uncontrollable rage and hatred suddenly came over Cruise and he picked Shard from Landon's still warm, dead hand and grasped it tightly.

'You really are a disgrace to your ancestry, did you know that?' said Cruise, 'I'm going to make you pay for what you've done,' said Cruise as he looked at Zane, his cruel smile still on his handsome face.

'Come on then, loser,' gritted Zane, flipping the sword's handle in his strong hand, 'let's see if you're a better fighter than your friend.'

Cruise lunged at Zane and the crowd witnessed in awe as Zane and Cruise displayed an extraordinary sword combat, both skilfully deflecting and parrying each other's blows.

The gold and silver blades pinged and clanged against each other as they collided, sending sparks flying.

Cruise swung for Zane relentlessly, but Zane seemed to be getting the better of Cruise, and quickly disarmed him.

Cruise took a step back and caught his heel on a protruding rock and fell backwards onto the ground.

Zane was about to bring down the festival blade onto Cruise when Thomas appeared from the crowd and grabbed hold of Zane's arm.

'That's enough, Zane,' said Thomas, 'leave him be.'

'I always knew that you were a traitor,' snarled Zane, 'here, you can join him.'

Zane gripped Thomas by his tunic and forced the festival blade through his gut then shoved him to the ground.

Zane turned back to Cruise and advanced towards him, his blade dripping with Thomas's blood.

'Zane!' cried Talia, 'just take a look at yourself. Please stop this madness!'

'You'll be next if you're not careful,' said Zane, 'you traitorous bitch, I'll stick you with this blade, still warm and dripping with your cousin's blood. Would you like that?'

'Hey, Zane,' said Cruise.

Zane turned around and felt a forceful shot hit

his eyeball.

While Zane was threatening Talia, Cruise had got a hold of his slingshot that had fallen out of his strewn pack of belongings and shot Zane in the eye with a small stone he had picked up from the ground.

Zane cried with pain as he held his eye with his free hand. Cruise wasted little time as he flicked open his pocket knife and stabbed Zane in the thigh.

As Zane fell to one knee howling with pain, Cruise picked up Shard from the ground. Zane rose and he charged towards him as he bent over to retrieve it.

Cruise turned quickly and blocked Zane's attack, then he slid Shard down the length of the festival blade, cutting off Zane's sword hand. Cruise punched Zane across his face with the hilt of his sword, and he fell onto his behind.

Zane was down, his nose broken and bloodied, and he had nothing left to defend himself with.

Zane scrambled for the festival blade, but Cruise stepped on it and pointed Shard at his face.

'Humphrey!' yelled Zane, 'Oram! Finish him off!'

Humphrey and Oram just looked at each other, and then diverted their gaze to the ground.

'Go on then,' snarled Zane, 'finish it.'

'Tie this filth up and send him to the Capital for trial,' said Cruise, 'the King can decide what to do with him.'

At that moment, Amber ran over to Zane crying out loud.

'Don't worry Amber,' smiled Cruise, 'you can still

write and visit him in his prison cell.'

The village militia restrained and took Zane away, as he shouted threats at Cruise, Talia, Humphrey, and Oram.

Humphrey and Oram both approached Cruise and shook his hand, while Talia wept over Thomas's dead body.

Cruise walked over to Landon's corpse and laid his head on his shoulder.

Chapter Thirty-Four

Home Sweet Home

Cruise returned to his home the evening after the race. There would be no ball this year, as a sign of respect for Landon and Thomas. Cruise heard a voice call out from behind him.

It was Talia.

'What are you doing here, Talia?' said Cruise, 'you'll miss your coach back to the Capital.'

'I didn't get a chance to congratulate you properly,' said Talia, 'and I wanted to come and say goodbye to you, until next year.'

'Thanks,' said Cruise, 'I'm so sorry about Thomas.'

'It's all right,' said Talia, 'at least Zane will get what's coming to him after everything he did.'

'Thomas didn't deserve to die like that,' said Cruise, 'neither did Landon. They both died protecting me. It's all my fault.'

'It's not your fault,' said Talia taking his hand. 'Zane was out of control and you stopped him. Who knows who else he might have been harmed if you hadn't acted when you did. He even said he was going to kill me.'

'I'm glad he didn't,' smiled Cruise.

'I have no reason to race anymore,' said Talia, 'Thomas

meant everything to me. He was the real reason why I raced.'

'You still have to race next year, Talia,' said Cruise, 'it's in your blood, and I have to race somebody who will give me a decent challenge.'

'Come back to the Capital with me,' said Talia, 'we can train together and you can come and live with me while we train.'

'I'd love to,' said Cruise, 'for now my place is here with my family, but I'll be sure visit you soon.'

'I hope you do,' said Talia.

They both stared at each other for a while, then they both leant in to each other and shared a kiss and a long embrace.

'Goodbye for now,' said Talia.

'Goodbye, Talia.' Cruise smiled.

He watched as Talia disappeared down the forest path.

Cruise turned and walked back towards his home.

Cruise stopped short, and stood still and silent, staring towards the golden horizon from the porch of his front door. He was fumbling with his pendant, and it hummed with suggestive awareness.

Something was drawing him to the west.

His fluffy black cat, Cicada, purred loudly and rubbed against his legs between intervals of sharp gazes with her bug-green eyes.

'Come on Cicada,' smiled Cruise, as he picked her up and retired into his home, 'you stupid cat.'

About the Author

I have been interested in writing stories ever since I was old enough to form words onto a page..., and even before then, I would make up stories in my head.

It proved challenging in the beginning, learning a new language during primary school (English being my second language), but my writing and storytelling was always told through the English language and word.

My passion continued into secondary school where my favourite subject was English.

When I entered the working world, I lost touch with my passion for writing as I experienced many different jobs from butchery to architecture and I took some time out to travel the world.

My love of writing stories returned sometime during my mid-twenties.

I live in a small peaceful village tucked away in a beautiful area of southwest Wales, and I write during any spare time I have between my day job working for the local police service.

My dream is to fulfil my dream of becoming a professional writer and am now writing a sequel to The Legacy of the Sky Pendant.

Twitter
Jonathan Crayford
@JonCrayford

Facebook
Jonathan Crayford Author

Website
www.JonathanCrayfordAuthor.co.uk

First instalment in the Sky Pendant trilogy

1. *The Legacy of the Sky Pendant*
2. *The Mystery of the Sky Pendant*
3. *The Origin of the Sky Pendant*